Amis

"Alan w

"A satisfyingly complex cozy." —*Library Journal*

"Alan captures Holmes County and the Amish life in a mystery that is nothing close to plain and simple."
—Avery Aames, author of the Cheese Shop Mysteries

"In the Amish Quilt Shop Mysteries, Isabella Alan captures the spirit of the Amish perfectly. . . . Throw in the *Englischers* living in Rolling Brook and the tourists visiting, and you have a great host of colorful characters."
—Cozy Mystery Book Reviews

"A dead-certain hit."
—P. L. Gaus, author of the Amish-Country Mysteries

"This is a community you'd like to visit, a shop where you'd find welcome . . . and people you'd want for friends. . . . There's a lot of interesting information about Amish life, but it's interwoven into the story line so the reader learns details as Angie does." —Kings River Life Magazine

"Cozy readers and Amish enthusiasts alike will be raving about this debut. It proves to be a great start for Isabella Alan." —Debbie's Book Bag

Titles by Amanda Flower

CRIME AND POETRY
PROSE AND CONS

PROSE AND CONS

A Magical Bookshop Mystery

AMANDA FLOWER

BERKLEY PRIME CRIME
New York

BERKLEY PRIME CRIME
Published by Berkley
An imprint of Penguin Random House LLC
375 Hudson Street, New York, New York 10014

Copyright © 2016 by Amanda Flower
Excerpt from *Crime and Poetry* copyright © 2016 by Amanda Flower
Penguin Random House supports copyright. Copyright fuels creativity, encourages
diverse voices, promotes free speech, and creates a vibrant culture. Thank you for buying
an authorized edition of this book and for complying with copyright laws by not
reproducing, scanning, or distributing any part of it in any form without permission.
You are supporting writers and allowing Penguin Random House to continue to
publish books for every reader.

BERKLEY is a registered trademark and BERKLEY PRIME CRIME and the B colophon
are trademarks of Penguin Random House LLC.

ISBN: 9780451477453

First Edition: December 2016

Printed in the United States of America
1 3 5 7 9 10 8 6 4 2

Cover art by Stephen Gardner
Cover design by Katie Anderson
Book design by Kelly Lipovich

For the Northeast Ohio Chapter of Sisters in Crime

Acknowledgments

Thanks to all my readers who have told me they wished Charming Books were a real place. I wish it were too and that we could all have a cup of tea with Grandma Daisy, Violet, Emerson, and, of course, Faulkner beneath the birch tree. I could never thank you enough for welcoming these characters into your busy lives.

Thank you also to my kind editor, Bethany Blair, and my beloved agent, Nicole Resciniti. I'm so blessed to have the opportunity to work with both of you.

Hugs to my super assistant and beta reader, Molly Carroll-Syracuse, who has a great eye, and my dearest friend, Mariellyn Grace, who is always there to talk me through the twists and turns in my plots and my own life. And special thanks to Sarah Preston, who helped me decide on the murder weapon for this book.

Thanks to Cari Dubiel for hosting *Crime and Poetry*'s tea party at the Twinsburg Public Library and to Kate Schlademan from the Learned Owl Book Shop for being the bookseller, and to my friends who made the party such a success: Molly, Samantha, Bobby, Delia, Suzy, Graham, and Preston.

As always, thank you to my family, Andy, Nicole, Isabella, and Andrew. I love you all very much.

Finally, thank you to God in Heaven. There is no guarantee that we will get everything we want in this life, but thank you for granting me this one big dream come true.

TRUE!—*nervous*—*very, very dreadfully nervous I had been and am; but why* will *you say that I am mad? The disease had sharpened my senses*—*not destroyed*—*not dulled them.*

—EDGAR ALLAN POE

ONE

A petite teenage girl stood in front of the display of sports biographies that was tucked away in a small corner of the bookshop Charming Books, which I co-owned with my grandma Daisy in the village of Cascade Springs, New York, and chewed on her lip.

I set a stack of picture books decorated with smiling pumpkins and mischievous squirrels on the top of one of the lower bookshelves a few feet from her. "Can I help you?" I asked in my most polite bookseller voice. The trick was to sound friendly and helpful, not too eager for a sale.

The girl turned to me, and tears glistened in her big green eyes. "I don't know. I'm supposed to pick up a gift for my boyfriend's father. It's his birthday, and the party starts in a half hour. I'm doomed!"

"I'm sure he would love any book that you give him," I said encouragingly. "It's the thought that counts, right?"

She shook her head and her brown hair covered her face. "You don't know his parents. They're horrible. Nothing I do is right. I just want them to like me or at least pretend to."

I straightened a row of books that sat unevenly on the shelf. I wouldn't be the least bit surprised if Grandma Daisy had moved the books just a little to drive me crazy. She and I had different ideas on the proper way to keep the books organized. I wanted everything in its place, preferably in alphabetical order. Grandma Daisy was satisfied if books were on the correct floor of the shop. She always said the books would find the person who needed them most no matter where they were in the shop, so precision didn't matter. That might be literally true in Charming Books, but still the alphabetizer in me couldn't handle the lackadaisical shelving method. After the books' spines were all sitting precisely at the edge, I said, "That sounds familiar."

She wrinkled her nose. "What does that mean?"

I gave her a half smile. "My high school boyfriend's parents didn't like me either."

"What would they have bad to say about you?" She blinked at me. "You're so tall and pretty."

I chuckled. "Being tall isn't everything. Neither is being pretty. That's sweet of you to say that I am, though. You're a beautiful girl, so if that argument didn't work for you, it most certainly wouldn't work for me."

She blushed at the compliment and said, "If your boyfriend's parents didn't like you, I really am in trouble. Maybe I should just go to his birthday party empty-handed. Why waste my money when it's not going to do any good?"

"Maybe you just need to let your subconscious pick the book," I said.

She lowered her eyebrows. "What do you mean?"

"Close your eyes and reach for the books. I think the right book will find you."

She gave me a dubious look.

I shrugged. "It's just a hunch. What do you have to lose?"

"Oh-kay." Her voice was still heavy with doubt.

While the girl's eyes were closed, a book flew across the shop from the history section and appeared in her hand.

Her eyes snapped open, and she stared at the tome with Abraham Lincoln on the cover. "How did this get in the sports section?"

"Oh," I said unconcernedly. "It must have been misplaced. Would you prefer a sports-related title?" I moved to take the book from her.

"No!" She jerked the book away from me and held it to her chest. "No, this is perfect. His father is a history buff, and I've seen a picture of Lincoln in his office. I'm only afraid he might have already read this one."

I fought to hide a smile. "I'm pretty sure he hasn't read it."

"How do you know?" She stared up at me with those big green eyes again.

"Call it bookseller intuition." I smiled.

She hugged the book more tightly to her chest. "This

is the right book. I just know it. Thank you so much. . . ." She trailed off.

"Violet," I said.

"You really saved my life with this."

"Happy to help. Let's ring you up, then, so you can make that party." I led her across the room to the sales counter.

Faulkner, the shop crow, walked across the counter. His talons made a clicking sound on the aged wood. I clapped my hands at him, and he flew over the girl's head, cawing, "Four score and seven years ago!"

She ducked, and her eyes went round. "Was the crow quoting the Gettysburg Address? Does he know about this book?"

I forced a laugh. "We've been playing a lot of historical audiobooks in the shop lately. He must have picked it up from that."

While she reached in her purse for her wallet, I glared at Faulkner, who landed on one of the low branches of the birch tree. The crow smoothed his silky black feathers with his sharp beak and ignored me. I wondered where my tuxedo cat, Emerson, had gone off to. He usually was able to keep the crow in line. Also it was never a good sign when Emerson wandered off. The cat was up to something or strolling around the neighborhood. I hadn't yet figured out how to keep my cat in the shop. His previous owner took him all around town.

She swiped her credit card through the machine.

"Would you like me to gift wrap the book for you?"

"Can you? That would be great and save me so much time. I'm already running late as it is."

"Of course." I cut off a piece of brown paper stamped with orange and red leaves from the roll behind the counter.

After the girl took the newly wrapped biography out the front door, I locked the door behind her and winked at the birch tree that grew in the middle of the bookshop. A spiral staircase led up to the second floor of Charming Books, where the children's fairy book loft and my one-bedroom apartment were. My ancestress Rosalee had built the original house around the tree after the War of 1812. "Nice work." I gave the tree a thumbs-up.

My seventysomething grandmother, who with her trim figure could easily pass for a woman half her age if not for the sleek silver bob that fell to her chin, came around the side of the tree, shaking her head. "Violet, my dear, you're becoming a little showy with helping customers choose books. What if someone else was in the shop when you pulled that stunt? It would not do for customers to see books flying across the shop." As usual, she wore jeans and a Charming Books sweatshirt, which was orange that day in celebration of the nearness of Halloween. To complete the outfit, she'd added a gauzy infinity scarf decorated with cheerful jack-o'-lanterns.

"Grandma Daisy, it's after seven. The shop was supposed to close fifteen minutes ago. There was no one else here."

"Still, you need to be careful." She tucked a lock of silver hair behind her ear. "Remember the most important job of the Caretaker is to keep the shop's secret. No one outside of the family can know."

"Four months ago you were arguing with me because

I didn't believe in the shop's essence. Now I'm in trouble because I do and make use of it." I couldn't keep the whine out of my voice. I knew I sounded like a stubborn four-year-old, and I knew it wasn't attractive on a woman nearing her thirtieth birthday.

Grandma Daisy adjusted her cat's-eye glasses on her nose. "You're not in trouble. I just want you to remember your duty as the Caretaker." She turned and headed in the direction of the kitchen, which was separated from the shop by a thick swinging door.

Like I could forget? Being the Caretaker of the huge Queen Anne Victorian house and its birch tree had been a duty of the women in my family for the last two centuries, ever since Rosalee watered the tree with the mystical and healing waters from the local natural springs. The water manifested itself in the shop and the books, and now the essence of the water was able to communicate with the Caretaker through cryptic messages sent through the books themselves. Trust me—I know how unbelievable that sounds.

My mother should have been the Caretaker after my grandmother was relieved of her post, but fate had other plans, stealing her from me when I was only thirteen. As a result, the Caretaker role skipped a generation and landed directly on my shoulders. Since I had no children, female or otherwise, it was unknown what would happen to the shop when it was time for me to pass it on to the next generation. I would love to have a child . . . someday. I rolled my eyes at Grandma Daisy's receding back. There was really no way I could forget my duty as the Caretaker of Charming Books even if I wanted to.

"I saw you roll your eyes at me," Grandma Daisy called over her shoulder.

"The essence doesn't give you the ability to see out the back of your head," I countered.

She glanced over her shoulder. "How do you know? You've only been the Caretaker for a few months. How do you know everything the essence can and cannot do?" Before I could think of a smart remark, she said, "Don't you have some cookies to be picked up from La Crepe Jolie for the Poe-try Reading tomorrow?"

I smacked myself on the forehead. "Oh, right, I forgot. I'll go collect them now."

She nodded. "The Red Inkers should be here by the time you return. Be careful. The traffic will be horrid on River Road with the start of the Food and Wine Festival tomorrow."

"I'll be careful," I promised.

The Cascade Springs Food and Wine Festival was the biggest event for the small village, which depended on tourism for its survival. It was held annually the third week of October. This year at Grandma Daisy's urging, Charming Books was participating in the festivities by hosting a Poe-try Reading, highlighting the work and life of the master of the macabre, Edgar Allan Poe. I couldn't think of a more perfect author to showcase this close to Halloween. Grandma Daisy and I were able to recruit the help of the Red Inkers, a local writers' group that regularly met in Charming Books after shop hours to discuss their work.

I grabbed my coat from the coat-tree by the kitchen door. "I should be going, then."

"Don't be too long. I know *everyone* in the group is looking forward to seeing you. . . ." she said in a teasing voice.

This time I rolled my eyes to her face, so there was no mistaking it. Grandma Daisy's bell-chime laugh rang through the empty shop, and Faulkner joined in on the chuckle fest. Her comment about the group wanting to see me was much more pointed than it sounded. She implied—not so subtly, might I add—that the village police chief, David Rainwater, wanted to see me.

The truth was I was looking forward to seeing him too.

TWO

Outside the shop, I walked around Charming Books to collect my bicycle. I wished that my grandmother hadn't brought up David Rainwater, even if indirectly. Now I knew I would be fretting over seeing him until the Red Inkers meeting. The police chief, who was an aspiring children's book author, was also a member. Seeing him wasn't a complication that I needed. I had enough to worry about between being the shop Caretaker, finishing my dissertation on Ralph Waldo Emerson and his Transcendentalist buddies, and teaching my adjunct courses at the local community college. Now was not a good time to think about finding a boyfriend, no matter how beautiful he was, and David Rainwater was beautiful. The female and even some of the male population of the village could vouch for that.

My aqua-colored cruiser bike leaned against the side of the shop. It had been my mother's, and Grandma Daisy had it refurbished as part of her master plan to convince me to stay in the village and accept my role as Caretaker of Charming Books. She had also had my bike helmet "improved" by asking a local artist to cover it in hand-painted purple violets. The helmet was beyond embarrassing, but it brought a smile to my grandmother's face every time I wore it, so I couldn't bring myself to buy a violet-free replacement. I lifted the helmet from where it dangled from the handlebars. As I fastened the chin strap into place, Emerson flew out from under Charming Books' wraparound porch and leaped into the bike's pink wire basket. The gerbera daisy on the front of the basket bounced with the impact.

"Emerson, you can't come with me this time."

He stared at me with his big amber eyes.

I put my hands on my hips, determined not to let him get the best of me. "How am I supposed to bring the cookies home with you in the basket? Do you want the cookies to be ruined?"

He flattened his ears and cocked his head. It was his most pitiful face, which caused me to cave every single time.

I shook my finger at him. "I mean it. You can't come."

The old-fashioned ironwork lampposts flickered to life as the sun made its downturn west. I didn't want to be biking cookies back to Charming Books in the dark. I didn't have time for Emerson's stubbornness.

The tuxie crouched lower in the basket and dug his claws into the towel I kept there to make the ride more comfortable for him. If the towel was any indication, Emerson and I both knew who would win this one.

I sighed. There was no arguing with the cat when he dug his claws in. "Fine, you win. Again."

He purred and settled into the bottom of the basket as I set off from Charming Books. At the curb, I paused to take a look at the periwinkle blue Victorian with its tower, delicate gingerbread, and wraparound porch. Sometimes, I still couldn't believe I was living and working there again after over a decade away. I smiled. It felt right. At some point over the last four months, I had accepted my prodigal return to the village and my place as the Caretaker of the shop. Grudgingly, I admitted to myself Grandma Daisy's warning had been just—I needed to be more careful not to reveal what the shop's essence could do. I kicked off from the sidewalk.

The ride between Charming Books and La Crepe Jolie was typically a short one. The village was so tiny that a bike ride from end to end took no more than fifteen minutes.

However, the evening before the Food and Wine Festival, the trip took longer than I expected as vendors and a few early bird tourists crowded River Road, the main street in Cascade Springs, which began in the shopping district where Charming Books was but then took a sharp turn to follow the path of the Niagara River.

A green space and trail on the river side of the street, called the Riverwalk, included a park, the local swanky spa, and the village pavilion. On the other side of the street away from the river, there were more businesses, like La Crepe Jolie, and the stately town hall.

White canvas tents operated by local restaurants and wineries dotted either side of the road and the filled park as vendors made last-minute preparations for the festival. The park boasted the premier food and wine tents, and I knew that was where Morton Vineyards' booth would be. I planned to avoid the park at all costs, and the town hall itself for good measure. I didn't want any impromptu meetings with the village mayor, Nathan Morton, the boy-now-man who'd broken my heart when I was seventeen.

In the months since I had moved back to Cascade Springs, I had expertly avoided Mayor Nathan Morton, my ex-boyfriend, which was no easy feat in a village with only a few thousand people. My best diversionary tactic was duck and cover. It was not uncommon for me to throw myself behind a bush or around the side of a building like an army private diving into a foxhole to avoid being seen by the village mayor.

I hit my bike's brakes as a pair of tourists stared up at the town hall and its domed clock tower. A large banner emblazoned in purple and gold script announcing "Cascade Springs Food and Wine Festival" hung just below the clock tower. With all the attractions New York's Niagara region had to offer, tiny Cascade Springs was the place to be this weekend, and we expected an influx of several thousand tourists.

Other small towns held Oktoberfests this time of year, but not Cascade Springs. The village fought for its reputation of high-class refinement. Because of this, while other towns touted brats and beer gardens, Cascade Springs brought out the wine and cheese.

With the maple and oak trees at their autumnal peak, it was easy to see why the Food and Wine Festival was held in the zenith of the season. It was as if the entire town was fringed in gold, bronze, and scarlet and any gap in color was more than made up for by the village grounds-keepers, who coddled the village's public green spaces with unadulterated devotion. The planters and gardens overflowed with mums and asters of every color. All year round, the village groundskeepers took immense pride in the upkeep of Cascade Springs' green spaces, but for the annual Food and Wine Festival, they brought their A game.

The question on my mind remained. Would the Poe-try Reading at Charming Books be attractive enough to the thousands of tourists to entice them away from the food and wine tents?

I chimed the bell on my bicycle's handlebars and the pair stepped to the side. I imagine Emerson, with his white forepaws braced on the front of the basket, gave them his signature smile as we passed. The two gawked at the cat and snapped photos of Emerson and me with their phones.

After his photo shoot, Emerson settled back into the basket.

I was just under way again when I hit the brake hard for two college-aged girls who stumbled directly in my path. They laughed and clutched plastic wineglasses close to their chests in order to avoid spilling any of the precious contents. It looked like they had scored a sample from one of the wine merchants a day early. I didn't look too closely at the two girls, afraid they might be some of my students from Springside Community College, where I was an adjunct English professor. In the student-professor relationship, it was sometimes better not to cross paths in the wild for everyone's sake.

Finally, feeling like I had just run a gauntlet, I parked my bike in front of La Crepe Jolie, a delightful French café. I gave a sigh of relief that the town hall was now behind me and dropped the kickstand on my bike, hopping off. In the same motion I removed my bike helmet in a practiced move.

"Violet, over here!" Lacey Dupont waved at me from the front door of La Crepe Jolie, which she co-owned with her French-Canadian chef husband, Adrien. Adrien had moved to Cascade Springs to open the café a little over five years ago, fallen in love with my old schoolmate Lacey, and, as far as I knew, never set foot on the other side of the border again.

I smiled at her, and Emerson jumped from the bicycle basket to my arms. The cat quickly latched himself to my right shoulder like he was a black-and-white fur wrap that I'd haphazardly tossed around my neck.

Lacey placed her hands on her ample hips. "Violet Waverly, I thought you were going to mow down those two girls on your bicycle."

I shook out my long strawberry blond hair, which felt like it was in a tangle of knots from being tucked under the helmet. "It wasn't even close."

She laughed. "That's good. It wouldn't do for you to crash into the tourists. I'm sure the town council and the *mayor* would have something to say about that."

I ignored her comment about the mayor. Lacey, my

grandmother, and half the town would love nothing better than to see Nathan and me back together like some kind of local storybook fairy tale. As much as they wished for that, it wasn't going to happen. I wasn't a storybook princess and didn't pretend to be, and Nathan was far from Prince Charming.

"Grandma Daisy sent me over to collect the cookies for our reading at Charming Books tomorrow," I said, hoping she would drop any more talk of Nathan. "It was so kind of Adrien to offer to bake them. You both must be terribly busy with the café and the festival. I hope the cookies weren't too much trouble."

White blond wisps of hair escaped the enameled barrettes on either side of her head and framed her rosy cheeks. "My Adrien loves nothing better than an all-night baking marathon. That's when my love is in his true element. Daisy called me when you left Charming Books, so I have the boxes right here for you." She pointed at the white metal tables with matching chairs. On one of the tables were four large bakery boxes. I blinked at the boxes. "Are those all for the Poe-try Reading?"

She gave the top box a loving pat. "You bet."

I blinked again. "Lacey, how many cookies did you give us?"

She held up her hands as if in surrender. "Don't blame me. It's all Adrien. You know when he gets to baking. There's no stopping him."

I still didn't take the boxes. "Don't you need some of these for the café or for your tent at the festival? There is no way we will have enough tourists at the reading to eat all of these."

She waved me away. "Oh, I have plenty more where those came from. Adrien made twice as many for the café and for the booth."

"What's in here?" I asked, nodding to the boxes.

"All Adrien's favorites: madeleines, sugar and lemon, macaroons, *Langues-de-Chat*, and three kinds of meringues. He included an extra dozen of the lemon madeleines. He knows those are Daisy's favorite." She smiled.

My mouth watered just from hearing all the names of the cookies. "Thank Adrien for us both. I should head back. There's a Red Inkers meeting tonight, and we are going over final preparation for the reading tomorrow."

She scratched Emerson on the top of his head. "How are you going to transport these cookies back to Charming Books with him riding shotgun?"

Emerson purred in my ear and shifted his weight on my shoulder. I could almost hear his thoughts. "Me? How could I ever be a problem?"

"That's a good question." I set Emerson back in his basket, and he propped his white paws on the basket's front rim as he did when he was ready for the next adventure. Since Emerson was always ready for the next adventure, he posed like that a lot. "If you have a sack," I said, "I can carry the cookies in the bag and Emerson can keep his spot."

"Are you sure that's a good idea in this traffic?" The space on her forehead between her eyes creased. She must have been remembering my near collision with the college girls.

Even with the population of the village tripling for the

festival, it was nothing compared with the rush hour I'd endured in Chicago. "I'll be fine," I reassured her.

With a shake of her head, she slipped inside the café. She was back in less than a minute with a large canvas bag. She carefully packed the boxes of cookies inside. "Still doesn't seem safe to me. If you get in an accident, I'm going to tell Daisy I tried to discourage you."

I chuckled. "She'll believe you. Don't you worry about that." I thanked her for the cookies one last time and kicked off the curb.

With my violet helmet securely on my head, a cat in my bicycle basket, and one hand on the handlebars, I pedaled down River Road in the direction of Charming Books. My other hand held the tote bag of cookies, which was so heavy that I had to lean in the opposite direction to avoid toppling over.

As I cruised around one of Cascade Springs' ubiquitous horse-drawn carriages parked in front of the town hall, I made the mistake of glancing up at the hall itself. Dusk had fallen in the time that I had been gone from Charming Books to retrieve the cookies. Despite the fading light, I could clearly see Mayor Nathan Morton standing on the hall's top step as if surveying the festivities of his town, but in reality, his gaze was locked on me. Under one of the village's streetlamps, I felt like a spotlight shone on me, and with no bush to dive behind in sight, I pedaled away as fast as I dared with my heavy load of cookies, feeling his eyes on my back the whole ride home.

I was so distracted by spying Nathan that I nearly hit a man who was marching across the road with a harmonica hanging from a stiff wire from his neck and an acoustic guitar strapped across his chest. He wore rectangular wire-rimmed glasses and had a full, well-kept gray beard. A long gray ponytail hung down his back over the lined flannel coat he wore. I had never seen him before, but that was to be expected. Most of the people in the village during the festival were visitors.

The man smiled at me in such a disarming way, I almost dropped the sack of cookies. Emerson crouched low in the basket as if he expected a crash.

"I'm so sorry," I called as I pedaled on.

I could have been wrong, but I would have sworn I heard him say, "That's all right, Violet," behind me. I shook the thought from my head. I must have heard him wrong, because there was no reason for him to know my name, no reason at all.

THREE

I made the turn on River Road toward Charming Books, and the crowds of tourists began to thin. The closer to home I drew, the more certain I was I'd misheard the man with the guitar. He didn't say my name, or if he did, was that really all that surprising? Grandma Daisy was one of the most prominent figures in the village. It wasn't impossible for people in the village I didn't recognize to know who I was because of my grandmother.

The strap of the cookie bag was biting into my fingers, so I hopped off my bike and walked it the last few feet to Charming Books.

Anastasia Faber, a Red Inker, stood under a streetlamp a few feet from the fence that surrounded Charming Books' small front yard. Anastasia had her back to me and she held a cell phone to her ear. "You aren't listening to me," she shouted at the person on the other end of the call. "I don't have time for your excuses!"

I inched closer, unable to squash my curiosity about her conversation.

Anastasia gripped her cell phone so tightly I was surprised it didn't crack as her knuckles turned white. "Fix it. Do you understand me? Find out who is behind this. I don't care how you do it, but fix it. If you can't, I will find someone who can." She ended the call, opened her large purse, and tossed the phone inside. She spun around and gasped when she found me just a few feet behind her. "How long have you been standing there?" she demanded.

Had any of the other Red Inkers greeted me like that, I would have been shocked and even a little hurt. However, for Anastasia, it was a pretty standard greeting. It was her way of saying "hello."

I held up the bag from La Crepe Jolie. "I just picked these up from La Crepe Jolie. They're cookies for tomorrow."

She curled her lip at the bag of cookies as if she thought I was just using them as a decoy. Maybe I was. I was insanely curious about Anastasia's phone call and felt terrible for whoever was on the receiving end of her rage. Anastasia was typically irritable and unpleasant, but I had never heard her furious before. It wasn't a good look for her.

She turned her glare on Emerson, who stared back at her in that impassive cat way that clearly said that he couldn't care less about her or her troubles.

I broke into their staring contest. "Anastasia, is everything all right?"

She smoothed back her silky brown hair with her

ever-present headband, which was rust colored today, perhaps in honor of fall. "Everything's fine, perfectly fine." She pursed her lips. "Let's hope it stays that way and the reading tomorrow isn't a complete disaster. Charming Books doesn't need any more poor publicity after your grandmother was accused of murder over the summer, does it?" With that, she marched into the bookshop, leaving me to carry in the bakery boxes myself. I refrained from sticking my tongue out at her behind her back, but only because a tourist nearby would have seen me do it.

"Nevermore!" Faulkner cawed from his perch halfway up the centuries-old birch tree as I stumbled into the shop with the tote bag of cookies in my arms. Emerson wove in and around my feet. It was a miracle that I didn't trip over him.

"Violet, let me help you with that." Grandma Daisy hurried toward me and took the bag from my arms. She set it on a side table.

"Thanks." I sighed with relief.

"Are all these cookies for tomorrow?" she asked as she unpacked the boxes.

I nodded. "Adrien may have grossly overestimated how popular the Poe-try Reading will be."

Grandma Daisy grinned. "If it's a flop, we'll have enough cookies to drown our sorrows."

I glanced around the main room of the bookshop. "Where's Anastasia? She came in the shop a few seconds before me."

"She ran into the kitchen," Grandma Daisy said. "She muttered something about needing to freshen up before the rest of the Red Inkers arrived. I just stepped out of the way. There's no point in engaging that woman until absolutely necessary."

"Grandma . . ." I said.

"Violet." She mimicked my tone. "You know as well as I do Anastasia is rearing for an argument. It was written all over her face when she stomped inside. I hope she doesn't cause a scene at the Poe-try Reading tomorrow. This event has great potential to drum up business for the shop."

I thought of Anastasia's argument over the phone, which I overheard just a few minutes ago. "I hope she doesn't either."

"Did he make lemon madeleines?" Grandma Daisy lifted the lid to one of the boxes and peeked inside. "Those are my favorites."

"Yes," I said, running my fingers through my hair as best I could to remove the bike helmet tangles. It was a futile act. "And Adrien made an extra dozen just for you."

"Nevermore!" Faulkner called again as he swooped down from the tree and onto his perch in the front window.

I gave the crow the hairy eyeball. "You're getting way too much mileage out of that quote."

Faulkner bobbed his head and repeated the famous quote from "The Raven." Ever since the poem was read aloud at the Red Inkers meeting the week before, the crow had been repeating "Nevermore" over and over again until I wished the word could be stricken from the English language forevermore.

Despite my annoyance, I didn't tell Faulkner that he

was a crow, not a raven. There was no reason to take the fluff out of his feathers.

Emerson jumped on the arm of one of the two couches that flanked the shop's wide fireplace and cocked his head at the crow first in one direction and then the other. It was almost as if the cat was assessing how much energy it would take to make the leap from the couch to Faulkner's perch.

Faulkner puffed his feathers, making him appear as large as possible. There was a war going on in Charming Books as the crow and the cat positioned themselves against each other: a fight for shop mascot. Both Faulkner and Emerson thought they were deserving of the title. Faulkner, who had been a resident of the shop longer, had seniority on his side, but Emerson had him beat in crowd appeal. No one ever came in the shop and cried, "How darling, you have a crow!" However, Emerson received daily compliments from customers about his adorableness; he lapped up the praise like cream from a dish. Those customers who noticed the big black bird in the tree usually gave him a wide berth and covered their heads as if they were afraid of bird droppings falling into their hair.

Grandma Daisy found one of the lemon madeleines and took a bite. "Oh!" she moaned. "It's like a lemon party in my mouth."

I glanced around the shop. Grandma Daisy and I were the only ones there. "Where are the rest of the Red Inkers? I thought you said they would be here by the time I returned from La Crepe Jolie."

Before Grandma Daisy could reply, someone knocked on the front door. There was a small four-paned window at eye level in the door, but even with the porch light, I couldn't make out the dark figure on the other side of the glass. Whoever it was looked like a massive blob. I mentally kicked myself for the comparison. Clearly, the nearness of Halloween was causing my mind to wander in a spooky direction.

Faulkner cawed from his perch. "Begone!" It was a welcome change from "Nevermore," but it certainly wasn't the friendliest greeting Faulkner knew.

"Shh!" I told the crow.

Emerson, who was far less vocal, sashayed to the door as if he were the Pied Piper. If he was the Pied Piper, I was a rat. It wasn't a comparison that I cared for. I went to answer the door.

The pounding came again, and Emerson seemed unconcerned by it, so I felt myself relax too. In the last few months since I had adopted the small tuxedo cat, I had begun to trust his instincts about people. He always seemed to know who was friend and who was foe. It was nice to have a feline litmus test, especially after my rough return to the village, which included a murder and almost getting killed. Twice. Three times if you counted the near bike accident.

I opened the door to see a pair of legs and then a huge pile of garment bags covering the rest of the carrier's body. I knew immediately whom the legs belonged to. There was only one person in Cascade Springs who would wear skull-and-crossbones-printed tights.

"Sadie?" I asked.

"Yes, it's me." Her voice was muffled by the impossibly high stack of garment bags. "A little help?"

I grabbed half the garment bags from her and carried them over to one of the shop's couches. I dropped the bags there and went back for another load. Holding only one bag now, Sadie stumbled into the shop and ran the back of her right hand across her forehead. "Those were a lot heavier than I thought they would be, and I almost got hit by a carriage crossing the street. Those drivers really need to watch where they're going." She said all of this with a bright smile on her face as if death by trampling might have been fun.

"Why didn't you call?" I asked. "I would have helped you carry these across the street."

She patted her high black ponytail to make sure not a hair was out of place. There wasn't. Even carrying half her weight in clothing the twenty or so yards from her vintage clothing shop, Midcentury Vintage, across River Road to Charming Books, Sadie looked adorable and perfectly put together in her own unique style. She wore a black skirt with a silver crow printed on it, an orange sweater, and silver Doc Marten boots to complement the skull and crossbones tights. Halloween was a little over a week away, but she was making the most of her Halloween wardrobe while she could.

"I guess I could have done that." She chuckled. "I was just too excited to think of it. You will not believe the pieces I found for the Poe-try Reading. Everyone is going to look incredible." She sighed happily. "This event is going to be amazing."

Almost every event in Sadie's life was "amazing." On

anyone else, I would have found that quality annoying, but Sadie was so sincerely cheerful that it was endearing.

"I brought a metal clothing rack across the street earlier today and Daisy stashed it in the stockroom. I'll just go grab it, so I can start hanging the garments. I can't wait for everyone to see them." She bounced off in the direction of the kitchen before I had a chance to warn her that Anastasia was back there.

The front door opened again and the remaining members of the Red Inkers trooped in. It was a small group. Other than Sadie, there was Trudy Conner, who was an eightysomething retired elementary school teacher; Dr. Richard Bunting, who was my department chair at Springside; and David Rainwater, Cascade Springs' chief of police.

My gaze glossed over Trudy and Richard and locked with the amber-colored eyes of the village police chief. As a member of the Seneca tribe, Rainwater had coal black hair, which he kept short, honey-colored skin, pronounced cheekbones, and eyes that were like pools of warm maple syrup. It went without saying that he was a handsome man. The fact he was an aspiring writer of children's books could topple a book-loving girl like me clean over.

Heat rushed to my face, and I broke eye contact to greet the entire group. "You're all just in time. Sadie brought over our garments for the Poe-try Reading."

Grandma Daisy locked the front door behind the Red Inkers. "That's just wonderful. I, for one, am excited to see everyone in their Edgar-inspired best. Sadie always discovers the most interesting clothes." Grandma Daisy hugged all three of the newcomers in turn. "Thank you for helping us out with this. Violet and I would never have been able to pull this off without the support of the Red Inkers."

Richard blushed slightly as he received the hug. As a stiff academic, he wasn't completely comfortable with PDAs, not even in the form of a grandmotherly embrace.

"It's the least we can do, Daisy." Trudy set her enormous leather pocketbook on the couch not covered by the garment bags. "You have let us meet in Charming Books for years at no charge and on most nights you even provide dessert."

"Hear, hear," Richard agreed, adjusting his satchel on his shoulder. Richard was the consummate college professor, from his perfectly side-parted brown hair flecked with silver and his wire-rimmed glasses to his worn oxford shoes.

Trudy settled on the couch next to her large purse. As she sat, her white pin curls bounced in place on the top of her head. The curls gave her a cherubic quality that most found disarming, but having had Mrs. Conner as my own first-grade teacher, I knew she didn't put up with any shenanigans. "I'm looking forward to it. It's high time that the Cascade Springs Food and Wine Festival added some cultural events to the week. The eating and drinking is all well and good, but there is a lot more to our little village than the vineyards and restaurants."

I glanced at the birch tree. *Don't I know that?*

Sadie and Anastasia entered the main room from the back kitchen. Anastasia carried a thick tome of Poe's works. Sadie pushed the empty clothing rack around the low bookshelves in the back of the shop and then around the staircase that encircled the birch tree in the middle of the store.

Sadie's usually happy face was drawn as if someone had just snatched the last vintage Chanel gown right out of her hand. Anastasia, who had been so furious the last time I'd seen her, was perfectly composed as if she didn't have a care in the world. Maybe she'd received word that whomever she had been yelling at on the phone had done her bidding. If Anastasia had been yelling at me as fiercely as she had to whoever had been on the other end of the call, I would have snapped to it just to get her off my back.

FOUR

I wanted to ask Sadie what was wrong, but she refused to make eye contact with me. She simply rolled the rack next to the couch with the garment bags and began hanging the garment bags one by one.

Rainwater seemed to notice Sadie's dark mood too, and he went to help her with the heavy bags. My heart melted a little at his quiet compassion.

"And," Trudy said from her comfy spot on the sofa, "I think a Poe-try Reading is undeniably clever. Poe's work is perfect material for an October event."

Grandma Daisy beamed at her as she removed her coat from the coat-tree and slung it over her arm. "Well, thank you, Trudy. That is high praise."

"You're most welcome." Trudy covered her mouth and coughed. "I'm so sorry. It's these dreadful fall allergies. They seem to act up every year."

I grabbed an unopened bottle of Cascade Springs water from behind the sales counter and handed it to her.

She smiled at me as she accepted the bottle. "Thank you, dear."

Anastasia sniffed. "I think this Poe-try Reading is an excellent idea. He is a true *literary* master in the craft of writing, but the idea of costumes is simply ridiculous. There is no reason that we have to dress up like a group of schoolchildren delving into their dress-up box."

Sadie's back stiffened. I wondered if Anastasia had insulted her costumes when they were in the kitchen. At the first chance to catch her alone, I would give Sadie a pep talk about the costumes. She took fashion very seriously, and she shouldn't let Anastasia discourage her.

Trudy's lips curved into a smile. "Is the Poe-try Reading not highfalutin enough for you, Anastasia, my dear?"

Anastasia glowered at the older woman. "I don't believe we should make a mockery of the master of the macabre."

Richard cleared his throat. "We would never make a mockery of any author's work. I'm sure the costumes are in good taste. I know Sadie has done extensive research into each and every costume. I've seen her countless times in Springside's library the last few weeks consulting with the librarian there."

I suppressed a smile because I knew Richard had seen Sadie in the college library so often since he spent all his free time there. He had a terrible crush on Springside's outspoken librarian, Renee Reid. As of yet, he hadn't worked up the nerve to ask her on a date, but I was hoping he would soon or I would have to don my Cupid wings and do it for him.

Grandma Daisy headed for the door. "Well, I'm looking forward to being surprised by all of your costumes tomorrow afternoon. I'm off to bake cupcakes for tomorrow's reading."

"Cupcakes?" I asked. "Why do you need cupcakes? Lacey and Adrien gave us enough cookies to feed the entire village and the city of Niagara Falls to boot." I gestured to the boxes of cookies from La Crepe Jolie still sitting on the end table.

"Violet, we will have to have more than cookies—even Adrien's scrumptious madeleines—to feed our guests at the reading. We need more options. Cupcakes are a must at any poetry reading. Sugar makes a person more appreciative of good literature."

"Hear, hear," Trudy said, mimicking Richard's serious tone from earlier.

After Grandma Daisy left to start her baking, Sadie and Rainwater finished hanging the garment bags and removing the costumes from the bags. Appropriate to Poe's material, there was a lot of black on the hanging rack.

"I guess you guys are stuck with just me tonight," I joked.

The police chief turned around and smiled. "I wouldn't say 'stuck.'"

I blushed, and with my fair skin, I knew I turned as red as the leaves falling from the maples on the street. The last thing I needed was another man in my life.

Nathan Morton was enough. Not that he was *in* my life, only the entirety of the village seemed to believe that he was. A girl could take only so much.

Anastasia settled on the other end of the couch from Trudy. "I say we get this show moving. I, for one, haven't reached my word count for the day and have some serious writing to do. As you all know, my work takes so much longer to craft than the rest of you because of the thought I must put into it."

Trudy held her leather handbag in her lap and snorted. "Our writing takes just as much time and energy as yours does, Anastasia. You don't have the monopoly on an author suffering for her art."

Anastasia gave her a withering glare.

All the Red Inkers were writers, but Anastasia wrote strictly what she called "serious literary fiction." Not for the first time, I wondered why she remained in the group when she so clearly thought what she wrote was a cut above what everyone else produced. I also wondered how the other Red Inkers had put up with her disparaging comments about their work for so long. I would have kicked her to the curb years ago.

Sadie straightened her back and removed a dress from the rack. "I think we should start with Violet's dress."

"My dress?" I squeaked.

"What selection will you be reading?" Rainwater asked from my right.

I jumped. I hadn't realized he'd moved across the room to join me. The man was as stealthy as Emerson. "There will be so much to do during the day between keeping an eye on the shop and the reading. I hadn't planned on reading anything at all."

"But you have to. I found you the perfect outfit," Sadie said, sounding so disappointed it nearly broke my heart.

I felt Rainwater watching me.

I smiled. "Since you have a dress for me, I suppose I must."

Sadie's face broke into her familiar smile. "You'll love the dress, Violet." She turned toward the rack and began sifting through the garments.

"That was a very nice thing you did," Rainwater said out of the side of his mouth.

I found myself smiling, but before I could respond, Anastasia cried out, "Ouch!" She popped her finger into her mouth.

"Are you okay?" I asked.

"I'm fine. It's only a stupid paper cut." She waved her hand in the air as if that would dispel the pain.

A single drop of blood fell from Anastasia's finger and onto the open book on her lap just below "The Tell-Tale Heart."

A shiver shook my body from the top of my head to the soles of my feet.

"Are you cold?" Rainwater asked me after my shiver finally stopped.

"There must be a draft. This is an old house." What I said was true, but the cool October air creeping through the cracks and crevices of the bookshop wasn't what caused me to shiver. It was the drop of blood on Anastasia's book.

I had lived in Charming Books and known about my destiny as the next Caretaker long enough to recognize that a drop of blood on a book page was a bad omen of things to come, but denial was a powerful tool. My brain immediately kicked it into gear, creating a counterargument against my subconscious. "It's just a paper cut," I whispered to myself.

The police chief's gaze darted in my direction. He heard me. He must have supersonic hearing in addition to cat stealth skills. Great.

I forced a smile, but I knew it didn't reach my eyes. I had never been very good at hiding my emotions, which was yet another reason I found being the Caretaker such a challenge. It was a secret I had to keep hidden for the rest of my life until I had a daughter of my own someday . . . if that ever happened.

"You should wash that out before it gets infected," Sadie said to Anastasia. "I had a great-great-great-uncle who died from an infected paper cut." She paused. "Or maybe it was four 'greats'? In any case, he got a staph infection and died. It was horrible."

"The poor man," Richard said, looking a little green. I noticed that he took care not to look at Anastasia's wound. It came as no surprise to me that the English professor was squeamish. However, at some point in his dual career as college professor and would-be author, he must have experienced a nasty paper cut or two of his own. It was unavoidable in his line of work.

Trudy scrunched her white eyebrows together. "We have to believe your great-uncle would have survived with today's modern medicine. Hardly anyone dies of paper cuts nowadays."

"Violet, do you have a first-aid kit?" the police chief asked, shaking me out of my daze.

I snapped to attention. "Yes, of course." I hurried across the room and retrieved the first-aid kit from under the sales counter and brought it to Anastasia.

Another drop of blood fell from her finger. "I'm sure it's not life threatening, but I will run it under cold water to stop the bleeding." She stood, took the first-aid kit from my hand, and hurried to the kitchen.

As she did, she dropped her copy of Poe's works on her empty seat, and the book remained open to the first page of "The Tell-Tale Heart." The second drop of Anastasia's blood had fallen on the line: "TRUE!—nervous—very, very dreadfully nervous I had been and am; but why *will* you say that I am mad? The disease had sharpened my senses—not destroyed—not dulled them."

Instinctively, I glanced up at the birch tree. Faulkner sat on his favorite branch, preening himself. He caught me looking and cawed, "Nevermore!"

Emerson walked over to me, and I scooped him up, cradling the cat in my arms.

"Violet, you're shaking like a leaf," Trudy said. "Are you sure you're not coming down with something? Do you want to borrow my wrap?" The older woman was wrapped up cocoon-style in a giant shawl that went around her small frame at least three times.

"No, I'm fine. Maybe someone was walking over my grave," I said with a forced laugh.

Anastasia rejoined the group. "As good as new." She waved her hand that now had a Band-Aid wrapped tightly around her injured finger.

"You really are all right?" I asked.

Everyone in the room stared at me as though I had just asked Anastasia if she planned to visit Mars any time soon.

I half-smiled. "I've never been one for blood."

Richard patted me on the arm. "A true humanities professor you are meant to be, then. We struggle with blood and gore, at least outside the literary world."

With that, Sadie launched into the tale of her ancestor's tragic death by paper cut, and I felt Rainwater watching me. I willed myself to remain calm. So what if there was a spot of blood on the first line in a story where a man is murdered? In almost every Poe poem or story a man is murdered. Besides, I reminded myself, no one in the room had a glass eye as the victim in "The Tell-Tale Heart" did. I told myself that there was nothing to worry about. Like Anastasia said herself, it was just a stupid paper cut.

Richard cleared his throat, interrupting Sadie's graphic description. "Now that that's settled, I believe we should go over the reading schedule for tomorrow."

"And don't forget the costumes," Sadie said, seemingly unconcerned that Richard cut her story short.

The rest of the evening flew by as Richard went over reading assignments for the next day and Sadie handed out the costumes. I accepted my dress, but barely looked at it as I was so distracted by Anastasia's paper cut. As much as I wanted to convince myself that the cut meant nothing, my intuition continued to nag to the point that I could no longer ignore it.

As the Red Inkers were packing up for the night, I walked over to Anastasia. "Are you sure everything is all right?" I asked her in a low voice.

She threw her garment bag over her arm. "Is this about the paper cut again? Honestly, I have never heard such a fuss made over such a minor injury."

Emerson meowed at my feet, and I bent over to pick up the small cat. He curved his lithe body around my neck.

"I'm just concerned," I said. "I happened to overhear the argument you had on the phone earlier this evening, and I thought you might have cut yourself because you were worried about—"

"*That* conversation is none of your business." Anastasia's eyes moved back and forth quickly as if she was looking for something or someone. "I'll kindly ask you to stay out of my personal affairs."

Emerson's warm body vibrated next to my throat.

"I'm sorry to intrude, but—" I paused before plunging in. "I think you might be in some kind of trouble. I'd like to help if I can."

She wrinkled her nose as if she smelled something foul and that something was me. "I don't have any idea what you are talking about."

Faulkner dove from the birch tree and swooped over our heads to his perch by the front window, cawing his favorite phrase as he went.

Anastasia screeched and covered her head.

"Faulkner," I admonished the bird, for whatever good that would do.

Anastasia licked her lips. "I really have no idea why I

keep coming here with these creatures and the complete lack of talent among the other writers—" She stared over my shoulder and stopped abruptly.

When I turned to see what had caught her attention, the only thing there was Faulkner, who was meticulously cleaning his feathers with his long black beak.

She shook her head as if to remove an aberration from her eyes. "It doesn't matter what I think of this place, does it? I'm just unnerved by the Halloween atmosphere. Aren't most writers sensitive to their environment?"

"Paranoid," I said barely above a whisper.

She narrowed her eyes. "I'm not paranoid."

I winced, not having realized I'd said the word aloud. "I was just thinking of Poe's story 'The Tell-Tale Heart.' Isn't it truly about paranoia at its core?"

She frowned. "I suppose." She edged around me and headed for the door. "Good night."

I inwardly groaned. I had royally messed that up. All I had been trying to do was to warn Anastasia without revealing to her how I might know she was in danger. No one could know about the springwater's essence and the impact that it had on the books.

"Something wrong?" Rainwater's deep voice brought me out of my dark thoughts.

I swallowed. "No, everything is fine." I saw that everyone else had left the shop. The police chief and I were alone.

Faulkner fluffed his feathers and Emerson placed a white paw on my cheek as if to remind me that he was still wrapped around my neck. Okay, we weren't completely alone.

Rainwater squinted at me until his amber eyes were just slits on his tawny face. "Why don't I believe you?"

I removed Emerson from my shoulder and set him on the arm of the sofa. "Don't know." I shrugged. "I'm very trustworthy."

He couldn't fight the smile forming on his lips. "I beg to differ there. I seem to remember you weren't one hundred percent forthcoming during my murder case last summer."

I swallowed again, knowing he was referring to Benedict Raisin's murder. Benedict had been my grandmother's boyfriend, and because of that, after he was murdered, she was the number one suspect in the crime. I butted into the murder investigation to make sure she wasn't falsely accused. Chief Rainwater had not been impressed with my detective skills, even though I was the one who'd figured out who the killer was. I didn't remind him of that fact, since I had nearly gotten killed in the process. I didn't think it would be a good argument as far as the village police chief was concerned.

"Do you feel ready to read tomorrow?" I asked, changing the conversation to a much more comfortable topic, books. I was always most comfortable talking about literature.

His smile broadened as if he knew all my diversionary tactics. "I'm happy Richard gave me a selection from 'The Murders in the Rue Morgue.'"

"It only seemed fitting that you would read one of Poe's great detective stories."

"'The mental features discoursed of as the analytical are, in themselves, but little susceptible of analysis,'" he quoted the first line of the story, in an officious tone.

I laughed. "You're a natural."

"I love Poe's work. I think he's one of the reasons that I went into police work."

"If that was the case, I'm surprised you're not a private detective. Poe gave a somewhat bumbling view of police or at least the Paris police."

His black eyebrows furrowed. "Sometimes being self-employed has its appeal. I could do without the village politics for one."

Village politics was something I definitely didn't want to talk about, so I led him to the door. "When are you going to let me read one of your books? All of the Red Inkers, even Anastasia, rave about your work. I feel a little left out."

"I will. I always keep my promises. It's just not ready yet. I want it to be the best it can be before you read it, you being a college professor and all."

I folded my arms. "Richard is a college professor, a full PhD in fact, and you've let him read it."

"I don't care much about impressing Richard, not like I want to impress you." He said it so smoothly I would have thought we were discussing the weather.

I felt another chill, but this time it was for a completely different reason from any darn paper cut.

He saved me from responding by saying, "My work is fiction for kids, true, but it's still a peek into my deepest thoughts. In a way, isn't that what all writers allow readers when they share their work, a window into another person's mind? Poe, the tortured soul that he was, was the perfect example."

"Maybe I should have you visit my freshman comp

class. I would love to express that idea to my students and it might be more impactful if coming from a true writer." I opened the front door.

He laughed. "If I can call myself such a thing." He hesitated before stepping out onto the porch. "It seems you had a delivery."

"Really?" I edged around him to find an enormous crate sitting under one of two outside lights flanking the door. "It's awfully late for a book delivery," I mused. "And all the deliverymen know to come to our back door. . . ." I trailed off when I saw the words on the wooden crate: MORTON VINEYARDS.

"There's a note," Rainwater said as he bent over and picked up the note. He handed it to me without reading it.

I opened the small envelope and read it silently to myself. "Vi, Best of luck on your Poe-try Reading tomorrow. It would not do for an event associated with the festival not to have wine. I took the liberty of dropping this off for you. Don't even try to return it. See you in the bushes, N." My face flushed bright red. Apparently, the duck-and-cover strategy to avoid Nathan had not been as effective as I thought.

I hid the note behind my back as if the police chief had the ability to read through the paper. Considering the other superpowers I suspected he possessed, it wasn't out of the question. "The mayor sent some wine over for the Poe-try Reading."

Rainwater's amber eyes were kind. "I gathered that from the name on the crate. He is a determined suitor, isn't he?"

"It's not like that," I said maybe a little too quickly.

"He's just supporting the shop. He's always cared about Grandma Daisy and Charming Books."

Rainwater gave me a sad smile. "I think that's exactly what it's like."

Before I could respond, he walked down the porch steps and through the front gate.

With a groan, I picked up the crate and clumsily carried it inside the shop. It was a crate of ice wine, Morton Vineyards' most expensive vintage. I knew Rainwater's estimation of Nathan's motives was much closer to the mark than mine.

I set the crate on the floor, shut and bolted the door, then leaned my back against it with my eyes closed. My head was swirling over all that had happened that evening: Anastasia's paper cut, Sadie's strange behavior, my conversation with Rainwater, and now the crate of wine. When I opened my eyes again, I found Emerson sitting at my feet on a stack of Edgar Allan Poe hardbacks, which hadn't been there a moment ago.

I banged the back of my head against the heavy antique door in defeat.

FIVE

By late the next morning, worries over Anastasia's paper cut and Nathan Morton's wine delivery flew right out of my mind as I bustled in and out of Charming Books helping customers select books from the shop and checking in with the last-minute preparations for the Poetry Reading. Sunday was always one of the busiest days of the week in the shop as city dwellers gravitated toward Cascade Springs on the weekends, but the business in the shop was even more brisk that day due to the influx of thousands of tourists in our small village for the Food and Wine Festival.

In my grandmother's prized back garden, a podium and microphone, borrowed from the community college, waited for the reading to begin. The village park with its woods adorned in autumn colors was the perfect backdrop for the reading.

Over the five decades that Grandma Daisy had been at the helm of Charming Books, she had been asked to sell the open acres surrounding the shop countless times. She always refused. When I was a teenager, I had thought she turned the offers down because she wanted to keep the land close to the springs clear of development. That might have been part of it, but I now knew the true reason. The Caretaker needed unobstructed access to the springs at all times to gather water for the tree.

The Poe-try Reading was to begin shortly, and a small crowd was already stopping by the refreshment table to partake of Grandma Daisy's cupcakes, the cookies from La Crepe Jolie, and Nathan's wine. Other attendees sat in the four dozen folding chairs we'd set up theater-style in the garden.

Sadie had taken it upon herself to adorn the garden in Poe-appropriate decorations. Pumpkins painted black, silver, and white were sprinkled throughout with arrangements of bloodred chrysanthemums. The color of the flowers brought to mind Anastasia's paper cut again.

After Chief Rainwater had left the night before, I'd collected the tomes of Poe that the shop clearly wanted me to study and took them to my apartment for the night. I'd flipped through the books, but they didn't guide me to read anything in particular. I fell asleep believing that the foreboding I had felt over Anastasia had all been in my head. Maybe the books were telling me only to study up for the reading the next day. I was an expert at denial after all.

The final decoration for the reading was Faulkner. We'd moved his perch into the backyard for the event.

The crow took to his part as the Raven like a duck to water. I knew he would lord this over Emerson at first chance. At present, Emerson, ever the social butterfly, was weaving his way in and around the rows of tourists. The visitors cooed and admired the cat. He drank up their praise and allowed them to scratch him between his two black ears.

"Violet," Sadie gasped. "What are you doing? Where's your dress? You need to change for the reading."

I peered down at my bookshop sweatshirt and jeans. "I was just about to go up."

Sadie was already dressed in a pewter gray silk dress with a deep V-neck. Her hair was twisted on the back of her head in an elaborate knot. I wasn't sure what Poe-esque woman she was going for, maybe Eleonora, but she was beautiful. Her raven black hair was the perfect complement to the dress. I doubted that my strawberry blond waves were what Poe had envisioned when crafting his stories.

"Is everyone else here?" I scanned the crowd looking for the other Red Inkers. Richard was at the podium in a black suit with a white gauzy tie wrapped around his throat. Usually clean-shaven, he had grown a mustache for the reading. He looked like he had stepped out of the pages of a Nathaniel Hawthorne novel, which I supposed for the majority of our guests was close enough to Poe.

Trudy sat in the front row, wearing a blue-and-white-pin-striped dress with puffed sleeves and a white straw hat decorated with matching flowers. "Hey, why does Trudy's dress have color, while mine is black?" I asked.

Sadie giggled. "Because Trudy refuses to wear black

even in the name of Poe. She claims it's morbid, and because that was the only time-period-appropriate dress that wasn't black in her size."

"I'm going to look like a corpse."

"Don't be silly. The black will complement your red gold hair and pale skin. You'll look like Poe's Ligeia herself."

I groaned. "That's just the impression I want to give: murdering ghost. I—" Whatever I was going to say next was cut short by the arrival of David Rainwater. The police chief wore a tweed suit and held a bowler hat in his hand. He carried himself with the assurance of C. Auguste Dupin himself, but unlike with Richard, no one would mistake the police chief for a nineteenth-century poet, and it wasn't just his ethnicity.

"What are you looking at?" Sadie asked as she followed my gaze. "Oh," she said, her mouth making a little O shape as she said it. "But what about Nathan?"

I blinked at the mention of the mayor's name. "What about Nathan?"

"You can't be making goo-goo eyes at another man when you are supposed to be dating Nathan." She folded her arms as if she was preparing to pout.

"First of all, I wasn't making goo-goo eyes at David. I was appreciating the outfit you picked out for him. That bowler hat is amazing."

She snorted.

A little more loudly, I said, "Second of all, Nathan and I are not dating. I can barely call us friends."

"But the wine?" she asked. "Grant told me Nathan gave it to you as a gift."

"Nathan gave it to Charming Books as a gift, not to me personally," I corrected. "You know that he cares about Grandma Daisy."

She rolled her large blue eyes. "While you were away for the last decade plus, Nathan never donated a whole case of ice wine to Charming Books. Now you're back and here's the wine," she said as if somehow that rested her case. Part of me was afraid that it had. "Besides, you have to date him," she went on. "You're perfect for each other. Everyone knows that. I've seen your yearbook pictures. You two were the golden couple of the village when you were in high school until . . ." She trailed off.

I sighed. Until my best friend, Colleen, died in a senseless accident and our lives were torn apart. Nathan stayed in the village after that. I fled, vowing never to return. I would have kept that vow if my own grandmother hadn't tricked me into returning with some made-up story that she was dying. Once she got me here, she revealed my destiny as the Caretaker and convinced me to stay. I didn't repeat any of these thoughts to Sadie; she knew the story except for the Caretaker piece—only Grandma Daisy and I knew that.

"*And*," she said even more earnestly, "you can't leave me to fend for myself against the elder Mortons. I need backup."

There was the real reason that Sadie wanted me to date Nathan. She was engaged to his younger brother, Grant. Nathan and Grant's parents could be . . . difficult. They were overachievers who assumed their sons should be the same way, and when the boys fell short, the elder Mortons did not hold back their criticism.

Grant Morton had more than fallen short of his parents'

dreams for his life. His mistakes and greed had almost landed him in jail. Sadie and Grant had postponed their wedding after the events of the summer, when Grant was caught in an embezzling scheme that had put the town's natural springwater at risk. The only way that Grant got off so easy was by giving up his coconspirators.

Against everyone's advice Sadie stood by her man through the whole ordeal, and according to Sadie, the couple was "taking time to work on their relationship." Now Grant was back working at the family winery and trying to pull his life together. I didn't begrudge him that, but I would have felt a lot better about the whole thing if Sadie had broken it off with him completely. I'd known Grant since we were kids and he always schemed to get ahead, from cheating on tests to organizing a smear campaign against anyone who even considered running against him for student council. It was difficult for me to believe he would completely change his wily ways after a few nights in jail, and I didn't want him to take sweet Sadie down with him.

"Now, go change," she ordered, giving me a gentle shove in the direction of the back door of the shop.

"Okay. Okay," I said, but I smiled, taking the bite out of my words, before I went inside. Instead of walking back into the main part of the shop and going up the spiral staircase that wound around the birch tree, I climbed up the narrow back stairs to my second-floor apartment. The stairs had been used by my ancestors' servants during an era in which it was common to have live-in help. The steps themselves were shallow, made in a time when people's feet where smaller. The only light for the staircase came from the children's book room on the second floor or the kitchen below. But I had been up and down the stairs so many times in my life that I didn't need light to navigate them. I knew every dip and crease in the old wood.

When I emerged in the children's room, it was empty. I peeked over the banister and through the limbs of the birch tree and was happy to see Charming Books' main floor full with customers. Jade, a college student who helped out at the shop when we needed an extra set of hands, stood at the register, checking out a long line of customers.

I smiled. To any shopkeeper, the sound of a cash register drawer opening and closing was welcome. I removed my keys from my jeans pocket and let myself inside the door in the back of the children's room, which led into my apartment. Emerson, who I hadn't known was on my heels, slid around my feet into the narrow living room and jumped on the long royal blue sofa, which had been a housewarming gift from Grandma Daisy. In fact, the entire apartment had been a gift from my grandmother. She had been so confident that I would stay in Cascade Springs after I learned I was the next Caretaker that she'd had the apartment completely remodeled.

As much as I wanted to pause in my living room and admire the space, I went straight for my bedroom.

My dress for the Poe-try Reading hung on the back of my bedroom door. It was black, fitting for Poe's work, and was made of satin. The sleeves puffed at the elbow and the dress was off the shoulder, which had been the fashion of the time. It looked terrifyingly itchy. When I touched the fabric, I was surprised that I found it to be as soft as cotton. The dress must have been an absolute nightmare to iron. I took care not to wrinkle it as I slipped it over my head.

Buttoning the dress by myself was a bit of a challenge, but I was able to reach all the buttons coming up the back except for that last one. I'd find Grandma Daisy or Sadie when I got outside and discreetly ask one of them for help.

I was pleased to see that Sadie had thought to include a black wrap with the dress. That was a welcome sight since the dress was off the shoulder and the reading was outside in October.

There wasn't much time to mess with my hair, so I twisted my wavy strawberry locks into a bun on the back of my head. That hairstyle seemed to be period appropriate to me.

Emerson jumped from my bed and as he did, I saw there was a thin paperback volume of Poe's works where he had been lying. It wasn't any of the volumes I had brought up from the shop the night before. I could say that Emerson had brought it into my apartment, but I knew that wasn't true.

I stepped toward the bed, and to my amazement the pages began to flutter and the book fell open to "The Fall of the House of Usher."

I swallowed. For some reason, the shop wanted me to read this story.

"Violet, are you ready?" My grandmother's voice carried up the stairs. "The reading is about to start."

"I'm coming down," I called back, and picked up the book. There was no time to read the story now, although I knew it well. Surely the blue Victorian that housed Charming Books wasn't as gloomy and cursed as the House of Usher.

There was nowhere in my dress to carry the book, but

it would not seem odd for me to be carrying a volume of Poe's work at the Poe-try Reading. I would fit right in.

When I reached the bottom of the back stairs, I discovered Anastasia in the kitchen, holding a garment bag and still in her street clothes. "Anastasia, we're about to start."

She glared at me. "I know that. I got held up. Where can I change? The public bathroom down here is so tiny that I might break something trying to put this on with no space to maneuver." She held up the bag. As she moved, I caught a faint whiff of strawberries. The scent was odd. Anastasia never struck me as one who wore perfume and if she did, it most certainly wouldn't smell like fruit.

I desperately wanted to ask her what had held her up, but I refrained. "There's no time to waste. I can hear that they've already started. You can use my apartment." I handed her the key. "It's at the top of the stairs. Just return the key to me when you're done."

"Fine." She grabbed the key from my hand and stomped up the stairs.

I watched her go before joining the others outside. I wasn't too enthused about leaving Anastasia alone in my apartment, but I didn't see any way around it. Richard was already giving opening remarks for the reading and I was the first one to read.

Sadie came up behind me and fastened the last button on my dress without being asked.

"Thanks," I whispered.

She smiled. "You're welcome, and you are as beautiful as Poe's Ligeia. Told you you would be."

I would have made a smart remark in return if I hadn't caught Rainwater in his Dupin outfit staring at me from across the lawn. Sadie gave me a little shove toward the podium, spurring me into action.

After I had finished reading my piece, Sadie was at the mic, reading "The Raven." Faulkner chimed in when his line was needed, and the crowd chortled in appreciation. Richard joined me on the sidelines. "Where's Anastasia? She's up next."

I pulled my wrap more tightly around my bare shoulders. "She hasn't come out yet? I gave her the keys to my apartment over a half hour ago so she could change into the costume for the reading."

He shook his head. "I haven't seen her at all. I didn't even know she was here."

My palms began to sweat, making me even more acutely aware of the thin paperback volume of Poe's works that I held in my hands. "I'll go look for her," I whispered. "She might need assistance with her dress and is too embarrassed to come down and ask for help."

He nodded. "I'll read next to stall for time." He returned his attention to Sadie at the podium.

"Nevermore," Faulkner cawed.

I slipped back into the kitchen and headed to the servants' stairs. At the foot of the staircase, I covered my mouth with my hand to stifle a scream. Anastasia Faber, wearing a black governess's dress that looked like it was straight from a production of *Jane Eyre*, lay in a crumpled heap at my feet, and she was most certainly dead.

SIX

I blinked as if to make sure I wasn't imagining the dead woman at my feet. Anastasia's neck was bent at a weird angle. I knew she couldn't possibly be alive, but I squatted beside her and checked her wrist for a pulse. As I did, I caught a strong scent of strawberry. It was much more powerful than it had been when Anastasia stopped me in the kitchen before the reading began.

I scrambled to my feet to escape the scent, which was sickly sweet. I knew it would be the smell that I would always associate with the moment of finding Anastasia's body for the rest of my life. I had left my cell phone in my apartment, since I had nowhere to carry it in my dress. There was a portable phone in the main shop, but I felt if the shoppers there saw my face, they would know something was very wrong.

"Meow," Emerson said at my feet.

I picked up the cat and set him on the kitchen counter. "Stay there," I said, and I slipped out the back door into the garden.

Sadie was no longer at the podium. Richard was at the mic reading a piece in his rich baritone. I immediately recognized it as from "The Fall of the House of Usher," the last story the books had wanted me to read before Anastasia died, the story I hadn't taken the time to read. If I had, would the writer still be alive?

"'My brain reeled as I saw the mighty walls rushing asunder,'" Richard read.

To my relief, Chief Rainwater was off by himself. Instead of a glass of wine in his hand, he held a mug I recognized from the Charming Books kitchen. I walked up to him and, without a word, took him by the hand, leading him back toward the house.

He stared down at our intertwined hands. "Violet?" He set his mug on a garden table.

I put a finger to my lips. "I have to show you something." I urged him inside the kitchen. I didn't stop pulling on his hand until I reached the bottom of the servants' stairs. He stared at Anastasia's body, and I released his hand, which fell limply at his side.

"I didn't want to make a scene with all those people out there," I squeaked. "Richard told me she hadn't come out of the shop, so I went to see if she needed any help with her dress, and—and I just found her there."

"Did you touch the body?" he asked.

I nodded. "But only her wrist. I wanted to make sure she was dead. I mean there is no way she's alive with her neck bent like that, but . . ." I rambled.

He squeezed my hand. "You did the right thing." Then he removed gloves from his jacket pocket. I was surprised he'd thought to put them there. I wondered what else he had inside that jacket. My money was on his badge and a gun. He checked for a pulse like I had and shook his head. "She's gone." He wrinkled his nose.

I knew that he must have smelled the overpowering scent of strawberries that I had.

His brow furrowed as he examined her neck. I finally had to look away.

After a beat, Rainwater stood and removed one of the gloves and took a cell phone from his pocket. "How did you find her?" His voice was all business.

"Just like that." I wrapped my arms more tightly around myself and, in my dress, felt like a shocked member of the cast of *Downton Abbey* when the script took an unbelievable turn. The discovery of Anastasia's body was starting to sink in. She was dead, and she was dead in Charming Books. "I need to tell Grandma Daisy what's going on."

He held up one finger. "Not just yet. I need to call this in. Can you wait in the kitchen?"

Dumbly, I nodded and shuffled into the other room. To my relief, Emerson was still sitting on the counter where I'd put him. I picked up the tuxie and held him under my chin, wrapping the black shawl from my costume around us both.

The kitchen window looked out onto the garden, and I could see what a wonderful time all the tourists were having. They ate cookies, drank wine, and listened with rapt attention to Richard's reading while Anastasia lay in a broken heap just feet away from them.

Despite my protests to Lacey that we would never be able to go through the number of cookies that Adrien baked for the Poe-try Reading, almost all the cookies were gone from the table. Grandma Daisy wove through the audience refilling wineglasses. The Poe-try Reading was a definite success, except for the dead writer at the bottom of the stairs, that is.

The police would have to investigate Anastasia's death. It would shut down the Poe-try Reading. But who was I kidding? The accident might shut Charming Books completely. The shop had insurance for accidents—at least I thought it did—but would it have enough to cover someone dying by tripping down the stairs? I didn't know, and I doubted Grandma Daisy knew either. Anastasia's accident had the potential to ruin us. What would that mean for the tree and the shop itself?

I gave my head a shake. What was I doing worrying about the shop when a woman was dead? At best, Anastasia had been standoffish, and at worst, she had been condescending and rude. But she didn't deserve to die.

Grandma Daisy looked up from the wineglass she was filling and saw me keeping vigil at the window. My face must have revealed something, because she came straight toward the shop.

Grandma Daisy stepped into the kitchen and set the bottle of wine on the counter. "Violet, what's going on? You're as white as a sheet." Before I could answer, she went on, "Where's Anastasia? Richard said that you went inside to fetch her. We need more readers. Sadie and Richard are getting hoarse from all the readings they're doing."

"Grandma, there's been an accident." As I said this, I could hear the sound of approaching sirens.

Chief Rainwater stepped out of the stairway. "No one goes back there until I say. The coroner is on his way."

"The coroner? Why is the coroner coming?" I asked. "Does the coroner usually come for an accident?"

Grandma Daisy's mouth fell open. She looked from Rainwater to me and back again. "Will someone please tell me what's going on?"

"It's Anastasia," I said. "It looks like she fell down the back stairs, and she's—she's dead."

Through the window, I could see that the sound of approaching sirens had distracted the audience from the poem that Sadie was reading. Rainwater went to the door. "I hate to do this, Daisy, but I'm going to have to make an announcement to the crowd. My officers will be here any second."

"What do you have to say to them?" Grandma Daisy asked.

"That there has been an accident, and I will ask them to stay where they are until my officers question them to learn if they witnessed anything."

"But I don't understand," I said. "If Anastasia tripped and fell down the stairs, why would you be concerned about anyone witnessing anything?" Clearly I was missing something and by Rainwater's grim expression it was something important.

"It's only a precaution," Rainwater said. "And so is the coroner."

"This is terrible. Poor Anastasia. Yes, you're right, David—the reading can't go on as if nothing happened.

Anastasia, for all her faults, was one of us." She placed a hand on her cheek. "That wouldn't be right to ignore this tragedy, but is it necessary to question them? Why, that makes it sound like you think there is something more to it than a tragic accident. Do you think it was more than just an accident?" Grandma Daisy said. "Someone could easily fall down the servants' stairs. They are narrow." Grandma Daisy twisted the end of the silk scarf around her index finger so tightly, I was afraid she might cut off the circulation.

"It's only a precaution," he repeated. "In any case, I have to say something. The audience will wonder why the police and EMTs are here."

"Wait," I said. "Let me do it. It will sound much more serious coming from the chief of police. Not," I added quickly, "that it isn't a serious matter, but I don't want to scare anyone."

The sirens were on top of us now and were suddenly cut off. Rainwater's cavalry was here. We couldn't delay any longer. Most of the Poe-try Reading audience were already out of their seats and leaning over the fence to see what the commotion was in the front of the house. We had no time to waste.

He nodded. "Fine. Just say that there's been an accident inside, and we need everyone to remain where they are and stay out of the EMTs' way."

"Should we cancel the reading?" Grandma Daisy asked. "What should we do?"

He glanced back at the narrow doorway that led to the stairs and beyond which Anastasia lay dead. "I think it would be best if you wrapped it up."

Grandma Daisy nodded with a determined set to her jaw. "You're right." She rubbed my arm. "You've had a terrible shock, Violet. Let me do the announcement, and I'll have Richard jump to the closing."

As terrible as I felt to let Grandma Daisy be the one to give the tourists the bad news, I was more than relieved I wouldn't have to do it. I fell onto a stool in the corner of the kitchen with Emerson still nestled against my chest. The cat didn't seem to mind in the least being confined by my shawl.

It was on that stool I had sat at the pinnacle of so many turning points in my life: when my mother died, when Colleen died, when I returned to Cascade Springs that summer my grandmother told me about being the Caretaker. Some Caretaker I had turned out to be. The books tried to warn me that Anastasia was in danger, but I wouldn't or couldn't understand what they were trying to reveal to me.

"Violet?" Rainwater asked softly. "Are you all right? Maybe we should have an EMT take a look at you when they arrive. You could be in shock. That's nothing to mess around with."

"I'm fine," I said, holding Emerson a little more closely. I was glad the thick wrap hid my trembling hands. "But I can't help but think this is my fault," I whispered. "I should have tried harder to warn her."

His amber eyes flashed. Their unusual color had a fiery quality to them that I hadn't noticed before. "Warn her? Warn her of what?"

I could have kicked myself that I'd let the comment slip. Maybe I *was* in shock to have said something so stupid. "Last night when she cut her finger, I had a bad feeling like something was going to happen to her." I met his amber-colored gaze. I broke eye contact and focused on the conversation. "I know that must sound silly to you."

Rainwater touched my arm and squeezed it. "It doesn't sound silly to me. I had the same feeling."

SEVEN

I met his eyes again and saw sincerity there. Before I could ask him what he meant, three police officers entered the kitchen through the shop. One of them was John Wheaton, an officer just a few years younger than me, and Wheaton and I had never been friendly. He had taken an instant dislike to me the moment we met. The police officer wore his hair buzz-cut. I suspected that he chose the haircut because it was reminiscent of the military and made him appear more intimidating. For all I knew, Wheaton might have been in the armed services.

Wheaton scowled at Rainwater's hand on my arm. "What do you have, *Chief*?" He said "Chief" with just enough edge to let it be known that he was certain Rainwater wasn't deserving of the title.

Rainwater dropped his hand from my arm and straightened to his full six-two height. Wheaton was only a couple of inches shorter than the police chief, but he seemed to get the message and took half a step back.

"Forty-five-year-old female dead on the back stairs." Rainwater's tone was all business. "The victim is Anastasia Faber. It appears she fell down the steps and broke her neck in the fall. Apparent accident."

"It's no wonder," one of the other officers said after peeking around the corner into the stairwell, "if she was coming down those stairs. There is no light and they are so narrow, I can't fit my entire foot on one of those steps."

A feeling of dread washed over me. Charming Books was going to be sued. There was no way around it. I tried to think of who in Anastasia's life would bring the case forward. No one came to mind. In fact, no one came to mind when I thought about Anastasia at all. I blinked back tears as the lonesomeness that Anastasia must have endured hit me. In the few months I had known her, I couldn't recall one mention of any family, not even in passing. Could it be possible that she didn't have any family? Would there be anyone left behind who might mourn her death? I felt woozy and settled back on my stool. I was afraid that if I stood up, I would topple over.

"Clear case of accident, wouldn't you say?" the officer who made the comment about the stairs said.

"Nothing's clear until the coroner makes his judgment," Rainwater replied. I felt his gaze on me.

What did that mean? What did Rainwater discover when he examined Anastasia's body that I had missed? I knew there must be something. I swallowed. It was like Benedict's death all over again. Colleen's death even. Was I never to escape this type of circumstance as long as I lived in Cascade Springs? And since being the Caretaker was a life sentence, that would be a very long time.

"Take another officer and collect the names and pertinent information from the Poe-try Reading audience. We don't have much to keep them here, and I want to get as many names as we can before they disperse. In case we need to speak to them again."

"Why would we need to do that, sir?" the young officer asked.

"It's just a precaution" was Rainwater's answer.

I was becoming very tired of that phrase.

"And," I heard Chief Rainwater say through my dark and hazy thoughts, "send an EMT over to check on Miss Waverly. She might be in shock."

"The EMTs are already here, sir. I will meet them outside and let them know about Miss Waverly." The officer moved toward the doorway where the staircase was. This was my chance to leave the kitchen. I didn't think I could stand any more talk about broken necks, and I knew Grandma Daisy must need my help dealing with the tourists at the Poe-try Reading, or what was left of it. I started to stand.

"Not so fast." An EMT carrying a medical kit entered through the back door. "We need to check you out before you can leave."

I frowned. "I don't need to be checked out. I'm perfectly fine."

"Sorry, miss," the EMT said, gently pushing me back onto the stool by placing his large hand on my shoulder. He had kind brown eyes set back in his dark skin. "The chief says we have to check you out, and he's the boss."

Emerson, who had concealed himself in the folds of my shawl, popped his head out right under my chin and meowed.

"Well, hello," the EMT said. "Who do we have here?"

Emerson lifted his chin, inviting the EMT to give him a scratch.

The paramedic obliged. "I'm afraid you're going to have to let go of the cat, so I can get an accurate reading with the blood pressure cuff."

"All right," I muttered, and reluctantly, I released Emerson. He jumped from my lap gracefully to the black-and-white checkerboard tiled floor.

The EMT read my blood pressure with a serious expression on his face.

"What's the prognosis, Doctor?" I joked.

"I'm not a doctor, and some of the MDs at the hospital would be alarmed you called me one." He grinned. His bright white teeth gleamed against his mocha-colored skin. "You can just call me Keenan." He removed the cuff. "Even though I'm not a doctor, I predict you'll be fine. You've had a shock. Your blood pressure and pulse are elevated, which is understandable, given the circumstances." He placed his fingers on my wrist again and looked at his watch. When he let go of my hand, he said, "Your pulse is already falling back to normal."

I smiled, grateful for his kindhearted teasing. It was what I needed at that moment. I glanced out the window again to see how Grandma Daisy was faring with breaking up the Poe-try Reading. Many of the members of the audience were out of their seats and whispering to one another. Clearly, they knew whatever had happened in Charming

Books was much more than a small accident to call the attention of so many police and EMTs, especially in the middle of the Cascade Springs Food and Wine Festival.

As Rainwater had ordered, two of his officers moved from person to person collecting names and information. They made notes on minuscule notepads. Some of the audience members were standoffish, while others almost seemed to enjoy talking to the police, or at least, that's how it appeared through the window.

I frowned when I saw the man with the guitar whom I'd seen while riding my bike the day before, standing just outside the white picket fence. He held the neck of his guitar and scanned the crowd as if he was searching for someone in particular.

"Violet?" Keenan asked.

I could tell from the tone of his voice that it wasn't the first time he had tried to grab my attention.

I turned away from the window. "Yes?"

The corner of his mouth tilted up. "I just told you to take it easy for the rest of the day."

Take it easy? How could I take it easy when one of the Red Inkers was dead in the back of Charming Books?

He rolled up his blood pressure cuff. "If you don't, David might come after me, and I don't really need that."

"David?" I asked, still feeling slightly dazed from seeing the man with the guitar through the window. There was something about him that gave me goose bumps. It was almost as if I thought that I should know him, even though I had seen him for the first time only the day before. When I looked out the window again, the man was gone.

"Chief Rainwater," Keenan said. "I suppose I should

call him by his official title when we're on the job. On Dungeons & Dragons nights he's just David."

My eyebrows shot sky-high. "Chief Rainwater plays Dungeons & Dragons?"

"Oh yeah, he's the one who started the club in the village. We play at least once a week. David can't make it every week between being the police chief and the fact that he spends every spare moment writing his book."

My eyebrows shot up a little farther with this new information about the chief of police. He sounded like a true Renaissance man. Chief, writer, role-playing game aficionado. It just seemed a little too good to be true. I wondered what else I didn't know about Chief David Rainwater. Every tidbit I learned made me that much more curious about him. Briefly, I wondered if that really was his appeal. Nathan I knew. I knew him better than almost anyone in my life. Rainwater was a mystery.

"Hey," he said. "Next time we play, you should join us. I think you would really like it."

"I've never played Dungeons & Dragons before. I'm afraid I would just slow you all down."

He gave me a lopsided grin. "I'm sure David would bring you up to speed in no time. Until then, put your feet up," he went on. "Read a book. You have plenty of those around here, I gather." He chuckled at his own joke.

His comment brought my thoughts back to the situation at hand. Read a book. That was just it. Had I read a book, the book that the shop had wanted me to read, Anastasia might still be alive.

EIGHT

After Keenan said I was free to go, I slipped out the back door of Charming Books into the garden. Despite Rainwater's officers' best efforts to question the crowd about what they might have seen or heard, many of them had left the Poe-try Reading. The few that remained watched the police coming and going from the shop with ghoulish attention. Perhaps they were hoping for an exciting story about their visit to Cascade Springs they could tell their friends and family back home. Grandma Daisy, Richard, Sadie, and Trudy huddled together. The man with the guitar was gone as well. I wondered if I'd imagined him being there in the first place.

Sadie waved me over to their group. "Violet, are you all right?" She gave me a hug so tight it nearly took my breath away. Despite her petite frame, she was strong from moving heavy dress forms around her shop. "I can't believe what has happened." There was a tremor in her voice. "Poor Anastasia."

Trudy sniffed. "Poor Anastasia, my eye."

We all stared at her.

Trudy folded her arms. In her pin-striped period dress, she looked like a geriatric Mary Poppins that was just about to break into song except for the scowl on her deeply wrinkled face. "I'm not saying I wished the woman dead, goodness knows, but I will not pretend I liked her now that she is gone. She was rude and uppity. I'm sorry she's dead, but I won't pretend I will miss her."

I winced at Trudy's harsh words. I wasn't necessarily a fan either, but I'd never be so blunt about someone who had passed. Truthfully, I found myself wondering if perhaps I should've been kinder or tried harder to see past Anastasia's cantankerous demeanor. Maybe there was a reason she was so guarded and quick to lash out at others.

"Even so," Grandma Daisy said evenly, "I have to echo Sadie's sentiments as to 'poor Anastasia.' It's just so terrible."

Richard nodded. "To fall down the stairs like that, to lose her life in such a senseless accident. Anastasia must be furious to know that was how she died."

If it was *an accident,* I thought. I hoped that I was wrong, but I suspected that Chief Rainwater didn't believe that it was. I cleared my throat, eager to change the subject. "Did you all see a man with a guitar wandering around here?"

Trudy adjusted her pocketbook on her arm. "You must mean Fenimore. I thought I saw him lurking about a little while ago."

"Fenimore?" I asked.

She nodded. "He's a troubadour. He floats from village to village playing his harmonica and guitar for tips. He is usually here every year for the Food and Wine Festival."

"I'd never seen him at the festival before," I said.

She waved away my comment. "Well, only in the last few years, then. I don't think I ever saw him before you left the village. Knowing Fenimore, he was here for the free cookies. He has a knack for sniffing out free eats."

"I've seen the man a few times myself." Richard touched his Poe mustache as if he was surprised to find it still there. "Does he just go by 'Fenimore'? What's his last name?"

Trudy shrugged. "Can't say that I've ever heard it. He's always introduced himself as Fenimore. There was nothing more than that."

"Violet, Daisy." Rainwater stood in the doorway of the shop. "May I have a word?"

I swallowed.

Grandma Daisy took my hand and gave it a little squeeze before we walked over to the chief together.

I linked my arm through my grandmother's to demonstrate that we were a united front. We could survive this. We had survived much worse. "What happened?" I asked. "Did she trip down the stairs?"

"It *appears* that's what happened. Everything points to that, but the coroner and I agree that something is off about her fall."

"What do you mean 'off'?" Grandma Daisy asked.

"I can't put my finger on it, but we've decided we will do a complete investigation."

"Like a murder investigation?" My pulse quickened.

He shook his head. "I wouldn't call it anything like that just yet, but it is most certainly a suspicious death."

"Are you saying someone pushed her down the stairs?" Grandma Daisy asked.

"No, no. There is no evidence of that."

"Then how else can her death be anything but an accident?" Grandma Daisy tightened her hold on my arm.

He pursed his lips together in a thin line. The police chief knew more than what he was saying. "I called you over to tell you that we will have to close down Charming Books while the investigation is going on." His brows dipped down as if in regret to have to share this news with us.

Grandma Daisy gasped. "But it's the festival. This is the busiest time for—"

Grandma's protest was interrupted by someone shouting my name. "Violet!"

My stomach dropped. I knew that voice as well as my own. Grandma Daisy's fingers dug into my arm as if she felt my body tense, ready to leap into the flight response. There was no way to escape.

Mayor Nathan Morton strode through the side gate. The autumn sunshine gleamed off the top of his blond, perfectly styled hair, and his suit was pressed and tailored to his body. He didn't wear a tie, but his shirt was open at the throat. As it was the weekend, I guessed he wanted to give off the impression of the approachable village mayor for the Food and Wine Festival. His dark brown eyes were focused on me. He reached me before I had the willpower to break eye contact. "Violet, are you all right? I heard there was an accident at Charming Books and someone was hurt." He took a deep, shaky breath. "I got here as soon as I could." He took a step closer to me. "Please tell me you're all right."

There was such naked and sincere concern in his eyes that something got stuck in my throat, and I couldn't speak.

"Mayor Morton," Rainwater said. His tone was respectful, but clearly he was not pleased to see Nathan there.

"Chief Rainwater." Nathan nodded in return and spoke in the same expressionless tone of voice. "Tell me what happened."

Rainwater was quiet for a moment as if he was trying to decide what to say. When it came down to it, Nathan was his boss, and he had to answer him. "Anastasia Faber fell down the back stairs of Charming Books. She broke her neck in the fall and died."

"So it was just an accident." Nathan exhaled a breath.

"At first glance, yes," the police chief countered. "But we need to do a thorough investigation."

Nathan's perfect brow wrinkled. "I don't think that is necessary if this was so clearly an accident."

"With all due respect, sir, both the county coroner and I agree that a suspicious death investigation is required."

"On what grounds?"

"I'm not at liberty to say, sir."

Nathan's jaw flexed. "Very well, but I am here to be of service to Violet and Grandma Daisy."

I swallowed as he called my grandmother by the

endearment. It shouldn't have bothered me. It was the name that all my childhood friends called my grandmother, and Nathan had been calling her that his whole life.

"Nathan," Grandma Daisy said, interrupting the two men scowling at each other. "David was just telling us we'll have to close Charming Books because of what happened."

"Is this a murder investigation, Chief?" Nathan frowned. "I see no other reason for you to ask the Waverlys to close their shop in the middle of the Food and Wine Festival otherwise."

Rainwater folded his arms. The fabric of his tweed coat strained across his chest as he moved. He was still wearing his Dupin costume, although the bowler hat was gone. "It is a suspicious death. The coroner will know more after he examines the body more thoroughly. It's always better to follow procedure in order to protect the rights of every citizen."

Nathan nodded. "I agree, but I don't see why you have to close down the entire store because of that. With a building of Charming Books' size, it should be no trouble to quarantine off the place where the woman fell."

"I respect your opinion, Mr. Morton, but the coroner and I agree that it would be best to close the shop for the day at least and do everything by the book."

Nathan shook his head. "That would never do. This is the Food and Wine Festival. Chief, there must be something that you can do. If you close the Waverlys down all weekend, you're putting their entire business at risk."

"I don't think it is as bad as that," I said, coming to Rainwater's defense. "One day won't put us out of business, and maybe we can open by tomorrow." I gave a hopeful look to the police chief, but his expression was impassive.

Okay, maybe not.

Nathan frowned at me like I was arguing for the other side. "If the Waverlys can't make sales from inside their shop, at least you can compromise and let them sell books outside."

Grandma Daisy clapped her hands. "That's a wonderful idea, Nathan. A sidewalk sale! In fact, I think it'll do even more to attract visitors, and there is nothing to be said that we couldn't continue the Poe-try Reading out front. It will be less formal, but that can't be helped. We will just tell the audience that there will be an intermission. We should be able to have everything moved and restart the reading in that amount of time."

"A great idea, Grandma Daisy." Nathan beamed at her.

Rainwater frowned. "I suppose there's no harm in that as long as my officers supervise what is taken from the shop."

"Good," Nathan said with a curt nod. "Why don't we go inside and start selecting the books you'd like to bring outside?" He waved the Red Inkers over. "Your friends can help, and I'm sure we can scare up a few more volunteers. You can't object to that, can you, Chief Rainwater?"

I glanced at the police chief. The hard lines of his face seemed to be sharper than before as he clenched his jaw. "I have no objection, but no one goes into the kitchen."

"Of course," Nathan said smoothly. "We want everyone to follow protocol."

A thought just dawned on me. I couldn't believe I hadn't thought about it before. "What about my apartment? Will I be allowed back into my apartment today?"

David shook his head. "That is a particular place of interest. Isn't it where Anastasia changed for the Poe-try Reading?"

"Yes, but—"

"In that case," Rainwater went on, "we need to search it as well. Do you know what room she changed in?"

"No, not exactly. I only gave her the key to my apartment. I would guess my bedroom. I told her to use my apartment. I didn't give her any more direction than that. It's small and there are only a few places that she could have comfortably changed her clothes."

"We found her garment bag and her other clothes on your bed," the police chief said.

I frowned. Why had he asked if he already knew the answer? A blush crept across my face when I realized I was still wearing the black dress. "I can understand why you wouldn't want me to go back into the apartment." I gestured to my dress. "But you can't expect me to wear this all day. Can't I at least change my clothes?"

Rainwater nodded. "If you go up through the front stairs and let yourself in that way." He paused. "And one of my officers will have to go with you."

"Not Officer Wheaton, I hope." I wrinkled my nose.

He shook his head. "I will ask Officer Clipton to accompany you."

"Have I met him before?" I thought that I had met everyone in the tiny village police department that summer when Grandma Daisy had been a murder suspect.

He smiled. "I don't think so. Officer Veronika Clipton is a new hire."

My face was hot again. Some great feminist I was by assuming that Rainwater's officer was a man. "Wait, I need my key to get into the apartment. Has anyone found it? Was . . ." I trailed off. I was about to ask if it was with Anastasia.

The police chief seemed to understand the direction of my questioning. "The key was in Anastasia's hand."

Something about this small detail of Anastasia's death turned my stomach. She had the key in her hand because she was going to return it to me. Had she fallen in her rush to return the key? That didn't sound like Anastasia. I couldn't imagine her being in a hurry for anyone other than herself. I internally winced at my uncharitable thoughts and was glad that no one else could hear them. I bit on my lip. I was the one who'd given her the key. If I hadn't and told her to change somewhere on the first floor of Charming Books, would she still be alive? Was her death at least in part my fault?

"Vi," Nathan said. "You're not responsible for that poor woman's death. It was a freak accident."

I stared at Nathan, surprised that he could so easily interpret my expressions like he had when we were teenagers. Back then, it seemed he always knew what I was thinking. At least he had until Colleen died.

Grandma Daisy removed her key ring from her pocket

and slipped off one of the silver keys from the ring. "Here, take my spare key to your apartment. You can keep it until you get yours back."

It would be a while before I got my own key back, since it was now evidence in a police investigation, and we all knew it. I folded my fingers around the key.

NINE

Officer Veronika Clipton was a petite woman who looked like she was fresh from the police academy with flushed cheeks and bright green eyes. Her blue police uniform did nothing to hide her shapely figure. She moved with the ease of an athlete. I suspected when she rode a bike, she never fell off it like I did . . . on a regular basis. I followed her up the spiral staircase to the second floor of Charming Books but couldn't stop myself from looking behind me. Grandma Daisy and Nathan were below, directing the Red Inkers and the volunteers they'd conscripted off the street as to what should be moved to the front yard for the sidewalk sale. I didn't spot the police chief. I imagined he had returned to the crime scene behind the kitchen.

"Oh my!" the officer said, and paused at the top of the stairs. She had stepped into the children's room, which resembled a woodland fairy paradise. "This is amazing." Her voice held as much awe as that of any child seeing the space for the first time.

"It's always been my favorite spot in the shop."

"I can see why." She shuffled into the room. "I would have loved this as a kid. I still love it as an adult, but as a child this would be pure magic."

Magic. It was funny that she chose the word.

I lifted my long black skirt and took the last few steps to join her on the landing. I couldn't wait to get the dress off. I hoped that I would never have an occasion to wear it again, because I was certain it would always remind me of Anastasia's death.

I crossed the children's room and unlocked the door that led into my apartment with Grandma Daisy's key, giving me an unobstructed view of my living room.

Slowly, I pushed the door inward. I don't know what I expected to find. The police had already searched my home. Everything was where it should be, but something felt off. I had a sense that my possessions had been moved or shifted, but I couldn't pick out which ones had been touched. Perhaps they all had been. I tentatively stepped into the room with Officer Clipton on my heels.

The stack of five Edgar Allan Poe books still sat on the coffee table in front of my couch. The pile was slightly askew. A rendering of Poe's face with his luxurious black mustache and penetrating eyes stared back at me, and I felt the guilt over Anastasia's death settle on my shoulders. It was a familiar feeling. I had carried Colleen's death with me for twelve years until I was finally able to let it go over the summer when I learned the full story of what had happened to her. I couldn't go back to that place of carrying someone's death on my conscience. I knew the only way to avoid that would be to find out what had happened to Anastasia, and if Rainwater discovered her death was the result of foul play, then that meant finding her killer.

I don't know how long I stood in my living room coming to this decision, but it must have been longer than I thought, because Officer Clipton cleared her throat. "I thought you wanted to change out of that dress, but if you want to keep wearing it, that's okay." She paused. "I guess you could say it makes a statement."

I looked down at the black satin dress with its intricate lace overlay. It was a beautiful dress, but I most certainly wanted it off.

Officer Clipton picked up the top volume of Poe books off the end table. "Why so many versions of the same book? Do they each say something different or something?"

"They are each different selections of his works, except the one on the bottom, which is Poe's complete works. The forewords are different, each commissioned by a different publisher to write them, but they all contain Poe's best-known works like 'The Fall of the House of Usher' and 'The Tell Tale Heart.'"

"I think the chief mentioned you were some kind of professor or something. Is that why you have so many?" Her question was casual and sounded friendly enough, but something about it put me on guard. Officer Clipton was gathering information about me through this casual exchange. Unlike Officer Wheaton, whose approach to questioning was downright hostile, Officer Clipton was subtle and got her quarry to trust her. I had no doubt she was an excellent police officer, but I had had enough dealings with the police to be wary of any questions and how I answered them, no matter how innocent they might seem on the surface.

"I wanted to make sure I had everything I needed for the reading." That explanation sounded lame even to me.

"If you say so. I'm not much for reading." She said this in a confessional tone as if she were admitting some great failing.

It was a tone I was used to as a college English professor. For some reason, students felt they needed to tell me that they didn't like to read. Some said it with trepidation like Officer Clipton had, and others stated it with bravado as if it were something to be proud of.

"You just haven't met the right book yet. I bet I could turn you into a reader." As the Caretaker, I knew I could.

She laughed. "I doubt that." She set the book back on the table.

Seeing the stack of Poe collections made me wonder what had happened to Anastasia's copy of Poe, the one she'd cut her finger on the day before. "Did Anastasia have anything else with her when she fell down the stairs other than my key? She should have had a copy of Poe's works with her. I could have sworn I saw it in her hand when she arrived along with the garment bag." I closed my eyes briefly, trying to think back to that moment when I almost ran into Anastasia in the kitchen.

Officer Clipton's face clouded over, and I knew I had pushed my luck too far. "You'll have to take questions like that to the chief." She changed the subject. "You had better get changed. The chief doesn't want us up here very long. The crime scene guys will need to process your bedroom."

"Process my bedroom?" I asked.

"Anastasia's garment bag and clothes were on your bed. We need to see what else she touched in here."

I wrinkled my nose at the thought of Anastasia poking her nose into my things. Not that I owned anything of real value. There was some costume jewelry that had been my mother's, but that was sentimental to me. It certainly wouldn't impress Anastasia.

Rather than argue, I went into the bedroom with the female police officer on my heels. I felt Officer Clipton watching me as I collected the jeans and the sweatshirt with the shop's logo on it that I'd had on earlier in the day. I carried them to the adjoining bathroom.

"Where are you going?" she asked.

"You really don't expect me to change in front of you. I mean isn't that taking this a little far?"

Her face turned a slight shade of pink that would have been beet red on my pale skin. "Right. Go ahead."

In the bathroom, I quickly changed out of the dress and hung it on the back of the bathroom door. I was relieved to have the dress off. I felt lighter not being weighed down with so much fabric. I slipped into my jeans and sweatshirt, feeling much more like myself. I removed the band holding my hair in a tight bun and allowed my long wavy strawberry blond hair to fall to my shoulders. That was more like it.

Back in my bedroom, Emerson sauntered into the room through the open door that connected to the living room.

The police officer blinked at him. "How did that cat get in here?"

"He's my cat, and he lives here. He has free run of my

apartment and of the shop." I didn't say "and of the town," because I feared Officer Clipton would enforce leash laws if there was such a thing for cats in the village.

She sniffed. "We can't have him creeping around up here. He could contaminate the crime scene."

There wasn't much Officer Clipton and I could do to keep Emerson out of a place that he wanted to be. He was a determined feline and a master at breaking and entering, but I thought it was best not to share any of this with the young police officer. "I'll take him with me."

She edged around Emerson.

"Are you afraid of cats?" I asked, noticing that she was more than a little alarmed every time Emerson came within three feet of her.

"Not afraid." She sneezed. "Allergic."

I plucked a tissue from a box on the nightstand beside my bed and handed it to her. Then I picked up Emerson to stop him from leaping on Officer Clipton and sending her to the emergency room with an allergic reaction.

She sneezed. "Do you have everything you need?"

The cat wriggled in my arms so fiercely I had to let him go to avoid being scratched.

I grabbed my cell phone from the nightstand and shoved it into the back pocket of my jeans. I was happy she didn't say I had to leave it behind. Not that I thought she saw me with Emerson circling her like a shark on the hunt. If I didn't know better, I would say my tuxie was purposely distracting the police officer so I could grab my phone without being noticed.

TEN

After Officer Clipton, Emerson, and I left my apartment, I locked the door after me, and Officer Clipton went down the spiral staircase first. I followed her with Emerson in my arms.

I noticed there were a number of the smaller bookcases missing from the shop.

By the time I got outside, Nathan had already mobilized the Red Inkers and some passersby to move the books and shelves that Grandma Daisy wanted to use for the sidewalk sale into the front yard. With the village mayor at the helm, Charming Books was all set up.

"What do you think?" Nathan asked me.

"I'm impressed," I said. "I can't believe you did all this so quickly."

He shrugged. "Getting people to do what I need them to do is one of my gifts."

How well I knew.

Nathan watched me for a moment. "The only person my charms don't work on is you."

My body tensed. I needed to keep this conversation on the shop. It could too easily veer into other topics that I didn't want to discuss with the village mayor. "I know Grandma Daisy appreciates the help. Thank you for the wine as well. Grandma Daisy was thrilled to get it."

"And you? Were you thrilled?"

"It was very kind." I kept my voice neutral.

"Violet, I don't think we can go on like this. At first, I thought it was adorable you were playing so hard to get. You were punishing me, I understand that. I know I deserve it after what I put you through when we were kids, but—"

"I'm not punishing anyone," I interrupted him. "Least of all not you."

"Oh?" He arched his eyebrow at me.

Was Nathan right? Was I punishing him? I told him months ago that I forgave him for everything that had happened between us after Colleen died. I lowered my voice. "I'm not punishing you." I bit my lip, not sure I could explain how I felt. "I don't know what to do with you."

"I'm not asking you to do anything with me. All I'm saying is I miss you. I didn't realize how much until you reappeared this past summer as if out of thin air. In all that time, no one ever replaced you to me."

I didn't know what to say. No one had replaced Nathan in my life either, but there was the small fact he had been willing to let me go to jail for a crime I didn't commit just because he didn't want to get involved. Forgiving and forgetting were two very different things. I cared about him still, but I didn't know that I could trust him. "We can talk about this later. I should help Grandma Daisy. The yard is filling up with customers."

"All right," he said, if not conceding the war, at least conceding the battle. "But the next time I see you jump into the bushes, I might just dive in there after you."

I turned away so he couldn't see the flush that filled my cheeks.

"Violet!" a voice called.

I turned to see Lacey running up the street, holding a bakery box. Her face was flushed red, and one of her silver barrettes dangled beside her ear.

I met her on the sidewalk. "Lacey, are you all right?"

She bent at the waist, trying to catch her breath. "I'm fine," she gasped. "Adrien and I just heard the news about Anastasia, and I came running at the first chance I had to make sure you were all right."

"We are okay, Lacey. Thank you," I said, touched by her concern.

She gave a sigh of relief. "I'm so glad." She held the bakery box out to me. "Adrien boxed up some more cookies for you. He copes with bad news by feeding people."

I took the box from her and smiled. "Since I cope with stress with sugar, we are well matched."

"I need to get back to the festival. We're so incredibly busy. It's hard to keep up." She glanced around. "You will tell Daisy that we're thinking of you two?"

"I will," I promised.

She squeezed my free hand. "You know you can come

to Adrien and me any time you're in trouble. We're there to help."

"I do," I said, making another promise.

When I turned back to the sidewalk sale, I found Nathan had gone. I wasn't sure if I was relieved or disappointed to see he'd disappeared. The fact that I found myself conflicted at all as far as Nathan was concerned was truly worrisome.

I set the new box of cookies on the refreshment table. A young couple stood a few feet away from me poking at the books. I saw them as the perfect escape from this conversation.

"What are you looking for?" I asked the couple.

"A gift for my father," the woman said. "He's retiring and he likes books. At least I always see him reading something. I just never paid much attention to what he read."

"I'm sure we have just the book for your father here. What are his interests?"

She made a pained expression. The man beside her, who I assumed was her boyfriend because neither of them wore any rings, appeared bored. If I wanted to make this sale, I would have to do it fast before he convinced her to leave Charming Books and head to the food and wine tents on the Riverwalk.

"Let me see," I murmured. We stood in front of a bookcase of romance fiction. I didn't know the girl's father, of course, but I was betting this wouldn't be his first choice for reading. Nevertheless, I ran my finger along the spines. As I passed one of the books, it popped off the shelf.

A travelogue about Ireland fell to the grass at the girl's

feet. She bent to pick it up. "This is perfect. Now I remember that Dad said he always dreamed about going to Ireland after he retired." She hugged the book to her chest. "He will think I'm the most thoughtful daughter in the world for remembering that, and to think it was mixed in with the romance novels. I never would have found it if I had gone to the travel section. How strange. It was meant to be."

How strange indeed.

The girl grabbed her boyfriend by the hand and dragged him over to the makeshift sales table that Grandma Daisy had set up near the front gate.

"That's interesting that there was a travel book shelved with the romances," Trudy said.

I jumped. I hadn't even known she was there. I covered my surprise by straightening the books on the shelves. "Well, the books were moved out into the yard in such a rush, it's not surprising a few titles might have been misplaced."

Trudy frowned as if she was suspicious of my story. My former first-grade teacher had a knack for sniffing out a liar. I had seen her make children confess to all sorts of crimes when I had been in her classroom. I squirmed under her scrutiny, but I didn't crack. I came close, but I couldn't reveal my family secret even to my first-grade teacher.

Faulkner swooped over our heads and landed on the bookcase. "Nevermore."

Trudy nodded. "Well then, I had best get back to your grandmother and help her save what is left of the Poe-try Reading."

I gave a sigh of relief as she marched away. Although she held an old wooden cane in her hand, she carried it above the grass. She didn't need it to keep her back straight and her stride strong. I hoped that when I was Trudy's age, I had half her gumption and energy.

Within a half hour, I had to admit that Nathan had been right to suggest the sidewalk sale. Business in Charming Books' front yard was brisk. Part of that could be attributed to the extra traffic on River Road from the Food and Wine Festival, and maybe some of the shoppers were there to sneak a peek where there had been an accident. However, from the customers' chatter it appeared most of the shoppers were blissfully unaware of Anastasia's demise.

A clean-shaven man stepped through the opened gate. He clearly wasn't from the village. His clothes had an expensive look to them. The collar sticking out of his cashmere sweater appeared to have been starched to within an inch of its life. I suspected he was from the city, and not Buffalo, which was the closest large city to Cascade Springs. He was from the Big Apple. More than the clothes, it was his shoes that gave him away. They were just too shiny to be from around here. There were many wealthy vineyard owners in the village, like the Mortons, but no one in the village had shoes that shiny because everyone was so accustomed to walking.

It wasn't the likelihood that the man was from the city that piqued my interest in him. It wasn't uncommon for visitors to come to Cascade Springs for a long weekend to visit the natural springs themselves or visit the wineries.

No, what caught my attention was the way that he held the book he had plucked from the shelf in his hand. He was staring at the back as if engrossed in the book's description, but the book was upside down.

I sidled over to him. "Can I help you find something?"

He shook his head. "No. I'm just deciding whether or not I would like to read this book."

I took the book from his hand and turned it around the right way. "It might be easier to make the decision if you can read it." I smiled. "Unless you have a knack for reading upside down. That would be a pretty good trick."

His face flushed as red as mine ever got. "Right."

I examined the book. It was a movie starlet's biography. I wouldn't have pegged him for a celebrity follower, but something I had learned from Charming Books is you can never know what a person would like to read just by appearances. The most docile grandmother might want the horror novels, and the goth teenager might be looking for cookbooks. Outward appearances were deceiving when it came to reader preferences.

"If you like this biography, I can suggest a few others that you might also like. It might help you make your decision."

"No, I don't need any help. Thank you." He pursed his lips together in a tense line, and I knew it was time to back away. It was never a good idea to go in for the hard sale with a New Yorker.

"Just let me know if you need anything, then." I started in the direction of another customer, who looked completely bewildered by the adult coloring book collection.

He stopped me. "Actually, you might be able to help me."

I turned back to face him.

He put the book he held back on the shelf. "But not with a book."

I arched an eyebrow. "Books are my specialty, but I can try."

"I'm looking for my friend E—I mean—Anastasia Faber. I heard that she might be here today. There was some type of event going on at this shop she was involved with." He glanced around and seemed to note the police presence. "I thought it was a reading of some sort. I have to say the village seems to be very secure. I was surprised to see so many police cars on this road."

"The village takes the Food and Wine Festival seriously." My pulse quickened. If he was looking for Anastasia and didn't know why there were so many police cars parked near Charming Books, he must not know she was dead.

"How do you know Anastasia?" I asked, stalling before telling him the news.

He frowned. "I told you she's a friend of mine. I'm visiting from out of town for your festival, and I wanted to drop in and see her while she was here. She was the one who told me about the reading. Where will it be? I must have written the time down wrong."

I shook my head. "You didn't write it down wrong. The reading should be starting up again at any moment. We took an"—I searched for the word Grandma Daisy had used—"intermission."

"Is Anastasia inside, then?"

He claimed to be Anastasia's friend. Was he her boy-friend? I wondered. I supposed that it was possible. The man was at least ten years younger than Anastasia, but that was no reason to disregard the possibility. "Are you a close friend of Anastasia's?" I asked, testing the waters and watching for his reaction.

"Not a very close friend. I'm more of—a family friend."

He was lying. A family friend had to be a euphemism for something else, but I didn't think there was a romantic attachment either. I couldn't keep pumping him for infor-mation all the while knowing that Anastasia was dead. "I actually have some bad news. There's been an acci-dent." I paused. "Anastasia died earlier this afternoon. It was completely unexpected. I know the police must be trying to notify her family. Maybe you can help them since you are a close friend of the family."

"She's dead?" He staggered as if the news were some type of physical blow. "That's not possible."

"Maybe you should talk to the police." I stepped toward him with my hand outstretched to keep him from falling.

He dodged out of the way. "No—no. I have to go."

Before I could stop him, he ran through the gate, his black scarf flying behind him like a cape. Part of me wanted to run after him, but I knew I would never find him as he melted into the crowded street. I needed to tell Chief Rainwater about my encounter. I was kicking myself that I hadn't asked the man his name.

Grandma Daisy waved me over to the cash register, where she was ringing up another sale.

I scanned the yard for Rainwater or another of his officers I could tell about Anastasia's friend, but the only officer I saw was Wheaton standing on Charming Books' wide front porch with his arms folded across his chest genie-style, watching the activity in the front yard. I most certainly didn't want to talk to him. He had thought Grandma Daisy committed murder that summer. Even when it was obvious Grandma Daisy had nothing to do with Benedict's murder, Wheaton was determined to prove she did it because he disliked me so much. The feeling was mutual.

"Violet, Richard and Trudy have everything together to resume the Poe-try Reading." She pointed to the far side of the yard where the podium and microphone now stood in the corner. "We were wondering if you could draw the crowd's attention."

I grimaced. As a college professor, I wasn't afraid of speaking in public, but I didn't know why Richard couldn't grab the crowd's attention.

"All right," I agreed. Before I crossed the yard, I turned back to my grandmother. "Grandma Daisy, did Anastasia have any family? I can't remember her speaking of anyone. You've known her much longer than I have."

Trudy overheard my question. She was still wearing her pin-striped dress, which was perfectly suited for her. It was like she stepped out of a garden party on Martha's Vineyard over a century ago. The only thing that ruined the image was the tourists milling about in jeans and sweaters. "She has a brother. He doesn't live in the village any longer, but I imagine her estate would go to him unless she wrote a will cutting him out of it."

"Would she do that?" I asked.

Trudy sniffed. "If he upset her for some reason. I wouldn't put it past Anastasia to cut family out of her life and her will."

"Do you know him?"

She nodded. "I knew him. I had both he and Anastasia in school. She was two years ahead of her brother. Coleridge lit out of the village almost as fast as you after he graduated high school."

I grimaced. "You had Anastasia in school?"

"Of course, I did. I had everyone in my class if they grew up in the village while I was in the classroom. I taught the first graders for over forty years. They finally had to force me to retire to get me to leave the students. Being a teacher is what I excelled in."

"But now in retirement you have time to fulfill your lifelong dream of being a published author," Grandma Daisy said. "You wouldn't have time for that if you were still teaching."

"No, I wouldn't. Everything seems to work out just as it should." Trudy stamped the end of her cane in the grass as if for emphasis before joining Richard near the microphone.

"Where's Sadie?" I'd just realized I hadn't seen her since I changed out of my dress and that had been several hours ago.

"She asked if it was all right if she went back to Midcentury Vintage for the rest of the day," my grandmother said as she adjusted the bookmark display on her makeshift sales table. "I think what happened to Anastasia really shook her. I told her that Trudy and Richard would have no trouble keeping the reading going. You know, those two love the spotlight."

I glanced across the street at the yellow cottage that was Midcentury Vintage. Tourists went in and out of the shop, and it seemed to me that the ones leaving were carrying shopping bags. It would make sense if Sadie wanted to focus on her own business during such an important weekend for commerce in the village, but her absence made me edgy. I still couldn't get out of my head how upset she'd been last night after being alone with Anastasia in Charming Books' kitchen.

Grandma Daisy shooed me over to the side of the yard where the microphone was. Behind the mic, I cleared my throat. "Thank you all for coming out here today. After a break, we are about to resume our Poe-try Reading, where we share with you the works of the literary genius Edgar Allan Poe. Poe has been credited with being the first man to pen a true detective story as well as being best known now for his terrifying work. . . ." I trailed off as Chief Rainwater followed by Wheaton and Clipton marched down the front steps of Charming Books and walked through the front gate and into the street.

I turned to Richard, completely forgetting what I had to say about Poe. "Dr. Bunting will be able to share much more about Poe's life and work than I ever possibly could." I stepped away from the mic. "Richard?"

He gave me a curious look, but I ran after the officers before he could protest. Just as Rainwater and his officers hit the sidewalk on the other side of the street, I dashed across the road, nearly getting run over by a horse and carriage in the process. Sadie was right. Those carriage drivers need to pay more attention to pedestrians.

The three officers had just reached the gate around Midcentury Vintage's tiny yard when I caught up with them. "David!"

Chief Rainwater turned around to face me, and I gasped for breath. I hadn't run very far, but my heightened anxiety made it hard to breathe. "Where are you going?"

The corner of Officer Wheaton's lip turned up in a sneer. "We don't have to tell you anything."

"I wasn't talking to you," I snapped.

Officer Clipton started to open her mouth, but then she caught the chief's eye. She closed it tight.

"We need to talk to Sadie," Rainwater said. By his tone I knew it wasn't a casual call. "Now, go back to Charming Books." He turned and he and the two officers headed for Sadie's store.

Go back to Charming Books? Like that was going to happen.

ELEVEN

Completely ignoring his direct order, I followed them through the gate. "Sadie? Why do you need to talk to Sadie? You already took her statement. She didn't see anything or speak to Anastasia before she fell down the stairs." I jumped in between Rainwater and Midcentury Vintage's front door.

The police chief sighed. "It's part of the investigation. Now, step aside, Violet. Please."

He sounded so tired by the task ahead of him that I did what I was asked, but I still had a horrible feeling in the pit of my stomach.

Grandma Daisy joined me in Sadie's front yard, holding a hand over her heart like she was caught in the middle of giving the Pledge of Allegiance. "What's going on? What is David doing marching toward Midcentury Vintage like he's leading Pickett's Charge?"

"I don't know," I said. "He said they have to talk to Sadie. It has to be related to Anastasia's death."

"What are you doing standing here, then?" Grandma Daisy gave me a little shove. "Go find out what's going on and see if you can help her."

Grandma Daisy was right. I half ran, half stumbled across the yard and through the open door into Midcentury Vintage.

Sadie stood by the sales counter. Her blue eyes were the size of dinner plates as she stared at Rainwater and his officers. "B-but I don't know anything about what happened to Anastasia. I told you that I was outside when she fell down the stairs. I hadn't seen her since the night before when we were all together at the Red Inkers meeting."

"At Charming Books when you gave her the dress she was to wear at the Poe-try Reading," Rainwater said as if he was trying to clarify something.

The hairs stood up on the back of my neck.

"Y-yes," Sadie stammered. "You were all there. All the Red Inkers were there."

"Tell me about the dress," he said.

"Are you trying to tell me the dress is the reason she is dead? Did she trip over the hem and fall down the stairs? Anastasia was a tall woman. The hem should not have even touched the floor, but I can understand how her heel could have gotten caught if she wasn't careful." She covered her mouth with her hand. "How terrible! I feel responsible if that's what has happened."

Rainwater held up his hand. "No, she didn't trip on the hem of her dress. That is not what caused her to fall."

"Then, I don't understand. Why would you ask me about the dress if it's not related to how she died? Was the dress damaged somehow when she fell? Because, please know, I don't care. I don't want it back, if that's what you think. I don't want it back after what happened. It's just too morbid. I could never sell it."

"The dress Anastasia was wearing when she died, was it a new acquisition for your shop?" Rainwater asked in a calm and steady voice.

Sadie shook her head. "No, I have had that dress well over a year. When I heard about the Poe-try Reading, I knew it would be perfect for the event. It does have a very goth look to it and it was approximately Anastasia's size. I had to do some alterations, but they were very minor."

Rainwater's amber gaze narrowed. "What alterations did you make?"

"I let out the middle a little bit, not much, just enough so that she could breathe comfortably while wearing it, and the dress was short, so I let out the hem a little. There wasn't enough fabric to make it the perfect length considering how tall she was."

"Was Anastasia present when you made the alterations?" the police chief asked.

She shook her head. "I had her measurements from some tailoring I'd done for her a little while back."

"Where did you keep the dress?" he asked.

"Why, here, in the shop. That's where I keep all my clothes to sell. If someone came in asking to buy that dress, I would have sold it and found something else for Anastasia to wear. I can't take a chance on missing a sale."

"You never took it anywhere? A customer never borrowed it for a special event?" He asked these questions as if he wanted her to tell him that someone had borrowed the dress.

"Did someone tamper with the dress?" I asked, speaking for the first time since I had stepped into Midcentury Vintage. "Is that what you're implying?"

Rainwater's eyes slid in my direction, but he didn't seem the least bit surprised I was standing in the doorway.

"Is Violet right?" Sadie's lips trembled.

He pursed his lips. "It does look like someone did something to Anastasia's dress."

"I told you I made some alterations, but I can hardly believe that the dress itself was related to what happened to Anastasia." Sadie looked as if she was about to cry.

"I'm afraid that it might," Rainwater said. "Would it be all right if we searched your shop?"

"Don't you need a warrant for that?" I asked.

"A—a warrant," Sadie stammered.

"Not if Sadie says that it's okay." He didn't look at me as he answered the question.

"Sadie," I began. "I think—"

"I have nothing to hide." She cut me off. "Go ahead. Look." Tears gathered in her eyes. "But I thought you were my friend, David."

The police chief looked pained, and for the first time since he walked into Sadie's shop, I felt sympathy for him. Just a little, but it was there.

"At least tell us what you are looking for," I said. "You can do that much."

"For a substance that the coroner found on the dress."

He turned to Sadie. "My officers will start searching while we talk—would that be all right?"

She nodded mutely. Officers Clipton and Wheaton started moving around the room. Wheaton stared at the ceiling while he circled the shop, and Clipton stared at the floor going the opposite direction. The synchronization would have been humorous if I didn't know that they were in the process of searching for evidence, evidence that might implicate Sadie in Anastasia's death.

"What kind of substance?" I asked, moving next to Sadie. "You can at least tell us that much."

He frowned but finally said, "Liquid nicotine."

Beside me, I felt Sadie tremble. I wrapped my arm protectively around her shoulders if only to hide her shaking from Rainwater. I knew it was a futile act; he must have noticed it just as I had.

I scrunched up my nose. "There was liquid nicotine on her dress? That doesn't make any sense. How did it get there?"

Rainwater watched his officers over our heads. "That's what I would like to know."

"If there was liquid nicotine on her dress, how could that cause her to fall? The dress got wet or something?"

He made a face as if he thought he had said too much already. "The dress was dry. There was nicotine on the inside of it. The coroner thinks that someone purposely poured liquid nicotine onto the inside of the dress and let it dry. When the liquid evaporated, the toxic nicotine remained on the dress. When Anastasia put on the dress, it was absorbed through her skin."

"Could it have spilled accidentally?" I asked.

"We don't believe so. There was too much all over the garment. It looks intentional."

"Why would anyone do that?" I was still confused.

"To disorient her, make her stumble or act strangely. At least that is my working theory."

"You mean murder her," I said.

"We don't know that. She died from falling down the stairs and breaking her neck, but she probably would not have fallen, though, if there wasn't so much nicotine in her system."

I shivered. Beside me I noticed that Sadie had stopped trembling and gone very still.

Rainwater turned to Sadie. "Sadie, do you have access to liquid nicotine?"

"I—I—" It didn't seem like she was able to get the words out.

"Chief!" Officer Clipton called out. "I found something!"

He glanced at Sadie before heading to the back of the shop to see what the officer had discovered.

"Sadie," I hissed. "What's going on? What did she find?"

She wrapped her arms about herself. She looked so young in her patent leather shoes and Peter Pan collar dress. She couldn't and wouldn't hurt a fly. She couldn't have done this.

"She probably found my e-cigarettes," she whispered.

Immediately I understood. E-cigarettes required liquid nicotine to work. "I didn't know that you smoked."

"I don't," she said defensively. "I mean I haven't for a very long time. I started in high school and gave it up in college because Grant didn't like it. I just started with the e-cigarettes after Grant was arrested this summer. It was so stressful not knowing what was going to happen to him, not knowing what was going to happen to our relationship, that I had the urge to smoke again. You know, just to take the edge off. I thought the e-cigarettes would be better. They say they are healthier."

I wasn't going to debate the health aspects of e-cigarettes with her. "You've been using them since the summer?"

She nodded. "No one knows. Not even Grant. Please don't tell him. He hates cigarettes, and he wouldn't like it if he knew."

I promised her I wouldn't, but there was no way for us to keep the secret if it became part of the murder investigation. Murder investigation. Chief Rainwater hadn't come right out and said that Anastasia had been murdered, but if someone purposely dosed her dress with liquid nicotine and it led to her death, it was the obvious conclusion.

As if she read my mind, Sadie grabbed my arm and said, "But I never spilled any of the liquid from my cigarettes on Anastasia's dress. I've never even used my e-cigarette in the shop."

"How could it have gotten on the dress, then?"

She shook her head. "I have no idea."

I squeezed her hand. "Maybe it wasn't from your e-cigarettes at all."

Rainwater rejoined us. In his hand he held a clear plastic bag with a bottle inside. The bottle resembled the type that would have contained eye drops, but instead of a clear liquid the remnants at the bottom of the nearly empty bottle were a sickly yellow color. "Sadie, is this yours?"

"It's strawberry flavor," Officer Clipton announced as if she were talking about some sort of candy.

The chief gave her a withering glance. "Sadie, can you please answer the question?"

"Y-yes. It's mine. Where did you find it?" Her grip on my arm tightened.

"In your wastebasket in the back of the shop," Officer Clipton answered, happy to help.

"I don't know how it got there," Sadie said. "I wouldn't have thrown it away in the shop. I wouldn't want anyone to find out about my habit, and it's mostly gone. I haven't even opened the strawberry one that I have."

"So what are you saying?" Rainwater asked.

"I—I don't know what I'm saying other than I didn't empty that bottle and I didn't throw it away in my shop." Her tone was emphatic, and I couldn't speak for Rainwater or his officers, but I believed her. Sadie would never throw the bottle away in her shop if she wanted to keep her habit a secret from her fiancé, Grant. There was too great a chance he might see it.

Then I remembered smelling strawberries when I met Anastasia at the bottom of the stairs when she first arrived at Charming Books that afternoon and again when I knelt beside her body. I had thought it was strange because it wasn't a scent I would have expected from her. It was too juvenile, like candy. I definitely wouldn't associate Anastasia with candy of any kind. It had been the dress that I'd smelled, not Anastasia.

"When I met Anastasia inside Charming Books before she went upstairs to put on the dress, I remember she smelled like strawberries," I told the others. "I thought it was strange at the time, but I didn't ask her about it because the Poe-try Reading was about to start."

"Are you sure?" Rainwater asked.

I nodded. "I remember it perfectly."

He rubbed his chin. "All that would lead us to believe is that the nicotine was placed on the dress before Anastasia put it on, but it does narrow the timetable as to when the crime may have taken place, however slightly."

I frowned. So that didn't disprove Sadie did it? She could have poured the nicotine on the dress and allowed it to dry before giving it to Anastasia. I tried to remember the night before when all the Red Inkers were together in Charming Books. Had I smelled anything resembling strawberries? All I could remember was the scent of the cookies as I rode my bike home from La Crepe Jolie.

The police chief turned to Sadie. "I'm going to have to take a look at the rest of your shop and your apartment."

"But I told you that I never took the dress from the shop. The only time I ever took it from this building was when I carried it and the other garments for the Red Inkers across the street to Charming Books." Sadie bit her bottom lip.

I grimaced. I didn't think that statement helped her case in the least.

I grasped Sadie's arm. "Sadie, I suggest you call a lawyer before you let this go any further."

Rainwater's eyes slid in my direction and back to Sadie. "That is Sadie's right."

"And," I said, "I suggest you come back with a warrant if you want to search any more."

Sadie's eyes filled with tears. One giant tear spilled over and ran down her flawless cheek. "But I can't afford a lawyer. Every penny I have goes back into the shop or is being saved for the wedding." She choked up when she said this. "If there ever is a wedding. Grant has called it off so many times."

I ground my teeth as I thought of Grant. He should be here now at Sadie's side supporting her through this. She had been with him every step of the way through his troubles with the law over the summer when he had been admittedly guilty. Sadie was innocent, and he was nowhere to be found.

"I can make a call," I said. "You don't worry about the cost right now. We'll sort it out."

"Is that what you want, Sadie?" Rainwater asked.

She looked to me and I gave her a slight nod.

"Yes," she squeaked.

"All right." He held up the evidence bag. "But we're going to have to take this."

Rainwater explained to Sadie he would go to the courthouse and request a warrant and would need her to meet him at her apartment within the hour with her lawyer. As he spoke, I stepped behind a mannequin and dialed the last number in Cascade Springs I'd thought I would ever call.

~•~

TWELVE

~•~

Nathan Morton strode up River Road from the direction of the Food and Wine Festival with a phone attached to his ear. He was a man on a mission. He was still wearing the suit he wore to his official duties as the mayor of Cascade Springs during the Food and Wine Festival, of which there were many. Despite the lateness in the day, the suit was still pristine as if he'd just put it on a few minutes before. His eyes bored into mine as he made his way up the sidewalk toward Midcentury Vintage until I was forced to look away.

Just as Nathan reached me, Chief Rainwater stepped out of Sadie's shop. He also had a cell phone attached to his ear, but I knew by the way his eyes narrowed ever so slightly he had noted Nathan's arrival.

"Violet, I came as quick as I could. How is Sadie?" He touched my arm.

I tried to ignore the feeling of his warm hand through my sweatshirt. "She's all right. I think. Where's Grant? I told you to bring him with you."

Nathan pressed his lips together. "He couldn't get away from the family wine booth. The place is packed with people lining up for dinner."

"But . . ."

Nathan just shook his head. I suppressed a frown. I knew there was more to it than just Grant's inability to escape the family's booth at the festival. Nathan was able to escape the festival, and he was the mayor, who was required to be there all day to schmooze with the visitors and villagers alike.

Grandma Daisy, holding Emerson in her arms, watched us from across the street. As it was close to dinnertime, the crowd partaking in Charming Books' impromptu side-walk sale and Poe-try Reading had dwindled significantly as the many tourists had headed down to the Riverwalk for something to eat. My grandmother waved to me and her silver eyebrows dropped low in worry. I knew I should cross the street and tell her what was happening, but there was something important I needed to take care of first. "What about the lawyer?" I asked Nathan. "The police want to search Sadie's apartment after discovering the liquid nicotine in her shop. I told them that she needed a lawyer and they needed a warrant."

"Mayor," the police chief said as he tucked his phone into the inside pocket of his tweed coat and approached us. I wondered when the chief would have time to go home and change out of his Dupin outfit. "What are you doing here?"

Nathan dropped his hand from my arm but not before Rainwater took note of it being there for so long.

"I'm the mayor of this village and as such I am your superior as far as the village government is concerned. You're required to share with me what you know about events, especially crimes that happen in *my* village."

I stared at Nathan. I don't think that I had ever seen him so angry before. I tried to think of a time I had heard him speak so harshly, but nothing came to mind. Nathan had always been the easygoing kind of guy, the guy whom everyone liked and who was popular without even trying.

The chief's tawny-colored skin flashed burnt red. "Before Violet Waverly returned to Cascade Springs, you had very little interest in law enforcement in the village, Mr. Mayor. I can't help but think that your sudden interest and her return to the village isn't a coincidence."

"What is that supposed to mean?" Nathan balled his fists at his sides.

Rainwater's jaw twitched. "I will not let you hinder my investigation because of your personal relationships that have nothing to do with your position as the mayor of Cascade Springs."

Nathan looked like he wanted to argue more, and a small group of tourists began to cluster around us on the sidewalk. I was sure this was not the entertainment they'd expected to find when they decided to come to the Cascade Springs Food and Wine Festival for the weekend, but they were more than happy to watch.

"Nathan." I grabbed Nathan's hand, pulling him away from the gate, and he intertwined his fingers with mine as if it was second nature. The familiarity of his touch even after all this time took my breath away.

"Sadie Cunningham's lawyer is on his way here, and please leave the poor girl alone until you have a warrant," Nathan called over his shoulder.

"It's on its way," the police chief said through gritted teeth. Rainwater's amber eyes noted our intertwined fingers. He stepped around us and through the gate leading into Midcentury Vintage. Officer Clipton followed with an annoying half smile on her face. I was glad she was finding all of this so entertaining.

I pulled my hand away from Nathan's grasp. "Call that lawyer again. I think Sadie needs him right now."

Nathan nodded and removed his cell from the lapel pocket of his jacket. He tapped the phone's screen and placed it against his ear.

"And call your brother too. Sadie will want him here," I added. "I don't care what excuse he makes up. She needs him."

He frowned but gave the slightest nod to acknowledge he'd heard me on that account too.

"Henry Baskin, please. Tell him this is Mayor Nathan Morton," he said into the phone.

Nathan had no sooner finished his call to Baskin's office than the lawyer himself ambled up the sidewalk from the direction of the Riverwalk.

Henry Baskin, Esq., reminded me of Eeyore the donkey from *Winnie-the-Pooh*. If the man had a tail, it would be half-pinned to his bottom, threatening to fall off, and if it fell, the droopy attorney wouldn't even have the energy to care. He was a huge man, over six feet tall and heavy. His ample stomach hung over the waistband of his pants, but he didn't seem as large as he actually was. He held himself in a slouching manner that made him look smaller and less imposing.

Nathan saw my expression. "He's the best. He's the one who got Grant off with such a great deal after his embezzlement scheme."

I frowned. To me, it didn't look like Baskin could fight for much of anything, let alone weasel Grant Morton out of all his crimes with barely more than a warning.

As the lawyer lumbered up the sidewalk, Grandma Daisy ran across the street. Emerson was no longer in her arms. "Can someone please tell me what's going on?"

Baskin was moving at such a slow pace I was able to give her the highlights of the last hour before he reached us.

Grandma Daisy gripped the end of her scarf. "Poor Sadie."

As she said this, Sadie stumbled out of the front door of her shop. The typically bubbly girl looked as droopy as her lawyer. This was not going to be an upbeat duo.

"Who is the suspect under investigation?" Baskin asked when he finally reached us.

"Suspect?" Sadie cried. Another big tear rolled down Sadie's cheek. "I wouldn't hurt anyone ever."

Grandma Daisy wrapped an arm around her shoulders. "We know that, dear. No one thinks you did anything wrong. Not even David."

I wasn't so sure about that last statement. It seemed that my grandmother had unfailing belief in her friend the police chief. She had made a similar claim about

Rainwater when she had been a murder suspect over the summer.

Baskin ambled over to Rainwater, where he stood with Wheaton and Clipton. "Chief Rainwater, might I have a word?"

Rainwater scowled but finally nodded. He and Baskin moved out of earshot from not only us but also his officers. I was dying to hear what they were saying but saw no way to move over there without being seen by Rainwater or his officers. Wheaton, in particular, appeared to be keeping an eye on me.

Instead I turned away from the chief and the attorney in the direction of the Riverwalk, hoping to see Grant striding up the sidewalk. He never came. Apparently, Grant Morton was still too busy to come to the aid of his wife-to-be. I made a mental note to tell him just what I thought of that the next time I saw him.

"Thank you for your time." Baskin shook Rainwater's hand. "Sadie and I will meet you at her apartment."

Rainwater nodded. Without looking at me, he and his officers left—I imagined in order to retrieve the search warrant they needed from the judge. My only hope was it would take time to track down Judge Bickle to sign the warrant. He had a reputation for loving the Food and Wine Festival, especially the wine. If luck held, he'd be snoozing under a table somewhere in the big dining tent.

Baskin tugged at his collar as if it were fastened too tightly around his throat even though it was open to the third button. "The police confiscated the bottle they found in Sadie's wastebasket before I arrived. They also took a sampling of her liquid nicotine."

"Are you sure that's all they took?" Grandma Daisy asked.

"Yes. They have to tell me what was taken, and Rainwater is a by-the-book sort. He wouldn't lie. He wouldn't risk ruining his case in court by not doing everything by the letter of the law."

"In court?" Sadie squeaked.

He turned his sorrowful Eeyore face in her direction. "I'm sure it won't come to that. After talking with Rainwater, I got the distinct impression he doesn't believe you're guilty, but the man has to do his job."

"See there," Grandma Daisy said, giving Sadie a side hug. "I told you there was nothing to worry about. This will be over soon enough."

The lawyer shook his head sadly. "When there is a murder case, there is always something to worry about. Until the real perpetrator is found, Sadie is in a whole mess of trouble."

Grandma Daisy scowled at the lawyer for undoing all her good efforts to cheer Sadie.

Sadie shivered. "I don't know if I can go back to my apartment for the night and sleep there knowing someone invaded my space and framed me for murder." She took a breath. "Usually I would go stay with Grant, but he moved back into the big house at the winery with his parents after this summer. . . ." She trailed off.

It came as no surprise that Sadie would not want to stay at the Mortons' home. Grant's parents had made it no secret they disapproved of Grant's engagement to her. A jaded part of me wondered if that was why he'd asked Sadie to marry him in the first place, to upset his parents.

It was interesting to learn he was living in the big house on the vineyard again, though. I didn't know about this latest turn of events in Grant's life. It seemed the elder Mortons wanted to keep a closer eye on their younger son. I knew Grant must hate the extra attention.

"Don't be silly. You will stay with Violet and me. Violet isn't allowed back in her apartment tonight because of what happened. We'll have an old-fashioned sleepover." Grandma Daisy rubbed her hands together. "We'll make Rice Krispie treats, do each other's hair, and have a pillow fight. I should warn you my pillow-fighting skills are fierce."

Sadie smiled in spite of her tears. "I would like that. Rice Krispie treats are my favorite."

Grandma Daisy squeezed Sadie's shoulders. "Let's pick out a few outfits from your collection to dress Violet up in tonight. I keep telling her to make time to shop and dress up her professional wardrobe. After so many years in graduate school, she still dresses like a coed. Now that she is a professor in her own right, she needs to dress the part. I think you will know just what will make her stand out in the classroom."

Sadie's trembling smile blossomed. "I do like to dress up Violet. She has the perfect coloring and figure for vintage clothing."

Nathan listened to their exchange with a bemused expression on his face. I would be their fashion guinea pig if it made Sadie and my grandmother both happy even for the briefest of moments.

Grandma Daisy winked at me over Sadie's head before she guided the girl back to Sadie's shop.

"Please be quick about it," Baskin said. "We need to meet the police at your apartment."

Sadie's shoulders drooped again, but she let Grandma Daisy lead her into Midcentury Vintage.

The lampposts up and down the street began to flicker on as the sun dipped lower in the sky. I shivered at the loss of sunlight and wished I had thought to throw a jacket over my sweatshirt. Then I remembered I most likely would not be able to grab my jacket, since it was part of a crime scene. Music floated up the street from the direction of the Riverwalk as the evening entertainment began for the festival.

I turned to Baskin again. "How much trouble is Sadie really in?"

"It doesn't look good for her," he said in his melancholy way. "She's a viable suspect. The only reason she hasn't been arrested yet is because of the police chief's goodwill. It's hard to determine how long that will hold out."

"There must be others who wanted Anastasia dead," Nathan said. "I'm sorry if that sounds harsh, but she wasn't a very nice woman."

"Sadie doesn't have motive." I wrapped my arms around my waist to conserve warmth.

In my peripheral vision, I saw Nathan shrug out of his suit jacket. The next thing I knew, he draped the jacket over my shoulders.

"Nathan, you'll freeze," I protested.

"I'll be fine," he said quietly.

I swallowed, but rather than argue with him, I wrapped the jacket more closely around myself. As I did, the scent of his aftershave wafted around me. The smell made it difficult to concentrate on the conversation with Sadie's lawyer.

The lawyer arched an eyebrow at me. "Are you sure she doesn't have a motive? I haven't been alone with her to ask her myself. I do plan to ask her. It would be much easier for me to keep her out of jail if I knew what motive she might have. I can't help her if I don't know everything she knows."

I shook my head. "I still can't believe that she has a motive, but I'll see if I can find out." I adjusted the shoulders of Nathan's jacket.

"Or another suspect," Nathan said.

Baskin nodded. "It would be most helpful to find another suspect." He shifted his feet. "But like I said, I do believe Chief Rainwater is not convinced Sadie did this, but she was in the best position to apply the poison to the dress. Who else would have been alone with the dress, not only to apply the nicotine, but to also have enough time for it to dry without Anastasia knowing?"

I frowned. He had a point.

Our conversation ended when Grandma Daisy and Sadie reappeared in Midcentury Vintage's doorway. Sadie had several dresses slung over her arm, and they all had intricate beading and lots of sparkle. If wearing one of those cocktail dresses would help her get through this, I was willing to do it . . . or at least I thought I was. Sadie locked the door of her shop and tested it before she and Grandma Daisy joined Nathan, Baskin, and me on the sidewalk.

"I don't even know why I bothered to lock it. It didn't keep out whoever tampered with Anastasia's dress before."

"Do you want me to go with you to your apartment?" I asked. "I can be with you while they search the apartment."

Sadie began to nod, but the attorney shook his head. "It would be best if Sadie and I went to her apartment alone. When the police finish their search, I'll drop her off at . . ."

"My house," Grandma Daisy said, and rattled off the address.

"My car is parked in the public parking lot near the courthouse," Baskin said. "I can go fetch it and drive back here to pick you up. It might take me a little time with this crowd, though. It's never easy to drive a car up or down River Road during the Food and Wine Festival."

"No." Sadie shook her head and her sleek black pony-tail dusted her cheek. "I'll walk with you. I think it will help clear my head."

I took off Nathan's jacket and handed it to him before I took the dresses from Sadie's arms. "We'll be waiting for you at Grandma Daisy's when you're done. I can't wait to play dress-up."

She laughed. "You're lying, but I appreciate it."

"Miss Cunningham," Baskin said. "We should go. I expect Rainwater will have his warrant soon."

She nodded and joined Baskin on the sidewalk. Grandma Daisy, Nathan, and I watched them walk away in silence.

Thirteen

After Sadie and Baskin left, Nathan helped Grandma Daisy and me put the impromptu sidewalk sale back inside Charming Books under the watchful supervision of another of Rainwater's officers. Richard pitched in too. By the time Grandma Daisy and I reached my grandmother's two-story row house that night, it was dark.

Grandma Daisy's house was still in the historic district, but there weren't very many tourists this far away from the Riverwalk this late at night. The street, normally active in the evening with neighbors dropping in on one another and children's laughter floating out of the windows, was silent as the entire population was either working at the festival or checking it out for themselves.

I parked my bike beside Grandma Daisy's garage, and Emerson leaped from the basket. The only one missing from our little family was Faulkner. Grandma Daisy had tried to convince him to come, but the crow wasn't having it, and since Rainwater's officer seemed to be absolutely terrified of the big black bird, he didn't argue with Grandma Daisy when she said that Faulkner was to remain in the bookshop.

Grandma Daisy was just unlocking her front door when a dark sedan stopped in front of the house. Sadie got out of the car and removed a small rolling suitcase from the backseat.

I met Sadie in the driveway. "How did it go?"

She shook her head. "The police took my e-cigarettes and all my liquid nicotine from my apartment. The strawberry-flavored one I had was gone. I swear I put it with the rest of them, but I couldn't find it anywhere."

I bit the inside of my lip. "That still doesn't prove it was yours."

"It does, I think." Tears gathered in her eyes. "I bought it from a company online."

"Did you tell him it was your bottle?" Grandma Daisy joined us in the driveway.

Sadie shook her head. "Not outright, no."

"Thank heavens for that," Grandma Daisy said.

"But he's going to figure it out," Sadie said glumly. "I bought the nicotine with my credit card."

Sadie was right. Rainwater would figure it out if he hadn't already.

Sadie swiped a tear from her cheek. "David said I could stay in my apartment and that I didn't have to leave. He doesn't consider it a crime scene, but I don't think I can stay there. Not tonight."

I hugged her. "You can stay here as long as you need."

"I suggest we discuss this more inside," Grandma Daisy said. "We need a nice pot of tea, and those Rice Krispie treats are calling my name."

"Mine too," I agreed.

Sadie and I followed Grandma Daisy to the house. Grandma Daisy opened her front door, and Emerson ran inside like he thought he owned the place, which in his mind he did.

"Let me start the tea." Grandma Daisy held the front door open for us. "That will make all of us feel better. I'd call for a pizza, but I doubt there is anyone to deliver it with the festival going on."

Sadie parked her suitcase by the front door and wrung her hands. "I don't want you to miss out on the festival because of me."

"Pish," Grandma Daisy said. "I've been to the festival every year for over sixty years. There's nothing there I haven't seen before. Don't you worry. We have the leftover cookies from the Poe-try Reading and I have some lasagna in the freezer we can heat up. Now, you take a seat and I'll go make that tea." Before she left the room, Grandma Daisy gave me a look. I interpreted it to mean "Find out her motive."

Sadie perched on the edge of my grandmother's sofa, and I sat across from her in an armchair.

She buried her face in her hands. "I can't believe this has happened. How did I get tangled up in this?"

"Why do you think someone would frame you for Anastasia's murder?" It was a question that needed to be asked.

She lifted her face from her hands. "I don't know."

"This wasn't a random act." I leaned back in the chair, and Emerson leaped into my lap. The tuxedo cat curled into a black-and-white ball of fur and went immediately to sleep. "Someone must have tampered with the dress while it was in your shop, unless they did it after Anastasia took it home. Those are the only options, and in any case, someone took your liquid nicotine from your apartment and put it on the dress. That is a very well-planned crime."

She wrapped the end of her long ponytail around her finger. "But why? Why me?"

"At last night's Red Inkers meeting, you seemed upset after being alone in the kitchen with Anastasia. What happened while you were in the kitchen? Did she say something to you that upset you?"

"I wasn't upset. Maybe you thought I was because I was nervous about everyone liking their clothing for the Poe-try Reading. You know how seriously I take my clothes." She wouldn't meet my gaze.

I shook my head. "It was more than that. I saw it and I know David saw it too."

Sadie concentrated on the floor. "I don't have anything to tell you."

I leaned forward, and Emerson made a snuffling sound to let me know that he disapproved of the minor disturbance to his slumber. "Sadie, I know something happened. You looked like someone told you Versace was going out of business."

She hugged a throw pillow to her chest.

"What happened in the kitchen the night of the Red Inkers meeting?"

She squeezed the pillow even more tightly. By how closely she was holding it, I wouldn't be the least bit surprised if it burst and feathers flew all over the room. Emerson appeared to have the same opinion because he jumped off my lap and onto the sofa next to Sadie. His gaze was focused on the pillow as if he was hoping for those feathers to emerge.

I was about to ask her the question again when she said, "Anastasia dug up something from my past and threatened to use it against me."

I blinked at her. Of all the things she could have said, that was the least likely to come to my mind. It was just too hard to imagine sweet Sadie having skeletons in her closet. "What was it?"

As I asked my last question, Grandma Daisy stepped into the living room with a tea tray. "I made peppermint tea. It will soothe us after this day, and it's too late for caffeine." The lemon madeleines from La Crepe Jolie were in a place of honor in the center of the tray. She set the tray on the coffee table and studied our serious faces. "It seems that I walked into the middle of a conversation. I'll let you girls talk and start dinner."

Sadie shook her head. "Daisy, please stay. I want you to hear this too."

"If you're sure." Grandma Daisy sat on the couch next to Sadie with two madeleines in her hands.

"Sadie, what secret did Anastasia know about you?" I asked, trying to put the conversation back on track.

My grandmother's eyes widened ever so slightly, but she didn't say anything.

Tears gathered in Sadie's eyes. "I plagiarized," she said

barely above a whisper and with so much guilt, you would think she was confessing to the murder.

I gaped at her. "Your book?" Sadie was in the process of writing a romance novel. I had read an early draft of it. It was very good. She was an extremely talented writer, but what if those words weren't really hers?

Her face flushed red. "No, no, I would never do that. It was on a paper back in college during my junior year. I borrowed a friend's paper. She wrote a paper on the same topic but went to another university. My friend let me use it, not that it made it right," she added quickly. "I was having such a terrible semester. Grant would have nothing to do with me. I was in love with him even back then. I was in the middle of an emotional breakdown and the paper was due the next day. My friend offered me her paper, and in a moment of weakness, I took her up on her offer."

"How did you get caught?" I asked.

"I'd had the same professor for a couple of classes before, and she knew my writing style. When my paper didn't sound like me, she confronted me. I cracked under the pressure of her interrogation and confessed everything."

"What was your punishment?" I asked.

Most colleges and universities had the option of expulsion for any student caught plagiarizing. It was considered an unforgivable sin in academia, at least in theory. I knew that most institutions would give a student who was a first-time offender a second chance.

"She failed me and I retook the class in the summer. I was so afraid I would get thrown out of the university."

Grandma took the pillow from her hands and handed

her a cup of peppermint tea. Sadie nodded gratefully and curled her fingers around the teacup.

I selected a cookie from the tray. "You weren't expelled from the university. How could Anastasia use this against you? It was so long ago. I don't know what it has to do with anything now." My brow wrinkled in confusion. "You would not believe the number of undergraduate students I have caught plagiarizing since I've been teaching, sometimes intentionally and sometimes unintentionally. It hasn't ruined them, and it won't ruin you either."

"Violet, you don't understand. I'm a writer, and I'm trying to find an agent for my book. If Anastasia spread rumors to writers' Web sites that I have a history of plagiarism, it could ruin my chances of being signed by an agent or selling my book to a publisher." She took a shuddering breath. "She even threatened to e-mail the agents I planned to query and tell them not to sign me because of it."

"They couldn't possibly take her seriously. They don't know her."

She wouldn't meet my eyes again. "With the number of unpublished authors trying to grab agents' attention, why would the agents take a risk on a writer with baggage?"

Maybe she had a point. With all the thousands of unpublished writers in the world, why would an agent or a publisher take the risk on one with a questionable writing background when there was a surplus of other equally talented authors querying at the same time? "How did she find out?"

"I'm not sure exactly. My best guess is that she talked to someone at my university in Kentucky who knew about it. She never said who, but she did know about it. When she told me she had the information, she said the name of my professor, the class that I cheated in, and the name of my friend whose paper I used. She had all the facts."

"Grant," I said. "He must have known."

She pulled back as if she was trying to melt into the sofa. "Grant would never tell anyone. He's my fiancé."

I bit my tongue, holding back the question on the tip of my tongue, which was, where was he now?

Grandma Daisy poured another cup of tea and handed a cup and saucer to me. "That was so long ago. I don't know what power that information has over your life now. What did Anastasia plan to do with it?"

"I don't know exactly." Again she wouldn't meet my eyes.

Sadie was holding something back again. Rather than push, I said, "This makes no sense. Why would she go to so much trouble to find this dirt on you and why would she threaten to use it against you? You haven't done anything to her."

She bit her lip. "I know. I was completely shocked when she told me all this in the kitchen. She was absolutely furious with me."

Her mention of Anastasia being furious brought back to mind the phone conversation that I had overheard Anastasia having outside Charming Books. With all the commotion around Anastasia's death, I hadn't thought to mention it to Rainwater, but now I knew I should. Whoever had been on the other side of that line was another murder suspect and if Sadie was the primary suspect, we needed alternatives, the more the better.

"Anastasia said she was in the process of gathering

information on all of us," Sadie said. "She said it was some kind of insurance. I don't really know what she meant by that."

Grandma Daisy stopped her teacup halfway to her mouth. "All of us? Who is all of us?"

"She didn't say specifically, but I could only guess she meant the Red Inkers, as well as you and Violet."

I frowned. There wasn't much that she could use against me. The entire village knew my history with the law because of Colleen's death when I was a senior in high school. Since it wasn't a secret, it robbed Anastasia of any power that the information might otherwise wield. But then, I felt the color drain from my face. That wasn't my only secret, not anymore. I glanced at Grandma Daisy. The teacup in her hand shook ever so slightly. We had a much larger, much more valuable secret than any of the Red Inkers could imagine.

FOURTEEN

I bit the inside of my lip. If Sadie thought Anastasia had
the ability to ruin her writing career before it even
began, and Sadie's greatest dream was to be a published
writer, that gave Sadie a very strong motive for murder.

"You should talk to Baskin about this before you talk
to David again," I said.

She blinked at me. "But David is my friend."

"I know that," I said, softening my tone. "But he's also
the chief of police and this is the second murder in the
village in less than six months. He's going to give this
investigation his full attention and follow every lead, even
those that incriminate his friends."

She held her teacup a little more tightly before setting
it, still full, back onto the tray. "I think I'll go and try to
call Grant again." Her face clouded over. "I know he's

busy and things between us have been strained since this summer, but I need to speak to him."

I reached across the coffee table and squeezed her hand. "That's a good idea. We'll figure this out, Sadie. I promise. Calling the lawyer was only a precaution."

"You think so?" She looked so hopeful.

I nodded. "Someone as caustic as Anastasia must have many enemies. The question is who hated her enough to kill her." I squeezed her hand again. "We'll find out who."

"Violet, you have to help. You have to find out who did this."

I thought about the story that the books had wanted me to read, "The Fall of the House of Usher." Maybe the bookshop had wanted me to go to Anastasia's house.

"I wish I could sneak inside Anastasia's house. Maybe then I would be able to understand why she was trying to gather information about the Red Inkers," I mused aloud.

"I can help you with that," Sadie said. "I have a key."

I blinked at her. "You have a key to Anastasia's house?"

She nodded. "She gave it to me the last time she went out of town and asked me to water her plants. I never gave it back to her. I kept forgetting to return it to her when we had Red Inkers meetings."

Anastasia had a lot of nerve to hold a secret over Sadie's head and then ask her to water her plants while she was out of town.

"I have done it for her before." As if she could tell what I thought about it from my expression. "It was not a big deal. She goes out of town quite a bit. I didn't mind."

Of course she didn't mind, because she was Sadie and just about the kindest person on the planet.

Sadie pulled a key ring out of her skirt pocket and removed a silver key from the ring. She held it out to me. "Here is the key."

The key sat in the middle of her palm. I stared at it. Was I really going to break into Anastasia's house? No. That would be stupid.

"Take the key," Grandma Daisy said. "If the police find it in Sadie's possession, things may become worse for her."

"If you plan to go in there—," Sadie began.

"I'm not going to Anastasia's house," I cut her off.

"I know." She chewed on her lip. "But if you did happen to go in there, she has a security system. The code to deactivate it is eighteen sixteen."

"Eighteen sixteen?" I asked. "The year the village was incorporated?"

She shrugged. "I guess. Anastasia never told me why that number was the code." The key still sat in the palm of her hand.

I took the key and pocketed it, promising myself I wouldn't use it. "What does Anastasia do?" I asked, picking up my own teacup and saucer and leaning back into my chair. As I did, Emerson hopped from the couch to my lap. I held the tea high to avoid spilling the steaming liquid on either of us. The tuxedo spun three times before settling on my lap again.

Grandma Daisy frowned. "What do you mean?"

"What's her job?" I sipped my tea.

Grandma Daisy frowned. "You know, she has never mentioned a job other than writing."

Sadie picked up her teacup, but she still didn't drink from it. It seemed she took comfort in its warmth. "I don't think she needed to work. She lives in a huge house deep in the woods near the springs."

"A lady of leisure?" I asked, surprised by the news. Maybe this was why Anastasia could afford her high-minded ideals of writing only literary fiction. She didn't have to make a living off her work like other writers did.

"But if she's never sold a book to a publisher, how can she live like that?" Grandma Daisy asked.

Sadie shrugged. "All I know is the house is huge and expensively furnished. Anytime I go over there, I break out into cold sweats because I'm afraid I will knock over one of her expensive pieces of art. Maybe she has a rich uncle or something."

"I think the answer as to why she was killed might be in that house," I said.

Grandma Daisy gave me an appraising look. She knew the books must have told me something, but I couldn't tell her what that was in front of Sadie without risking revealing the Waverly family's best-kept secret. Instead she asked, "Are you thinking about using that key?"

"You should go," Sadie said. "It might be the only way to find out what Anastasia knew about all the Red Inkers."

I laughed. "The place must be crawling with police. If there is anything to find, David would have found it by now." I felt Anastasia's house key burning a hole in my pocket.

The key reminded me about something else that I'd forgotten. The tree. I stood up abruptly, which sent Emerson and my empty teacup falling to the floor. Emerson hissed. I scooped up the teacup, which thankfully was unbroken, and set it back on the tray.

"Violet?" Sadie asked, sounding alarmed. "Are you all right?"

"I'm fine. I just remembered something I have to do," I said. "It's nothing to worry about." I shot a glance at my grandmother.

Grandma Daisy seemed to get my message. "Sadie, dear, why don't you try to call Grant again? Violet and I will give you a minute so you can talk to him in private." Grandma Daisy gave me a nod toward the kitchen. I refilled my cup from the teapot before I followed her out of the room.

"Violet, what's wrong?" Grandma Daisy asked, setting her own teacup on the counter.

I started to pace. "I forgot to water the tree."

"What do you mean you forgot to water the tree?" my grandmother hissed.

"I was supposed to water it last night, but that was the night the Red Inkers were there. I was too tired after the meeting to walk out to the springs and collect the water. I thought that I would do it tonight."

"You forgot to water the tree!" My grandmother stared at me as if she had never heard such a thing.

"Do you think it can hold on for another night? Maybe it will be all right? What will happen if the tree isn't watered on schedule?"

Grandma Daisy frowned. "I don't know if any Caretaker has forgotten to water the tree before."

Great. I was the worst Caretaker in the history of the Waverly family and Charming Books.

"Then, I'm going to have to go over there and do it. The police are gone by now and everyone is at the festival. No one will see me. I'll be in and out before you know it."

Grandma Daisy nodded. "You have to go. I'll stay here with Sadie."

I said a quick good-bye to Sadie as I left the house. She barely nodded. She was staring at her cell phone in her hand. It looked to me like she didn't have much luck getting ahold of Grant. I added having a talk with Grant about neglecting his fiancée to my growing to-do list.

~❧~

FIFTEEN

~❧~

Sometimes I do something really stupid and even while I'm doing it, I know that it's stupid, but I do it anyway. In college my attempt at a pixie haircut—stupid. Later in grad school when I had a crush on one of my professors and told him about it—double stupid. I knew that this breaking and entering into Charming Books would be right up there, pushing the professor crush to a distant second.

I wished Grandma Daisy were with me. Grant should be the one with Sadie and comforting her after her long day. My grandmother should be with me committing a felony. That's what family was all about, wasn't it?

I parked my bike behind Charming Books and walked over to the gardening shed. Thankfully, it was unlocked. Grandma Daisy was forever forgetting to lock the shed after tending to her flowers. The spare watering can was on the top shelf, and I grabbed it. As I did, a trowel sitting on the same shelf clattered to the wooden floor of the shed. I froze, expecting police with guns drawn to charge toward me. I held my breath for a full minute. When nothing happened, I gave a sigh of relief and carefully set the trowel back on the shelf from where it had fallen. I had a feeling that Chief Rainwater had thoroughly searched this shed. He would notice if one garden tool was out of place.

I poked my head out of the shed, looking left and right. I couldn't believe I was moving like a thief on my own property. I kicked myself, not for the first time, for not watering the tree the day before. Now the situation was dire and I didn't have any choice in the matter.

I took a deep breath and headed for the woods and the path that led toward the springs. Dappled light from the moon streamed through the branches, giving the autumnal-colored leaves an eerie glow. An owl hooted somewhere high in the trees. There was a rustling under the brush to my right. I told myself it was a mole or a chipmunk, not a snake. The snakes should be hibernating soon for the winter or at least I consoled myself with that theory.

The springs were a quarter mile from Charming Books. I could grab the water and return to the house in less than a half hour, maybe twenty minutes if I ran. I tripped over a root and almost face-planted in the middle of the path. Okay, running wasn't a good idea.

The closer I came to the springs, the more the path widened. I could hear the water bubbling down the side of the springs' rocky face and into the pool at the end. Moon-light shone on the surface of the water. Even though I couldn't afford the time, I paused to take in the view. The moon's rays reflected off the moss and the golden maple leaves and the silver birch leaves, giving everything a glow that was both beautiful and haunting. Even if I hadn't already accepted and known what the water in the springs had the ability to do, I would have believed all the stories about its mystical and healing properties in that moment.

A twig snapped behind me, and I jumped behind a birch tree. The tree trunk was narrow, so it didn't afford much cover. Even this late at night, with so many visitors in town, it was possible a tourist who had drunk a little too much wine at the festival had stumbled into the park. Every year, it seemed some tourists wandered off and the police had to go look for them.

A doe tiptoed up to the spring and drank from the cool water. I let out a sigh of relief. It was only a deer and a deer wouldn't reveal my secret.

I let the animal drink its fill, and then took a step forward. The doe watched me and calmly walked back into the trees.

Kneeling beside the springs, I dipped the watering can inside and collected some of the water. My action caused ripples to run across the silvery surface in tiny waves.

I filled the watering can and hurried back into the trees. As much as I wanted to stay and admire the beautiful place, I knew I had to hurry back to Charming Books and water the birch tree.

The trip back to the shop was short with no incident. I knew better than to go into the shop through the back door, which led into the kitchen and was too close to the crime scene. The problem was the only other door to Charming Books was the front door, a place where anyone could see me enter the shop.

Like a thief, I crept around the side of the bookshop. I stuck my head out around the corner and looked in both directions. Near the point where River Road turned and began to follow the Riverwalk was a small cluster of people laughing and talking so loudly they were almost shouting. Clearly, they had enjoyed the festival. I doubted that if I did backflips across Charming Books' front yard, they would remember seeing me.

They were causing such a scene, I suspected they would distract anyone else who might see me too, which was just fine with me.

I ran up the front steps of the shop with my shop key in one hand and the full watering can hugged to my chest in the other arm.

The old lock stuck just as it always did, but finally it gave way. With a sigh of relief, I slipped inside. Ambient light poured in from the skylight above the tree and from the streetlamps through the front windows. It was enough light to see Emerson sitting at the base of the tree with his black tail swishing back and forth across the floor

"How on earth did you get over here?" I demanded. "You're supposed to be home with Grandma Daisy and Sadie."

"Stowaway!" Faulkner cawed from somewhere in the tree.

Emerson looked up and squinted at the bird.

"Okay, never mind how you got here," I said. "I'll just

water the tree, and then you and I are heading back to Grandma Daisy's, no arguments." I shuffled toward the tree and poured the water into the ring of dirt that surrounded it.

The first time I'd watered the tree under my grandmother's instruction, I had expected something to happen, like the tree to move or shimmer or something. Nothing happened. Nothing ever happened when I watered the tree.

I shook the last droplets from the watering can and stepped back. My foot bumped into something. I turned around and found a hardback volume of Poe's work at my feet. In front of my eyes, the cover opened and pages flew until they settled to a particular page near the middle of the book. "The Fall of the House of Usher."

Even in the moonlight it was too dark to read the words of the story. I picked the book up from the floor and carried it to the window and read the first page. As I read, I felt Anastasia's key in my pocket. Did the book want me to go to Anastasia's house? Was I taking this interpretation of the shop's cryptic messages too far? According to Sadie, Anastasia lived alone. There would be no one there at this time of night. The police would have been and gone.

I held the book to my chest. Emerson looked up at me and meowed. "Maybe we will swing by there on the way home just to look around. If it's anything close to the House of Usher, going inside at night is a really, really bad idea."

Emerson meowed again and Faulkner swooped down from the birch tree onto the sales counter. As he walked across the polished wooden surface, his talons clicked. The pair of them seemed to agree with my plan. I was taking advice from a Houdini cat and a talking crow—I had come a long way since I'd moved back to the village.

When Sadie had described Anastasia's house, I'd recognized the description of the home immediately. There weren't many houses close to the natural springs. The area was protected, and the village took the zoning to an obsessive level, but there was one mansion that had been built not far from the spring in the 1920s. The original owner had been a robber baron in New York City. Becoming chronically ill, he heard about the healing waters of Cascade Springs and moved to the village to retire. The man had lived well into his nineties.

The robber baron's home had to be Anastasia's house today. There wasn't another large home close to the springs. By car, it would have taken me fifteen minutes to reach the house, even longer with the festival in full swing. However, on bike I could ride on the trails passing the springs and cut through the park to make it there in half the time.

I stared down at my tuxedo cat, who sat by the front door of Charming Books. His tail swished back and forth over the floor, and he focused on the doorknob, a not-so-subtle hint that he was ready to leave. That was a problem. "Emerson, you are going to have to stay here with Faulkner. I'll come back for you."

The tuxedo cat arched his back in an impressive Halloween display and plopped down in front of the door again.

I stuck my hands on my hips. "Emerson, I don't want you to get lost. You'll be much safer if you stay here with Faulkner."

He got to his feet again and marched back and forth in front of the doorway like a panther prowling in a cage.

I sighed. There wasn't much point in arguing with the cat. If I refused to take him, he would find his way to Anastasia's house on his own. "Fine. You can come, but you have to be on your best behavior."

He stopped pacing and looked up at me endearingly, twitching his long white whiskers.

I pointed at him. "That face is how you get away with so much."

He swished his tail in agreement.

I scooped up the cat, said one final good-bye to the crow, and slipped out the door. The street was still quiet. The small cluster of festivalgoers who'd been at the corner were gone. I hurried down the porch steps and to my bike.

Again I was thankful for the moonlight to guide my way through the woods. Emerson sat in my bicycle basket with his paws on the edge of the basket's pink wire rim.

The bike path through the woods came to an end on the other side of the park, leading onto a paved street. There was a stone lamppost in the middle of the woodland road, indicating the end of a driveway, the driveway I knew led to Anastasia's house. I couldn't see the house from the road, between the dense woods and the dark.

Emerson looked back at me from his basket as I hesitated at the end of the driveway. His amber eyes glowed. I swallowed and put my feet back onto the pedals and started down the driveway.

As I rolled down the paved drive, the first lines from "The Fall of the House of Usher" came to mind again.

*During the whole of a dull, dark, and soundless day
in the autumn of the year, when the clouds hung
oppressively low in the heavens, I had been passing
alone, on horseback, through a singularly dreary
tract of country; and at length found myself, as the
shades of the evening drew on, within view of the
melancholy House of Usher.*

Okay, I wasn't on horseback and this wasn't the House
of Usher, but the similarities were creepy. I stopped in
front of the house. Other than some of the estates that were
attached to wineries like the Mortons', the stone house in
front of me was the largest in the village. The house—
mansion would have been a better word—was three stories
high and had a widow's walk on the third floor. Thick ivy
snaked up the right side of the house and even in the dark,
I could see the huge brass knocker on the front door that
was in the shape of a lion's head. Stone lions flanked either
side of the front door, and more ivy wound around their
bodies like serpents taking hold of their prey.

I let out a deep breath. "All right," I whispered to
myself. "You've seen the house. Now it's time to go home
and have one of those hard-earned Rice Krispies treats
that Grandma Daisy and Sadie were making." I started
to turn the bike back in the direction of the street. As I
did, Emerson jumped out of my bicycle basket and dashed
toward the mansion.

"Emerson! Come back," I yelled at the cat.

He didn't even glance over his shoulder as he disappeared around the side of the house.

SIXTEEN

As Emerson disappeared around the side of the house, I raced after him. I wouldn't have been able to pick him out at all in the dark if it weren't for his bright white markings on his tuxedo coat.

When I rounded the side of the enormous house, I called the cat again, but he sprinted away. I ran after him, just in time to see him shimmy up a drainpipe and wriggle through a half-opened window on the second floor.

My arms fell dejectedly to my sides, and I stood there for a moment digesting the enormity of what my cat had just done.

"This is bad," I said to myself. "This is really bad."

I had two options. I could call the police and tell them my cat was running loose in a murder victim's house, or I could go in there after Emerson. I felt in my jeans pocket. The key was there. Did I have much of a choice?

I couldn't leave Emerson in Anastasia's house, and if I told the police, it would most certainly reach Chief Rainwater that I was trespassing on a crime scene. There was a back door near the window where Emerson had disappeared. Before I could change my mind, I put the key in the lock and turned. The door swung inward.

My heart thundered in my chest as I saw a security system's console blinking on the wall to my right. The tiny red light blinked in tandem with an incessant beeping noise. Sadie had warned me about the security system. I should have remembered it before I stormed into the house. *Eighteen sixteen.* The date jumped into my head. That was the pass code that Sadie had told me. Wincing the entire time, I typed the number into the keypad and hit enter. The light turned green and the beeping stopped. I went weak with relief. My relief didn't last long, however. I needed to find Emerson and leave Anastasia's house as soon as possible. It was always possible the police would be back at her house later that night for another look. I didn't want to be here when they arrived. And—although I didn't want to even think it—there remained the fact that disarming the alarm would leave a digital footprint on the house; match that with my literal footprints, and my fingerprints on the alarm's keypad. Things were not looking good. Rainwater was going to know I was in Anastasia's house. There was no way around that. I decided to find Emerson first and worry about the repercussions of running headlong into Anastasia's mansion after I collected my cat.

Just to be safe, I called out, "Hello! Hello, is anyone home? I'm just looking for my cat who ran off."

The only answer was Emerson's meow from somewhere deep in the house. I remained in the mudroom. "Emerson, come here."

It would be much easier if the cat came to me. I wasn't keen on the idea of taking one more step into the house.

"Emerson!" I hissed. "Here, kitty kitty. If you come here, I will give you a whole can of tuna for dinner, and we can go to the pet boutique on River Road and pick you up a new toy mouse. You would like that, wouldn't you?"

He meowed back. This time it sounded even farther away. Apparently, the can of tuna and the new toy weren't as enticing as the opportunity to explore Anastasia's mansion.

I groaned. He wasn't leaving me much choice. I had to go in, but I didn't know how I had any hope of finding the small cat in a house of this size. He could be anywhere.

Straightening my shoulders and giving myself a pep talk, I crept into the kitchen with tentative steps. I don't know what I expected. For someone to jump out and cry *boo*? It wasn't lost on me that this wasn't the first time I was trying to find Emerson in a murder victim's house. The last time, Chief Rainwater caught me in the act of trying to find the cat. I didn't want that to happen again.

Emerson's meow came again. It was more haunting and drawn out this time, closer to a yowl than a conversational chirp. I stopped worrying about making noise and hurried through the large kitchen into a narrow hallway. The hallway opened into an extensive great room. At the end of the great room, I saw an archway that must have led to the formal foyer. To my left there was a curved staircase with a polished wooden railing. At the top of the stairs there was a huge Palladian window that cast enough moonlight onto the staircase and foyer to see by.

Again, I wondered how Anastasia could afford such a grand home. True, in the village a home this stately would cost much less than it would in other parts of the country, but I was willing to bet that—between the house, the amount of land, and the location close to the park and springs—the property was worth well over a million dollars.

What exactly did she do? I supposed that it wasn't out of the question she had inherited the money or the home or made a savvy investment with the money she did have.

But this wasn't the time to mull over Anastasia's financial situation. I had plenty of time to do that when I was safely back at my grandmother's house enjoying a cup of tea and those promised Rice Krispies treats.

"Emerson!" I called the cat for the umpteenth time.

Nothing.

I shivered. As spooky as his meows sounded in the empty house, I was more creeped out by the silence. "Emerson?"

Much to my relief, a meow answered me. It seemed to be coming from the second floor. Great. Emerson was determined to have me tramp all over the house. Had I known that I would be breaking and entering this evening, I would have worn gloves to avoid leaving fingerprints behind.

I walked to the bottom of the stairs. "Emerson, you can't just go running off by yourself all the time. This is not working for me. If you keep it up, I might start walking you on a leash."

A terrible yowl answered me from the second floor. It was an ungodly sound that forced my heart into my throat. Without another thought, I ran up the stairs two at a time. "Emerson! Emerson!"

I tripped at the top of the steps and landed on my knees with a thud. There would be bruises later. Emerson gave that terrible yowl again, and I jumped to my feet as if I were hit with a bolt of electricity. The sound came from my right. I moved into yet another hallway. At the end of it was a sitting room. The furnishings were clean and modern. Dark leather couches dominated the room, and a glass and chrome coffee table sat in between them. The ebony shelves were lined with books, many of them classics.

A yowling came from the other side of the wall behind the shelving and I placed my hand on my chest. It came again. I stepped over to the bookcase that seemed to be at the heart of the cry. Poe's story "The Black Cat" came to mind as I stood in front of the bookcase. If some feline ghost came floating through the shelves, I was out of there.

Emerson meowed softly now and my pulse dropped closer to normal. "Emerson, are you behind the bookcase?"

The tip of his small white paw with claws extended curled around the side of the case about two feet from the floor. There was just enough room for his toes to poke out. I had no idea how he'd gotten back there in the first place when it was clear he couldn't even fit his full paw through the opening.

Did the bookcase move?

"How did you get back there?" I asked the white paw.

He wiggled his toes in reply. This would've been a great time for him to have learned how to speak English. The bookcase had to have moved. It was the only way I could see he might have gotten behind it. I ran my hand down the side of the case and couldn't see any way to open it. I tried to pull the large bookcase toward me, conscious of the dozens of heavy books on the shelves. It didn't budge. I was about to try again with a little more force when I saw it. There was a small groove in the back of the bookcase near where Emerson's paw appeared. I never would have seen it without him. It was impossibly small. I couldn't get more than two fingertips behind it.

Using my two fingers, I pulled forward and felt a latch. The latch clicked and the bookshelf moved. I stumbled backward as the moving bookcase revealed another room. Emerson sat on the other side in the middle of the floor. His black tail swished back and forth across the geometric rug.

"What is this place?" There were no windows, and I could see only a few feet inside. I ran my hand along the wall, searching for a light switch. I found one and switched on the overhead light. I blinked against the sudden glare. As I looked around, my jaw hit the floor.

I had stepped into an office, a writing office. I had expected such a room in Anastasia's house. That wasn't the surprise; the surprise was what else I found there. The bookcases were full to bursting with romance novels. Many of the novels were multiple copies by the same author.

There were framed romance covers on the wall. The

covers had attractive male models with smoldering eyes. Some wore shirts; others did not. Each cover was for a book, like the majority of the volumes on the shelves, written by Evanna Blue. Being a bookseller, I immediately recognized the author's name. Even if I weren't a bookseller, I would be hard-pressed not to have at least heard of her. Evanna Blue was one of the top romance writers in the country at that moment. Her books regularly debuted in the number one slot on the *New York Times* best seller list, and at least three of her novels had been turned into major motion pictures. Despite her popularity, she was also a reclusive author. There were no pictures of her on the dust jackets of her books or in the press. Ever. In the publishing industry, the identity of Evanna Blue was one of the best-kept secrets. Over the years, rumors as to her identity had run rampant. Some said she was a man, which was why her identity was hidden. Others said she was a made-up figure like Carolyn Keene, the author of Nancy Drew, who was in fact a fictional author, and a number of ghostwriters had written those books. Believe me when I say that I was crushed when I was a teenager and discovered the truth about Carolyn Keene.

However, that discovery was nothing compared with the one I had just made. There was a printed manuscript sitting next to a computer on the long, narrow desk across from me, and I inched toward it. Small corrections had been made in red ink and Post-it notes marked pages where more changes should be made.

There was a printed e-mail next to the stack: "Anastasia, we need to talk about the situation. I think it's very unwise to stop writing as Evanna. You're doing very well. Why change what is working? I understand you're disappointed the books you care most about aren't receiving the attention we both want from publishers. But you know as well as I do that literary fiction is a hard sell in today's market. I'm not telling you to give up on your passion project, but don't cast aside everything that you've accomplished as Evanna. Thousands of authors would kill for the success you've had."

Thousands of authors would kill for the success you've had. That line played again in my mind. Could it be that was what happened? One of Evanna's—I mean Anastasia's—rivals killed her out of jealousy?

The e-mail was simply signed "Edmund." The sender's e-mail address included the name of a top literary agency in New York and the name Edmund Eaton. Another startling discovery—Anastasia had a literary agent, a successful one too, but she would have had to have one if she was Evanna Blue. Finding a literary agent was always a popular topic of conversation with the Red Inkers. Never once had Anastasia let on that she had one. She wouldn't, would she? If she could keep it a secret she was Evanna Blue, international best-selling author, I supposed the secret of having a literary agent would have been a cakewalk.

I reread the e-mail. Anastasia Faber was Evanna Blue. It didn't compute. How was that possible? I removed my phone from the back pocket of my jeans and snapped a photo of the letter. It was proof of the unbelievable and it gave me Edmund's e-mail address.

I was about to leave when I remembered Sadie saying that Anastasia was gathering information on all the Red

Inkers, including Grandma Daisy and me. If she had that type of information, it would be in this office. If Anastasia had somehow learned Charming Books' secret, I couldn't leave it there for the police to find. Before I could talk myself out of it, I began to search her office for any mention of the Red Inkers, taking care not to move anything out of place. I started on the top of the desk, which was clean except for the computer and papers I'd found when I first stepped inside of the room.

The desk drawers were full of office supplies and little else. I moved on to the four-drawer black filing cabinet tucked in a corner of the room. I opened the first drawer and found a file labeled "Royalties." I pulled out her statement and whistled at the earnings Anastasia had made as Evanna in just a six-month period. I hadn't seen that many zeros, well, ever. Anastasia could definitely afford her home. She could also afford a yacht and her own Caribbean island. Briefly, I wondered why she'd remained in Cascade Springs, where she'd grown up, when she could have lived just about anywhere on the planet.

I put the statement back and moved on. I found what I was looking for in the back of the bottom drawer. The file was labeled simply "Evidence." Evidence for what? I sat back on my heels and set the file on my lap.

Inside there was a handwritten page that contained the names of all the Red Inkers. By each name there was a single word. Sadie's said "plagiarism," as expected. Beside Richard's name was the word "divorce." Richard was divorced? I didn't know that, but I didn't know why it mattered either. What about his divorce was blackmail-worthy, assuming that was Anastasia's plan with all this information? The spots beside Rainwater's and Trudy's names were blank. They didn't have any secrets? Or Anastasia wasn't able to discover them before she died? There was no way to know the answer.

I flipped the paper over and found Grandma Daisy's and my names. The word beside our names was simply "tree." The paper in my hands shook. Emerson placed a comforting paw on my knee.

SEVENTEEN

There was nothing else in the folder. I searched the rest of the office for any other mention of the Red Inkers and found nothing. "I can't leave this paper here," I told Emerson.

He meowed as if in agreement.

I folded the piece of paper and slipped it into the back pocket of my jeans. Guilt pricked the back of my mind. It might contain evidence for the murder, but I couldn't allow the police or anyone to find any mention of the tree—I just couldn't.

I picked up Emerson and backed out of the secret office. Now my question was, what should I do with this newfound information? Did Rainwater know Anastasia was Evanna? This changed everything. It had to be related to her murder. It just had to be. It could be the motive for the crime itself. I shivered as I remembered the last line of Edmund's e-mail.

I needed to go to my grandmother's house, where I had time to think this over. I turned out the light in the hidden office, still holding Emerson tightly to my chest with my other arm. He didn't squirm in an effort to get away from me again.

A loud crash came from the first floor. It sounded like someone knocked over a lamp and it shattered. My heart flew into my throat for a second time that night when I heard the sound of footsteps on the stairs. I closed the bookcase door, making sure it was secure, and looked for someplace to hide.

Outside the sitting room door, which I'd left open, I saw the beam of a flashlight run across the floor. I couldn't breathe. There wasn't much in the sitting room besides the floor-to-ceiling bookshelves and the two large sofas.

The beam of light turned into the sitting room, and I ducked behind the far sofa, which was perpendicular to the door. From behind the couch, I heard the approach of heavy footsteps. I didn't dare take a peek to see who it was, for fear I would be spotted.

The footsteps moved with purpose to the wall of bookcases. I sensed more than saw that the flashlight's beam was trained on the bookshelves, which were across the room from where I hid behind the sofa. Hoping that I was right, I dared to peek around the corner of the sofa. I saw the form of an average-sized man standing in front of the bookshelves.

He ran his flashlight along the shelves at eye level. He

stepped up to a bookcase and slipped his hand behind it. Nothing happened. He moved to the next bookcase and did the same. And then to the next and the next until he came to the bookcase I'd closed just moments ago. He hit the latch and the bookcase clicked open. "There you are, Evanna."

As much as I wanted to see what the man was going to do in Anastasia's secret office, I knew this was my chance for escape. With Emerson tucked close to my chest in one arm, I crawled behind the long couch. I could hear the man in the secret office moving things around. He didn't seem to make any effort to be quiet about it.

At the end of the couch, I stood and in my haste bumped the end of the couch with my hip. The impact made the slightest thud, but in the stillness of the old stone house it sounded like a gunshot.

"Is someone there?" the man called. "Who's there?"

The flashlight beam ran over my back. I jumped to my feet and fled down the long hallway to the curved staircase. I made no effort to be quiet now. I had to get out of the house. I hit the main floor and heard the sound of rapid footsteps coming down the stairs behind me. I spared half a second to catch a glimpse of the man's face. It was narrow and a scruffy goatee worn hipster-style darkened the lower half of his face, and dark-rimmed glasses dominated the upper half.

"Stop!" the man called.

His shout was just what I needed to spur me into motion again. I dashed back down the long dark hallway toward the mudroom and the kitchen.

"Stop!" he cried a second time.

Like that was going to happen. Outside, I dropped Emerson in my bicycle basket, jumped onto my bike, and flew down the driveway. I made the mistake of looking back just as I passed the lamppost at the end of Anastasia's driveway. The man stood in the middle of the drive. He held a piece of paper in his hand. I knew it was the e-mail I'd snapped a picture of. I saw him, but he saw me too. He knew what I looked like, but the reverse was true too.

I didn't stop pedaling until I made it all the way to the Riverwalk. I was so afraid the man with glasses and beard would follow me that I rode at top speed. Emerson hunkered down in the bicycle basket in front of me as the cold October wind whipped through his fur.

When I reached the Riverwalk and saw the festivities were still in full swing despite that late hour, I let out a sigh of relief. Emerson appeared to relax as well and dared to lift his black-and-white head over the edge of the basket.

I slowed my pedaling as I made my way down River Road along the Riverwalk. The presence of so many people made me feel safe. The full moon reflected off the surface of the Niagara River. The river curved in and around the Niagara's boulders, which were outlined by silver threads coming straight from the orb in the night's sky.

I slowed my bicycle even more as I took care not to hit any woozy pedestrians who took it upon themselves to sample every vintage the twenty-plus wineries at the festival had to offer. Finally, I gave up riding altogether as I came closer to the heart of the festival, and I jumped off my bike in front of La Crepe Jolie. The café was closed for the night, but I knew Lacey and Adrien also had a booth at the festival. I hoped they were still there.

I leaned my bike against the side of the café and scooped Emerson out of the basket. The cat hung over the back of my shoulder like a baby in need of burping.

After waiting for a carriage and two slow-moving cars to make their way down River Road, I crossed the street and headed to the cluster of white tents, which made up the bulk of the festival. Twinkle lights hung from the maple trees in the green where the tents stood, which made the trees' red and orange leaves glow like fiery torches against the night's sky.

More white twinkle lights hung from the tents themselves, where the food and wine vendors sold their wares. A much larger wedding-style tent sat on the far side of the green. A string quartet played music while clusters of people sat at round tables with seating for six and listened while they sipped their wines. The scene was so very refined, so very Cascade Springs. It was hard to believe there could be a murder in the village and only a block from this very spot.

I shook my head, and Emerson purred in my ear. I didn't have time to take in all the highlights of the festival. With over thirty matching tents, it would take me far too long to find La Crepe Jolie's tent, so I stopped at the first tent just at the entrance of the festival. "Can you tell me where La Crepe Jolie's tent is?"

"Hello, Violet," a prim voice said in return. "It is nice to see you." Her tone spoke to the contrary.

My stomach dropped. I should have read the sign before opening my mouth. Mrs. Nanette Morton, Nathan's mother, appraised me with perfectly made-up eyes. I could only guess that she'd applied her eye makeup that morning, but it appeared as fresh as if she'd just set down her mascara wand. Perfection went for everything about Nathan's mother, from her styled short hair to her pristine white coat, without a splash of wine on it, despite Mrs. Morton's working in the booth all day on the uneven grass.

EIGHTEEN

I mentally kicked myself. I should have known better and skipped to the next tent. Of course, Morton Vineyards would have the first tent at the festival's main entrance. It was the most successful winery in the village, not to mention that the owners' son and winery heir was the mayor.

Mrs. Morton was one of the last people I ever wanted to run into in the village. If I had to choose between bumping into Nathan or his mother, I would always choose Nathan, and that was saying a lot, since I threw myself behind bushes in order to avoid my ex-boyfriend.

I cleared my throat. "Hello, Mrs. Morton. I'm sorry to bother you. I was only looking for Lacey or Adrien Dupont. Do you know where I can find their tent?" I figured it wouldn't hurt to ask my question.

As if she didn't hear me, she asked, "Are pets allowed at the festival?"

Emerson tensed in my arms. He liked Mrs. Morton as much as I did. That was telling.

"Emerson is," I said.

She frowned. "And why would your cat receive special dispensation?"

"He's more like a mascot than a cat."

Emerson purred in my ear.

"Can you direct me to the café's booth?" I asked for the second time. I should find someone else to help me. It would go much faster if I did.

To my surprise, she handed me a half piece of paper with a map of the festival on it, listing all the tents. I glanced down at it. La Crepe Jolie's tent was near the big tent. Perfect. I just hoped that Lacey or her husband was still there. "Thank you." I turned to leave with the paper clutched in my hand.

"Nathan tells me that the two of you are friendly again," Mrs. Morton said. Her tone was ice-cold, so much so that it froze me in place.

"We're cordial." I hoped that she would leave it at that.

"As long as that's all it is. I think you would agree with me that it would not be a good idea for you to become involved with my son again. He is the mayor of Cascade Springs and needs to find a wife who can fill the role as first lady of the village. We both know you would never be comfortable in a role like that."

I clenched my teeth. I had no desire to be the first lady of Cascade Springs, but at the same time, I didn't want to be told I wasn't fit for the job.

"I had better go find the Duponts," I said, and walked away before I said something I might regret. I hoped my self-restraint would show Mrs. Morton how much more mature I was. As a teenager, it wasn't uncommon for me to mouth off to even an adult in Mrs. Morton's position when I thought I was in the right, which happened a lot, because what teenager doesn't believe she is in the right all the time? Nothing cured me from talking back to one of my elders as much as teaching college students. Every time I had a student make a sarcastic retort in class, I knew it was a form of cosmic payback from my smart mouth as a kid.

I made a beeline for the Duponts' tent. Both Lacey and Adrien were there. Adrien was flipping crepes with a practiced hand. As soon as the crepe was cooked through, he added ham and cheese and quickly folded it together. After just enough time for the cheese to melt, he whipped it off the crepe pan and wrapped it in paper before handing it off to the salivating customer.

My mouth watered too. Adrien's crepes were as good as—if not better than—any I'd eaten in Montreal or Paris.

Lacey handed the waiting customer a plastic cup of hot apple cider to go with the crepe. On the surface, the food combination seemed like an odd pairing, but on the cool October night with a biting breeze coming across the river from Canada, it was the perfect choice. The customer carried his meal over to the tables in the large dining tent.

Lacey spotted me first. "Violet, what's wrong? You're as white as a sheet."

"I think I might have seen Anastasia's killer, and it's possible that he is coming after me now." I said all of this in one exhaled breath. Now that I was among friends, I could allow the fear that I had felt while being chased through Anastasia's house seep out of me.

Both of their mouths fell open at my announcement. I couldn't blame them—it was an outrageous statement. The only problem was it might be a true statement. I started shaking and Emerson ever so gently dug his claws into the shoulder of my jacket. It was as if the cat was reminding me to keep it together.

Adrien thrust a goblet of wine into my hand. "Drink this."

Despite growing up in wine country, I wasn't much of a drinker myself. I'd never acquired a taste for alcohol. If I was given the choice, I would much rather eat my calories in the form of sugary baked goodness like the cookies from La Crepe Jolie than from a glass of wine. With no cookies in sight, this was an emergency situation where any form of fortitude was welcome.

I took a big gulp from the half-full goblet. It was ice wine, the region's specialty. Usually, it was a drink that was delicately sipped, not guzzled down. Now I knew why, as the sweet liquid nearly choked me.

Lacey's eyes were the size of Adrien's crepes. "Yikes. You just went for it, didn't you?" She took Emerson from my arms.

I coughed and spurted and Adrien pounded on my back. Adrien had enough muscles to crush me like a bug, so his gentle back taps made me stumble forward. He caught me by the arm before I brought down their entire tent.

"That teenager is clearly drunk. Terrible," a woman walking by said to her friend. "You would think in a place like Cascade Springs they would have better control over underage drinking."

I didn't know if I should be happy the woman thought I wasn't old enough to drink or upset she thought I was publicly drunk.

A customer approached the Duponts' booth ready to make an order. Lacey nodded to her husband, and he seemed to understand what she meant. He stepped into her place to take the order and speak to the customers.

Lacey led me to one of the empty tables in the big tent. She was sure to choose a table that was off by itself. I still had my glass of wine in my hand. I set it in the middle of the table. So much for fortitude when I needed it.

I glanced back to their crepe booth. Late-night customers were beginning to line up as they craved a warm crepe to stave off the cold. "I shouldn't be taking you away from your booth."

She waved away my concern. "Adrien can handle it for a little while alone. He relishes the fast pace. It reminds him of the time he was the head chef at his restaurant in Montreal."

"He was a head chef in Montreal?" This was new information. Not that I doubted it. Adrien's food was some of the best food that I had ever tasted. He certainly had the talent to make it in the cosmopolitan city, but it only made me wonder more how he ended up in the village.

She nodded. "Enough about Adrien. Tell me what happened. Were you serious when you said you were chased by Anastasia's killer? I thought her death was an accident."

"It's looking less and less like an accident by the

second." Quickly and as quietly as I could, I related the events that had led me to flee Anastasia's mansion. However, I held back the discovery that Anastasia was Evanna Blue. I would save that revelation for Chief Rainwater. Was it possible the police had found the secret writing office and he already knew? In that case telling him would only reveal that I was trespassing. I shook away my misgivings. I had to tell Rainwater whether he knew or not. He needed to track down the man in the beard and glasses, the man who might just be Anastasia's murderer.

After I finished telling my tale, Lacey's eyes misted over. "I'm honored that you came to me first when you were so frightened. I know that we weren't the best of friends in school. You and Colleen were joined at the hip and nobody could break into your impenetrable duo, but you both were so good to me. I missed you both after she died and you left. I'm glad that we can be close again as adults." She grabbed a napkin off the table and touched it to the corner of her eye.

In high school, Lacey had been nothing more than a friendly acquaintance in my mind. Sometimes my best friend, Colleen, and I would let her hang around with us at school, but there wasn't much more to the friendship than that. Now I was ashamed to remember that when I left the village after Colleen's death, I hadn't given Lacey another thought until I'd returned to the village and discovered she'd opened La Crepe Jolie with her new husband.

Her teary reaction took me by surprise. I hadn't run to Lacey and Adrien's tent for any other reason than I knew they were close and they would help me. Normally, I would have run back to my grandma Daisy at a time like this to ask for guidance as to what I should do, but with Sadie there in her fragile state, I didn't want her to overhear anything that might upset her more.

"Have you told the police any of this?" Lacey asked, seeming to have recovered from her tears.

Of course, this was the right question to ask. I should have called the police chief the moment I lost the guy who broke into Anastasia's house. There was just the small detail that I'd broken into the house first that held me back.

"I really don't want to be arrested," I said.

"Why would you be arrested, Violet?" a deep baritone voice asked directly behind me.

NINETEEN

Even if I hadn't recognized the man's voice when he spoke, I would have known who it was the instant I saw Lacey's face. Her eyes went wide again, and her hand covered her mouth.

I spun around on the white folding chair to find Chief David Rainwater standing behind me. He'd changed out of his Detective Dupin outfit and now wore his police uniform. As chief of police, he wasn't typically in uniform. I suspected he wore it now because there were so many tourists in town for the Food and Wine Festival.

Despite the day that I'd had, I couldn't help but notice how nice the uniform looked on him. A light blush crept across my cheeks. I hoped it was too dark for him to notice, although I feared the surplus of twinkling lights all around the tent gave me away.

Lacey snapped her mouth closed. "Violet was just

telling me she was chased by a killer. Can you believe that? She's lucky to be alive, if you ask me. You should find the man who chased her and string him up by his toes."

I inwardly groaned. I appreciated her desire to defend me, but that was not the way I would have broken the news to the Cascade Springs chief of police.

"Come again?" the police chief asked. He narrowed his eyes until they were slits. "She was what?"

Before I could answer, Lacey launched into my tale. "She and Emerson were chased out of Anastasia's house!"

"Violet and Emerson were at Anastasia's place?" Rainwater's voice was calm, but I knew that was deceiving. "They were inside Anastasia's house, you mean?"

"You didn't know that." Lacey paled.

"No," Rainwater said. His lips barely moved as he spoke.

Lacey shot me an apologetic look and mouthed, "Sorry."

I gave her a small smile and turned to Rainwater. "I can answer for myself."

The chief's amber-colored eyes bored into mine. "I have plenty of questions for you, Violet. Don't worry about that." He turned back to Lacey. "Lacey, I would like to talk to Violet alone if you don't mind."

I gave Lacey a pleading look, silently asking her to stay. Lacey hesitated. "I—"

"Lacey," he said a little more firmly. "I need to speak to Violet alone, and it appears as if Adrien could use some help."

Adrien was in fact backed up at the La Crepe Jolie tent. His line was ten-deep and growing. It seemed everyone at the festival had the same idea that a hot crepe would be just the thing to warm them up on such a cold night. Lacey knit her brow in apology to me. "I'll be just over there if you need me, Violet. You holler, and I'll come running." She hopped out of her folding chair and hurried over to her husband, where she immediately began taking orders.

I was in trouble. I could have counted on Lacey to distract Rainwater at least for a little while with her rambling. Now I was strictly on my own.

Rainwater sat across from me in Lacey's vacated chair. "Tell me what happened from the beginning and describe the person who chased you in detail."

I was relieved to see the police chief didn't think I was making up the story.

I told him what I could from the beginning, but before I could get to the part about what I found in the room and what the man took, the police chief stood up. "I need to call this in and send some uniforms over there to search the house and secure the scene."

I felt a twinge of guilt for that. If I hadn't already been inside of the house and turned off the alarm, maybe the police would have caught the culprit in the act of breaking and entering.

Rainwater stepped a few feet away and spoke into his cell phone in hushed tones. I'd much rather he was speaking to Officer Clipton as opposed to Officer Wheaton. The buzz-cut officer grated on my last nerve, and I knew the feeling was mutual. Rainwater turned away from me, making it clear he didn't want me to overhear his conversation.

Fine, I thought, and checked my phone for messages and e-mails while he was in the middle of his conversation. I had missed three text messages from Grandma Daisy asking what was taking me so long. I swallowed when I saw a text message from Nathan asking how I was and saying he would do whatever he could to make the police allow my grandmother and me to open Charming Books the next day. I knew it was Nathan because he signed the text message. I didn't have his number in my phone, and I hadn't given him mine for that matter. I didn't know how he'd gotten it. I suspected that a certain meddling grandmother was to blame. I was beginning to wonder why she seemed to be so dead set on forcing Nathan and me back together.

Rainwater returned to our table and clipped his cell phone onto his duty belt next to his gun. He sat. "I doubt they will catch the person who saw you. He is likely long gone by now. About what time did you see the man?"

"I had *technically* broken into Anastasia's house too. I didn't mean to," I added in a rush. "Emerson got loose and jumped through an open window."

"Open window?" His voice was sharp. "There weren't any open windows in that house when we searched the place earlier today."

I shrugged. "That's how Emerson got inside. The window was on the second floor. Emerson shimmied up the drainpipe like he was Tarzan on a vine."

A smile flashed across Rainwater's face, but came and went so quickly, I wasn't sure I had seen it there at all. "And you too? Did you follow him through the window?"

I winced. I couldn't see any way out of this other than telling the truth. "I had a key."

He held out his hand.

I stuck my own hand in my jeans pocket to retrieve the key and dropped it into his palm.

"Where did you get this?" The police chief turned the key over in his large hand.

I bit the inside of my lip. I had certainly made a mess of things. If I told him the truth, it would only look worse for Sadie. To the police, it would have given her even more opportunity to tamper with the dress.

When I didn't answer, he asked, "How did you get past Anastasia's security system?"

I winced. "I had the code."

The police chief's phone rang before he could question me further. Rainwater held his index finger up at me as he stood up. "I have to take this. Hold that thought." Again Rainwater turned away from me as he spoke on the phone in a hushed tone.

It took everything I had not to lay my head on the white linen tablecloth in front of me and go to sleep. The adrenaline that had been coursing through me while being chased by the bearded man seeped out of my body all at once. Emerson shifted from my shoulder to my lap, where he curled up and fell asleep. Oh, to be a cat, and sleep whenever and wherever you felt like it.

Rainwater returned to the table. "I'm sorry about that. Officer Clipton was just reporting they're on the scene. They found a broken lamp in the great room that must have been the crash that you heard."

I nodded wearily.

"You look exhausted."

I nodded again.

"Breaking and entering will do that to you, I suppose." He said this with just a hint of teasing in his voice.

I looked up.

"You do realize I could have you arrested for breaking and entering, trespassing, tampering with a crime scene, and even fleeing the scene of a crime if I felt like it."

"Do you feel like it?" I asked.

"I haven't made up my mind on that score yet."

I frowned and scratched a slumbering Emerson between the ears. "Well, I have information that might keep me out of jail."

He leaned forward. "What is it?"

I leaned back in my chair under his intense scrutiny. "Anastasia was none other than Evanna Blue."

"The author?" he cried, clearly shocked by this news.

TWENTY

The festivalgoers dining and drinking in the big tent glanced over in our direction at his outburst.

I knew Rainwater would immediately understand the implications of that news. Maybe another police chief wouldn't know what it meant, but Rainwater was a writer; he knew. He blinked as he processed this new information. He pressed his lips into a thin line. "My officers have been in and out of that house all day. I went over there twice looking for evidence that might help us determine what exactly happened to Anastasia Faber and how she was killed. You're telling me you went in there after we did and discovered she was an international best-selling author and keeping it a secret all this time?"

I nodded.

"How?"

"In a secret room."

He arched one of his black eyebrows at me. "A secret room?"

"On the second floor of the house behind one of the bookcases in the big sitting room at the end of the hallway. There is a latch behind the shelf. When you press it, the door opens and you're inside Anastasia's secret writing office."

"How did you find it?" he asked.

I patted Emerson's head. "I didn't. He did."

Rainwater looked skyward for just a moment as if asking the heavens for some type of relief. Instead, all he saw was the ceiling of the big tent.

"I can show you where it is," I offered. Some of my energy had returned with the idea of seeing Anastasia's hideaway again.

"Fine. I need to get to Anastasia's house as it is and see how the investigation is going. I will also need to know everything that you remember touching. Hopefully we can grab a print of this guy. Have you ever seen him before?"

I shook my head. "Never." I bit the inside of my cheek, well aware that my fingerprints were all over Anastasia's office because of my search for information about the Red Inkers. The piece of paper with that information remained in the back pocket of my jeans. I didn't bring it to Rainwater's attention.

He nodded at Emerson. "The cat is going to have to stay here. I can't have him running around and potentially contaminating the crime scene."

Emerson opened one eye at the chief's comment.

"I'll leave him with Lacey," I said, putting what I hoped was a soothing hand on Emerson's back.

Rainwater nodded and stood. Standing over me, he

extended his hand to help me to my feet. I hesitated, but finally put my hand into his and stood, lifting Emerson in my other arm.

"Thanks," I murmured, and removed my hand as quickly as was polite, although I had the residual feeling of his palm against mine.

Thankfully, Lacey was more than happy to watch Emerson. She said she and Adrien would be closing up the booth in a few minutes and would run the cat to my grandmother's house as soon as they were done.

Everyone seemed to be happy with the arrangement except for the small tuxie. Emerson meowed at me from her arms, but when Adrien shook a piece of ham at him, he decided staying with the Duponts for a little bit wasn't all that bad.

I followed the chief to his department car, which was a small SUV with CASCADE SPRINGS POLICE emblazoned on the back of it. He unlocked the car with his key fob.

"I'm not going to sit in the back, am I? There are enough people in the village who still think I have a criminal past. I'd rather not encourage the rumor mill."

He chuckled and opened the passenger-side door. "You can sit in the front. The only time I will ever make you sit in the back is if I arrest you."

"And you aren't going to arrest me for my transgressions tonight?" I asked.

He leaned on the opened car door. "Still haven't decided."

In the darkness, I couldn't tell if he was joking. Not that it would have made much difference in the light. The police chief had the most stoic expression I had ever seen.

"That's encouraging," I said. "I guess I will have to be on my best behavior from here on out."

"I'll hold you to that."

I climbed into the car, and he shut the door after me. I could be wrong, but I might have seen a hint of a smile on his face.

The passenger seat in the chief's department-issued SUV was small, because it was partly crowded by a small laptop computer that was bolted to his console. I knew it was there so that he could look up people's registrations during traffic stops or other arrests. Those were usually the worst of the offenses in our village, until recently. I wondered if I put my information in that machine, what would come up. I had a longer history with police interest than I wished to remember.

Rainwater saw me eyeing the laptop and snapped it closed, folding it up toward the dashboard. So much for that idea. He started the car. He beeped his siren to encourage festivalgoers to move out of the way as he pulled out onto River Road. When we were finally clear of the Riverwalk area, he turned the siren on at full blast.

The siren was loud but sounded muffled from inside the police vehicle, but it still made any conversation difficult, which was just fine with me. It gave me time to collect my thoughts and mull over what had happened in the last day. There was a lot to ponder, starting of course with Anastasia's death.

He glanced at me. "Did you get that key and the alarm passcode from Sadie?" he asked over the screeching of the sirens.

I had been prepared to tell Rainwater all about Anastasia/Evanna and my discovery. I had hoped he would have forgotten about the key and the security system code. I should have known better.

"Violet?" he asked when I didn't answer. "I know she watered Anastasia's plants when Anastasia was out of town. She would have needed a key and the passcode to do that. So answer my question. Did she give them to you?"

I sighed. "Yes."

He gripped the steering wheel a little more tightly as if he had expected this answer, but was disappointed to hear it.

"I know that Sadie didn't do this," I said. "She wasn't the one who was in Anastasia's house tonight. I'm certain of that."

He didn't say anything as he drove by the lamppost at the end of Anastasia's property and up the long driveway to the house.

There were two village police cruisers with flashers and headlights on in the driveway. Their blue and red lights reflected on the sides of the large stone house and the trees. It gave everything an ominous glow.

Rainwater parked his SUV behind the last cruiser, and Officer Clipton was already at his side by the time I climbed out of the car. The officer raised her blond eyebrows. "What is she doing here?"

Hello to you too, Officer, I thought, and just when I was starting to like her too.

"She's going to show us the location of Anastasia's secret room." His tone was matter-of-fact, and I relaxed a little. Despite his dozens of questions, the police chief believed me at least as far as Anastasia's secret writing office was concerned.

"There is no such thing. Officer Wheaton and I tore this place apart. Trust me when I say we would have found a hidden room if it was there."

Wheaton stood in the back doorway of the mansion and scowled at me.

Chief Rainwater gestured to the house. "Miss Waverly, after you."

The fact that he called me "Miss Waverly" in front of his officers wasn't lost on me. Without a word, I led the group of three officers into the house, through the kitchen, down the long hallway, and up the stairs. I walked with purpose up the curved staircase and directly into the sitting room. I was surprised to see that the bookcase was closed. After chasing me out of the house, the man must have run back upstairs and closed up the office. Why would he have done that? To cover his tracks?

"There's nothing here," Wheaton protested. "I have been through this room three times myself."

I ignored him and walked up to the bookcase that I had opened just a few short hours before. With an expert hand, I hit the latch behind the case and the bookshelf clicked open.

Behind me there was an audible gasp from the police, and I couldn't help taking a little bit of satisfaction in proving Wheaton wrong. I wasn't above that. I turned on the light.

Officer Clipton swore under her breath. "How on earth did you find that?"

"Emerson," I said simply.

She blinked at me.

"Emerson is her cat." Wheaton supplied the answer to the unspoken question.

"Like that is supposed to clear it up. Is knowing a cat told her about this room making this any clearer to anyone else?" Clipton asked.

"Violet, can you step back?" Rainwater asked.

I stepped out of the doorway.

Rainwater and Officer Wheaton went inside. There wasn't enough room in the small space for more than two people. Officer Clipton and I watched from the doorway. The office was just as I had left it. The only thing that was missing was the printed e-mail that had been on the desk. My phone sat in the back pocket of my jeans. The intruder had taken the e-mail. I knew that I should tell the police about the photo I had taken of the e-mail, and I was about to when Chief Rainwater said, "I want to know who was aware that Anastasia Faber was Evanna Blue. We need to contact her publisher. There must be someone there who knows. They might also have a list of the people who signed a nondisclosure agreement. This is the reason that she was murdered. I would put all my money on it."

"A nondisclosure agreement?" Clipton asked.

Wheaton glanced up from Anastasia's desk, where he was in the process of taking a picture. "A contract that people ask others to sign to keep a secret."

"In this case," I said, "a contract that kept Evanna Blue's true identity a secret."

"Evanna who?" the female officer asked.

"Clipton, you need to get out more," Wheaton said to the other officer before going back to taking photographs.

I found it quite interesting that Wheaton knew who Evanna Blue was, and I was just about to comment on it when Rainwater spoke up.

"Officer Clipton," Rainwater said. "Can you take Miss Waverly home?" He turned to me. "Thank you for your help tonight, but we've got what we need to take it from here."

I had been dismissed.

TWENTY-ONE

The next morning, sunlight was streaming in through the large window of the bedroom that had been mine in my grandmother's house after my mother's death. When I was in the pale yellow room with the ruffled gingham curtains, it was difficult not to remember that time and how many tears the pillows on the four-poster bed had absorbed. The light coming through the window was tinted ochre as it broke through the oak tree in my grandmother's front yard.

I peered at the foot of the bed for any sign of Emerson, but the cat was gone. My bedroom door was open a crack as well. I knew that the tuxie would be in the kitchen begging my grandmother for breakfast. My own stomach rumbled at the thought of one of Grandma Daisy's extravagant breakfasts. I wondered what she was making. Chocolate chip pancakes would be my request if I was given a choice. I could use a ruler-high stack of chocolate chip pancakes after the night I'd had. On second thought, Grandma Daisy could hold the pancakes and just hand over the bag of chocolate chips. Sometimes chocolate chips straight up was the only medicine that would do the trick.

I rolled onto my stomach and reached for my cell phone on the nightstand. I yelped as soon as I saw the time. It was after nine, and I had a ten a.m. class to teach at the college. If I didn't leave now, I would never make it, and if I didn't make it within the first fifteen minutes of the class session, my students would bolt and I would be even further behind in my lesson plan than I already was.

At least I'd had the good sense to bring my massive tote bag that I carried for class to my grandmother's house for the night. I'd had some grand plan of marking papers the night before. That hadn't happened. By the time I had gotten home from Anastasia's house, it was after midnight.

I tore out of my bedroom and into the bathroom, where I took the world's fastest shower, and ran back into the bedroom a moment later, throwing open the small overnight bag. I wriggled into jeans and a sweater, perhaps not professor-appropriate attire, but I hadn't thought about teaching when I threw together my overnight bag the day before. I had been distracted by murder at the time. Sadie would be aghast at my clothing.

I shoved my feet into ankle boots, selected by Sadie—at least I had those to show her—and dropped my cell phone in my tote bag.

"Violet?" my grandmother called up the stairs. "Is that you up there making that racket?"

I didn't even bother to answer. I twirled my wet hair into a knot on the back of my head. This was as good as it was going to get. As I stormed down the stairs, I remembered that I had left my bike parked outside La Crepe Jolie, and my car was parked by Charming Books. I didn't have time to retrieve either before class. My grandmother's car was the only option.

In the kitchen, Sadie sat at the round table by the window with a full breakfast in front of her: eggs, toast, bacon, juice, coffee, and, be still my heart, chocolate chip pancakes. Her meal was completely untouched.

My grandmother was at the stove flipping more pancakes. It smelled heavenly. I wished that I had more time to enjoy it.

"Grandma Daisy, can I borrow your car? I'm late for class and I don't have either my bike or car here."

She held her spatula in midair. "Of course, but won't you sit down for some breakfast? Sadie and I were just saying that we didn't know what time you got home last night. I thought you were only running out on an *errand*."

I knew she wouldn't say the name of the errand, watering the tree, in front of Sadie for fear of revealing our secret.

"I'll fill you in later. Right now, I have to run. I'm late for class." I grabbed a piece of bacon from the plate by the stove. It was still steaming hot as I popped it into my mouth and burned the roof of my mouth. That was just par for the kind of morning that I was having. With one hand, I ripped a paper towel off the roll and grabbed two chocolate chip pancakes from the stack at my grandmother's elbow. I shoved them into my tote bag. "For the road," I said as I snatched up my grandmother's car key from its hook on the kitchen wall.

Outside the house, I typed the code into the console bolted to the side of the freestanding garage to reveal my grandmother's ancient compact car. Grandma Daisy hardly ever drove. She rarely had a reason to. On those infrequent occasions she did drive, she went grocery shopping over in the next town, which had one of those grocery supercenters. Cascade Springs would never allow such a monstrosity within its borders. Or she would use the car when she had to pick up a shipment of books in nearby Niagara Falls. Sometimes it cost less to receive shipments there and then pick them up.

As the garage door recessed into the ceiling, I winced as I took in the sight of my grandmother's car. The compact was almost as old as I was and it still had only fifty thousand miles on it. It was the same car she had had when I was a child and it looked to be in perfect condition. Appearances could be deceiving, though. Over a decade ago, the lock on the driver's side broke in the lock position. The car was so old that it predated automatic locks and key fobs. Grandma Daisy had yet to have the lock fixed. She saw no reason to spend the money on the door, since she hardly used the compact to begin with, and she claimed that climbing through the passenger side and over the seat like a contortionist kept her spry.

I, however, saw the advantage of a working driver-side door as I yanked open the heavy passenger door, especially when I was so terribly late for class. I dropped my tote bag on the floor of the car, hoping the pancakes survived the impact, and scrambled into the vehicle. I banged the top of my head on the car's ceiling and rammed my knee into the gearshift. Under these circumstances, being tall was not working to my advantage.

Finally, behind the wheel and acutely aware of muscles that I hadn't known I possessed, I started the car, shifted into reverse, and backed out of the garage and onto Grandma Daisy's quiet street.

Springside Community College was a picturesque wooded campus that sat on the outskirts of the village along the Niagara River.

In my rush, I didn't have time to appreciate the beauty of the campus as I usually did. I semilegally parked outside the academic building where my class was being held, hoping that campus security would forgive my parking violation just this once.

I ran through the long hallway, grateful that my class was on the first floor, and I reached the classroom just as the students were packing up, ready to make their escape. The twenty or so students in the room groaned as I crashed through the door.

I caught my breath. "Sorry, guys. I'm here. Get out the response papers you wrote for homework and pass them to the left. We will have a short critique session to begin class." I tried to cover my panting.

The groans became worse. No one liked the critique sessions. I'd hated them myself as a student, but the fifteen minutes the students would take to read and comment on one another's papers would give me enough time to get my bearings.

As I heard the shuffle of pages being passed throughout the room, I fell into my chair at the front of the room and started to rummage through my tote bag for my class notes. With longing in my heart, I pushed the chocolate chip pancakes aside and pulled out a thin volume of Poe's works. My chest constricted. How had the book ended up in my bag? I distinctly remembered leaving the paperback of Poe's works on my unmade bed in my grandmother's house. The books had never appeared to me outside the shop. I didn't know that the magic could work away from Charming Books. I shook my head. The book must have appeared in the bag before I took it from Charming Books. Yes, that must be it. I didn't know if I could handle books flying around and appearing all over the village. I was just becoming used to it inside of the shop.

"Professor Waverly, are you okay?" one of the students sitting in the first row asked. She had a bar going through her eyebrow that gave her round baby face a little edge. I assumed that was the motivation for the piercing.

I looked up from my tote bag. "I'm fine. Why do you ask?"

"It's just your hair," she said as sweetly as possible. "You sort of look like you've been electrocuted. Was that what you were going for?"

I sighed and closed my bag. So much for class notes. It appeared that I would have to wing it. "Please return the response papers to the original owner. Would anyone like to read what they wrote?"

The remainder of the class we discussed sentence structure and active versus passive voice. Even I was bored with the lecture by the time my students filed out of the room.

"Don't forget. Midterms are next week. You should be halfway through *Huckleberry Finn* at this point in the semester."

There was another groan.

After the students left, I fell back into my chair to catch my breath. I was relieved that there wasn't another class scheduled until noon. It gave me a few minutes to collect myself. I removed the band from my hair, which was mostly dry by now. My wavy hair, now curled from being restrained in the knot, bounced around my face. I did my best to finger comb it into submission. It was a futile act.

I stuck my hand in the tote bag again and pulled out the volume of Poe's work and the now-cold chocolate chip pancakes. I took a bite of one of the pancakes. It was cold, but the chocolate was still good. I flipped open the book on the table and began doing what the books had wanted me to do from the start, reading. Remembering the strange events of the night before, I began with "The Fall of the House of Usher." As I read, I made notes in the book's margins. The House of Usher was a house with a secret, just like Anastasia's home.

"I have class in here in ten minutes," a deep female voice said, interrupting my concentration.

I looked up from my notes to find a heavyset woman pushing a full skeleton into the classroom. "I'm so sorry," I said, quickly gathering up my notes.

She pushed the skeleton to the corner of the room.

I dropped my last folder into my tote bag. "Decorating for Halloween?" I quipped.

She wrinkled her nose. "No," she said. "This is for an anatomy course."

Oh-kay. I sighed and gathered up my things as the anatomy professor's students filed into the room. I left the building shaking my head.

As I expected, there was a ticket from the campus police on my grandmother's car for my illegal parking job. I crumpled it up and shoved it into my bag. I had no intention of paying the ticket, since it was unlikely that I would ever again drive my grandmother's car onto campus, or at least I hoped that was the case.

"Violet!" A voice called my name just as I was about to climb into the car through the passenger side.

I dropped my bag on the car's floorboard and turned to see Renee Reid running toward me. Her owl-printed scarf trailed behind her, and she gripped a piece of paper in her right hand like her life depended on it.

Students heading to class moved out of her way. It was the most natural response when a librarian ran across campus.

TWENTY-TWO

Renee waved the paper. "Violet, wait!"

I closed the door to the car with a thud and met her on the sidewalk. "Renee, what's going on? You're going to give yourself a heart attack."

She bent at the waist. "Oh, I hate running. Why do people run for fun? They must be crazy," she gasped.

I had wondered the same a few times myself.

She took a deep breath. "I'm so glad I caught you. I've been waiting for you all morning."

"Waiting for me why?" I tried to remember if I had a research appointment with her that day. Renee has been an invaluable help to me in researching for my dissertation.

She straightened up and thrust the printout into my hand. "This!"

The paper was badly wrinkled from being held in her

hand so tightly. I smoothed it out as best I could so that I could read it. It was an article from a premier publishing magazine. I recognized it right away because Grandma Daisy subscribed to the magazine to keep up-to-date on the trends in publishing, so she would know what to stock in the store.

EVANNA BLUE UNMASKED, the headline read. The article went on to say that Anastasia Faber, a reclusive author who lived in the small village of Cascade Springs, New York, was in fact Evanna Blue. The author of the article claimed to have found undisputable evidence of Evanna's identity. Then the article went on to describe Anastasia's murder, naming Charming Books as the place of her death. Charming Books was noted as the location of a murder in a national magazine. Terrific.

"Can you believe this?" Renee asked, still slightly out of breath from her run across campus or from the excitement. "Evanna Blue was living here in our little village all this time, and no one knew it!"

I stared at the paper, trying to process what I had just read.

She ran a hand through her tangled auburn hair. "Why aren't you freaking out? Why are you not surprised?"

I looked up from the article. "I already knew."

"What?" she shrieked. "How could you have already known? According to this, it was the greatest secret in Western civilization."

A student strolling the sidewalk did an about-face when the librarian screeched at me. Perhaps a yelling librarian was even more alarming than a running librarian. Not that Renee was your typical librarian, with her tendency to be loud and her infectious laugh that could be heard all over the library building multiple times throughout the day. She wasn't one to whisper, and I had seen her shush a student only once, when a group of football players was especially rowdy.

"I haven't known for long," I said quickly, not wanting Renee to think I'd kept the information from her. "I just learned about Anastasia's secret identity last night." I wrapped my coat a little more tightly around myself. "I was surprised that I didn't see you yesterday in the village."

"I was out of town over the weekend visiting my sister and her kids. She has five boys under seven. If you ever need good birth control, I will give you her address." She shivered in mock horror.

I bit my lip. "They can't be that bad."

"Wanna bet?" She waved her hand. "Never mind all that. Where have you been? I've been waiting to tell you this all morning," she went on. "Usually, you come straight to the library after class. What happened?"

"I was jotting down some notes after my last class and lost track of time." I read the article. As far as I could tell, the journalist had gotten all the facts right. I glanced at the byline. The article was written by one "Daven York." However, it wasn't so much his name as his grainy photo that caught my attention. The picture of the article's author was tiny, but it was easy to make out the man's features, which included a beard and glasses. "It's him!"

"Him?" she asked, apparently distracted by my hair. "Him who?"

"The guy who chased me last night," I said. The piece of paper shook in my hands.

"Wait, you are going to have to back up and tell me that again. Someone chased you last night? Is that the reason for the crazy hair?"

"Please forget about the hair."

"Sorry," she said. "Tell me what happened."

So I did, telling her everything that had happened from the moment I reached Anastasia's home the night before.

She folded her arms across her chest. "You do know it was really stupid for you to have gone in there, don't you?"

"What was I supposed to do? Emerson was inside. If I left him there, David would have found him."

A smile twitched at the corners of her mouth. "David? Would you be referring to the chief of police?"

I frowned. "Yes. At the time, I didn't see any reason to risk getting more tangled up with the police than I was already. Anastasia died in Charming Books, you know. It wouldn't be good for me to be caught snooping at her house a few hours later."

Her smile was broad now. "But *David* and the police know now, don't they? What did he say when he found out?" She was just short of rubbing her hands together in anticipation of the news.

"He wasn't thrilled." I held up the article. "Can I take this?"

She sighed as if disappointed that I wouldn't tell her more about my encounter with Rainwater. "I e-mailed you a copy too. Do you think it is connected to the murder?"

I bit my lip. "I don't know, but since Sadie Cunningham is the police's main suspect at the moment, anything I can give the chief to distract him away from her is good."

"Sadie Cunningham," she yelled for a second time in our conversation, causing another student to change course.

If I ever wanted to clear the sidewalk, I would have to remember to bring Renee with me. She could really project her voice. If the librarian thing ever fell through, she could always try stage acting.

"How could the police chief possibly think Sadie Cunningham had anything to do with Anastasia's death? She is the least murderous person on planet earth. I saw her carry a spider out of her shop once like it was made of gold. A spider. In my book, if a spider comes into my domain, all bets are off."

I had to agree with her stance on spiders—I had seen *Arachnophobia* at a very impressionable age—and about Sadie too. Sadie wouldn't hurt any creature on earth.

"Does the police chief suspect Sadie because he's still upset that Grant Morton got nothing more than a reprimand from the DA after all the trouble that he caused last summer?"

Until Renee made that comment, I hadn't considered that, but the thought that David might be treating Sadie differently because of Grant's mistakes made me heartsick.

TWENTY-THREE

Faintly, I heard my phone ring from deep in the recesses of my tote bag. I dove into the car to grab it. It was Grandma Daisy. "I just heard from David," she said without a greeting. "He said it's fine for us to go back to Charming Books this afternoon. I'm heading over now to open up shop. He wants us to stay away from the back stairs and kitchen, but other than that, we have free rein of the shop. Thankfully the kitchen and stairs are away from where any customers would go anyway."

"That's great news. I'm shocked that he's letting us back in so fast."

"He gave me the impression that he was getting some pressure from the mayor. You might want to thank Nathan next time you see him."

Nathan. Of course Nathan was behind it, and I was grateful. I only hoped that he didn't expect anything in return.

"Can I go in my apartment?" I asked.

"Yes." She sounded so relieved, and I couldn't help feeling the same despite my misgivings about Nathan's involvement. The Food and Wine Festival lasted the entire week, and to be closed for any part of it could sorely hurt our business.

"I'm done teaching for the day, so I will head over there now."

"All right, dear," she said distractedly.

I slipped the phone into the back pocket of my jeans. "That was my grandmother. The police are letting us reopen Charming Books."

"That's great," Renee said. "But what are you going to do about that?" She pointed at the article in my hand.

I folded the piece of paper and dropped it into my tote bag. "I'll give it to Chief Rainwater and let him take it from there."

She cocked her head. "I don't doubt you will give it to the police chief, but I don't believe for a minute that you are going to let the case go."

"Private citizens shouldn't mess with police investigations," I said, having heard it a time or two repeated to me.

"Says you," she said with a laugh. "I suggest you go home and make yourself presentable before you see the police chief."

My brows knit together. "Presentable?"

Her eyes twinkled. "He's a handsome man."

"And your point is?" I dropped my bag back onto the floor of my car.

She pantomimed zipping her lips closed and throwing away the key.

I wanted to question her more about what *all that* meant, but I didn't have the time. The sooner I reached Charming Books, the better. I had a feeling my grandmother might have some grand plan to distract festivalgoers from the murder. That couldn't be good. "I'd better go."

She gave me a quick hug. "At least promise that you will be careful. I know Chief Rainwater will be keeping an eye on you, but you could have been killed last night. Cut down on the stupid, okay? For Rainwater and for me."

"I will," I promised, and couldn't stop myself from saying, "You do realize everyone else in the village, including my own grandmother, is pushing me toward Nathan, not David."

She clicked her tongue. "The mayor is all wrong for you," she said with conviction.

I arched my brow. "Really?"

She nodded. "You would never fit in with that family."

My cheek twitched. Renee had repeated what I had heard from Nathan's parents my entire life. The comment didn't hurt any less coming from her. In fact, it chafed a little bit more.

"Trust me. I'm a librarian, which means I'm all-knowing," she said, completely unaware how her comment had affected me.

"I didn't know that about librarians," I quipped, hiding my feelings from her.

She nodded seriously. "It's true. We get a badge and everything with our master's degrees."

I smiled and thanked her for the article. Renee turned to go back to the library. As she left, I spotted the troubadour, Fenimore, standing outside the library. He cradled his guitar in his arms, and he was watching me with such intensity that I looked away.

I shook off the creepy feeling that his persistent stare gave me and climbed into Grandma Daisy's car.

The traffic in the central part of the village was terrible due to the Food and Wine Festival. I would have thought that the festivalgoers would have tapered off on Monday. Apparently, I was wrong. Since I was making no progress by car, I turned off on a side street, opting to leave my grandmother's car at her house and walk to Charming Books. I pulled the car into the driveway. The house was still. Grandma Daisy and Sadie must already be on River Road, and I had no doubt Emerson had gone with them.

As I walked, I fashioned my long hair into a braid. It was the only thing that could be done with it when it was so unruly. The braid would restrain it for a little while at least.

I was a block from Charming Books when pedestrians and cyclists crowded the sidewalk. I wove through the throng as my unease grew. The congestion became worse as I came closer to the bookshop.

"She was killed in this very store," someone said in his best announcer voice as if he were telling the world that there was a sale on turkey at Thanksgiving.

"Do you think they will build a memorial?" another voice asked in the same tone. "They should," someone answered the question. "I can't believe she's gone. Who is going to write her books? She's the only author I read. Her work speaks to me. I don't know how I will go on."

I still couldn't see who was saying these things. There were just too many people on this section of River Road, more than there should be even in the middle of the Cascade Springs Food and Wine Festival.

I pushed through the crowd, muttering "excuse me" and "pardon me" as I went. Finally, I broke through the crush of bodies in front of Charming Books and my mouth fell open. There were at least a dozen reporters with microphones in their hands and video cameras pointed at their faces standing in the tiny front yard of Charming Books. The street was completely blocked by news vans. There was no way any traffic would be able to move an inch. I hadn't seen a snarl of traffic like this since I'd left Chicago.

Press from as far away as New York City stood on the sidewalk in front of Charming Books. I started when I spotted a cable news truck as well. The commentator from NBC New York recorded a sound bite. "International best-selling author Evanna Blue's identity has been revealed only through her tragic death. Murdered right here while she was participating at a reading in this small bookshop in Cascade Springs, New York."

Evanna Blue's true identity was news, national news, and my beloved Charming Books was smack in the center of it.

A man shoved a huge camera lens in my face and snapped a picture. Another man thrust a microphone in my face. "Miss, how do you know Anastasia?" he asked breathlessly. "Are you a family friend?"

"No comment," I said, and ducked away from them.

Officer Clipton stood in the middle of the street shouting at the news vans to move or they would be cited for blocking traffic.

"Excuse me." I stepped around a reporter who barricaded the gate into Charming Books' front lawn. Flashbulbs went off in my line of vision as photographers snapped pictures of me.

Officer Wheaton stood sentinel at the front door of the shop, stopping the press from entering. I broke free from the throng and stumbled up the steps. Wheaton stepped in my path. "Chief says no one gets in."

I glared at him. "This is my home and business, Wheaton. Get out of my way."

He scowled down his perfectly straight nose at me.

"Move," I hissed, ever aware of the photos being taken of me. I blinked away the bright lights, which hurt my eyes.

A strong hand reached out from inside Charming Books and around Wheaton. I yelped as the hand pulled me into the shop and slammed the door shut after me.

~ও

TWENTY-FOUR

~ও

My captor steadied me before releasing my arm.
"Sorry about that," Chief Rainwater said. "I just
didn't want to give them any more opportunity to snap footage of you."

I rubbed my upper arm where he had grabbed me.
"Thanks. I think."

He winced. "Did I hurt you?"

I shook my head. "What's going on out there?" I demanded.
"Is every reporter on the East Coast in our village? Did I see
a CNN truck? Please tell me I didn't."

He grimaced. "It seems that way, I know. I was just
about to go back out and help my officers clear the street."

I took in the shop. The lights were off and the cash register drawer stood open as we left it every night when we
removed the money. "Where's Grandma Daisy? She told me

she was coming straight here when you gave her the all clear to return to the shop. Does she know what's going on?"

He nodded. "She's out there somewhere, I'm afraid. As soon as the press showed up, your grandmother sprang into action. You know how she is."

I did. Unfortunately.

"And Sadie?"

His frown deepened. "I haven't seen her. She wasn't with Daisy when she arrived."

I bit my lip, wondering where my friend could be. I prayed she wasn't out on River Road in this mess. The press would eat her alive, especially when they discovered that she was the prime suspect in Anastasia's murder.

"What are all these people doing here?"

He ran a hand back and forth over his short hair. I noted that he was still in uniform and how the fabric pulled tight against his chest as he moved. I dropped my eyes to the floor, where I found Emerson lying across an open volume of Poe's works.

Rainwater didn't seem to notice any of this when he said, "The press got wind of Evanna Blue's true identity. Everyone wants a piece of the story. It's big news, or it will be for the next day or two until they find something else to move on to. I just don't know how they found out that quickly. I swore my officers to secrecy."

"I know how." I fished in my bag for the article that Renee had given me and handed it to him. "The story must be all over the Internet by now. There's something else that you should know."

He looked up from the article. "What do you mean?"

"Check out the byline." I pointed to the spot on the paper.

He read the name. "Daven York? Should I know him? Is he from the village?"

I shook my head. "That's the guy who broke into Anastasia's house last night. I'm sure of it. I recognize him by his picture."

Rainwater gripped the piece of paper a little more tightly and it crinkled in his hand. "Did you see him outside with the other reporters?"

"No, but there was such a crush of people that I could have easily missed him."

"I need to talk to Mr. York." The police chief's tone was as menacing as I'd ever heard it.

"He's the one who broke the story. He must have some type of informant," I said. "How else would he have gotten wind of Anastasia's death so fast, and how else would he have known where exactly her secret office was?"

"What do you mean?"

"Last night when he came into Anastasia's sitting room, I hid behind her sofa."

Rainwater grimaced as if the image pained him.

I forged on. "He went directly to the bookshelves and felt for the lever behind them. Someone would have had to tell him to do that. The only reason I found the lever was because Emerson showed me."

The tuxie meowed at that comment, not without a little pride, I thought.

"You make a good point. That could only mean that someone here in the village would be able to tell him that."

I walked across the room and dropped my tote bag behind the sales counter. The bag was heavy from all my textbooks from class. "I might have an idea," I said, and told him about the man who asked about Anastasia yesterday afternoon during Charming Books' sidewalk sale.

He followed me across the room and leaned on the counter. "Why didn't you tell me this before?"

"I forgot the moment you and your officers stormed Sadie's shop."

He folded the article by quarters. "We didn't storm her shop."

"Call it what you will, but the commotion made me forget. Everything happened so fast after that."

"Everything? Does that include breaking and entering into a murder victim's house?"

I gave him a look and was surprised to see humor in his amber eyes. I quickly glanced away.

"What can you tell me about this other man? Did you recognize him?" he asked.

I shook my head. "I've never seen him before either. Could it be the two men were working together?"

"I'm able to believe just about anything at this point."

My eyes fell to Emerson lounging like a lion across Poe's works. I wasn't so sure about that. I knew of at least one thing the police chief would not be able to believe.

"We can't rule out that Anastasia herself might have told the reporter about her secret room."

"Anastasia?" Rainwater asked.

"After she kept this secret for so long, and it was clear from the e-mail that I found that she was becoming increasingly agitated that Evanna's work was doing so well when she, Anastasia, was having zero success in getting her literary fiction published."

"What e-mail?"

Whoops. I had forgotten I hadn't told the chief about the e-mail that had been on Anastasia's desk when I entered her office for the first time either. I removed my cell phone from my back pocket.

"What e-mail, Violet?" Rainwater asked.

I held up a finger. "One second." I found the photo I'd taken of the e-mail in my photo gallery. I handed him the phone.

He pinched the screen for a better look at the image and his eyes widened. "Why didn't you tell me about this last night?"

"I had planned to," I said, half-fibbing. "But I forgot in all the confusion."

The police chief arched his eyebrows as if he didn't quite believe me. "You seem to forget to share information with me a lot."

I shrugged. "It was a busy night. I assume that you would have found this eventually in her e-mail, though."

He nodded. "Yes. One of the crime scene techs over in Niagara Falls is going through her computer now, but that takes time and we aren't the only case that the Niagara Falls PD has to worry about. We don't have the time or manpower to go through her computer ourselves with just a half dozen officers in the village, and we are still dealing with security for the Food and Wine Festival."

I held up a hand. "I wasn't judging you. I know you have your hands full."

"I know and I appreciate that." He tapped the screen and started to type on the touch screen.

I reached for my phone. "What are you doing?"

He stepped back out of my range. "I'm sending this picture to my phone and now I am deleting it." He handed the phone back to me with a smile on his face. "From your gallery and from your sent text messages for good measure."

I grabbed the phone back from him. "You can't erase it from my phone. It's my picture."

"You shouldn't be walking around with police evidence in a murder investigation on your phone."

I scowled. Just when I was beginning to think that Rainwater and I were on the same team too. It was a good thing I'd sent a copy to my e-mail the night before. I was an academic. I knew how to back up my work.

"I did it for your own good. You seem to be forgetting that this isn't a game. Anastasia was murdered in such a way that took premeditation and a good deal of hatred."

I shivered. "Do you think the reporter, York, is behind it? Would he kill her just for this story? Wouldn't it have been better to reveal who she was while she was alive, so he could interview her or something?"

He frowned so deeply that lines I had never noticed before appeared on the sides of his mouth. If anything, the lines gave his handsome face more character. "I have no idea what the press thinks will make a printable story. And thank you for this information. I know it will help us with the investigation."

I thought the police chief was trying to be nice after commandeering my phone until he said, "Stay out of it."

I shoved my phone into the back pocket of my jeans.

"Now," he said as if that was settled, "I need to go outside and help my officers clear the street." He walked across the room and placed his hand on the doorknob. He turned and said, "By the way, you might want to put that watering can back in the shed where it was yesterday afternoon."

My mouth went dry and I stared at the watering can that I had used the night before when I broke into Charming Books to water the tree. It sat on top of one of the low bookcases in the middle of the room as plain as day. Rainwater probably noticed it the moment that he set foot in the shop that morning, and he knew that I had been there.

He left the shop before I could utter a word about it.

TWENTY-FIVE

After Rainwater left, I went to the large picture window and stared out. Rainwater and Wheaton were marching toward the reporters with their hands outstretched in the universal stop sign. The newspeople didn't appear happy about the interruption to their sound bites. I searched the faces for Daven York, but I didn't spot him. I supposed he didn't have to be there with the others, since he was the one who broke the story. Everyone else was trying to catch up with him.

With a great *ca-caw*, Faulkner swooped down and landed on his perch next to me, causing me to jump. "Where have you been?" I asked.

"Nevermore!" he cried.

I scowled, but his comment of course brought to mind Poe and the books and how the shop's essence wanted me to read them. I turned away from the window back to Emerson, the birch tree, and the Poe book.

I sighed and walked over to the foot of the tree. Emerson pawed at my pant leg and meowed. I looked down at him. He ran to the front door and back to me. Lassie had nothing on my tuxedo cat.

"I thought you wanted me to read the book." I pointed at the book of Poe still sitting open on the floor.

He scratched at the front door.

"All right. I'll go. I need to find Grandma Daisy anyway and make sure that she's staying out of trouble, but you have to stay here."

He flattened down on his haunches with his black ears pressed back against his head.

"I know that you don't like this idea, but that's just too bad. I can't have you outside with all those people. There's too great a risk that you might get hurt. If you got hurt, I would never forgive myself."

He flattened his body even more and his whiskers turned down.

I sighed. There wasn't much I could do to keep the cat in the shop, especially when we finally did open for business and people began to come and go. Emerson had mad escape artist skills that would put the world's top magicians to shame. "Are you ever going to tell me how you got behind that bookcase in Anastasia's house?" I asked the cat.

He pranced back and forth in front of the door with his sleek black tail held high.

"Fine," I said as I stooped to pick up the volume of Poe. To my surprise, this time instead of falling open to

"The Fall of the House of Usher," the book opened to the first page of "The Purloined Letter." I wrinkled my brow—yet another direction that the books wanted me to investigate? I hadn't read the story in a very long time, but I knew it was about a stolen letter that was hidden out in the open. Did that mean that the answer as to who killed Anastasia was right in front of my face? I looked to Emerson and Faulkner as if they had the answer, but for the moment both were silent.

I set the book on an end table beside one of the couches, where another volume of Poe sat. This one was a thin paperback. I reached for it, and as I did, the book flew open. The pages fluttered and finally fell open to "The Purloined Letter" again. The shop essence most definitely wanted me to read this story, but that would have to wait. It had been well over fifteen minutes since Rainwater left the shop, and who knew what was going on outside? Who knew what my grandmother was up to?

I slipped the paperback into the back pocket of my jeans. It was tight, but I wanted the book close to me in case I got a spare moment to read Poe's famous detective story.

Emerson waited at the door. I picked up the cat and deposited him on the couch and then I ran full speed for the door before he knew what was happening. I heard his outraged meow through the closed door behind me. I would pay for that move later. I knew it.

"And how long have you known Evanna—excuse me—I mean Anastasia Faber?" a voice asked.

I stared openmouthed. Grandma Daisy reclined on one of the white rocking chairs on the porch across from a man in a rumpled suit. A second man in jeans and a Windbreaker stood a little off to the side holding a video camera with a fuzzy microphone attached to the top of it.

"I've known Anastasia for years," Grandma Daisy said regally as she rocked in the chair. "She was a regular customer in my bookshop, Charming Books, in Cascade Springs, New York, where the perfect book picks you," she added for the free advertising, I was sure.

A hand grabbed my arm, and I yelped.

The journalist in the rumpled suit glared at me.

The small fingers wrapped around my upper arm dug in a little deeper. "Shh," Sadie hissed.

"Sadie, let me go or I might need amputation because of lack of blood flow to my fingers."

"I'm sorry," she whispered, and lessened her grasp just a little bit, enough to restore feeling to my fingers at least. "Violet, you have to help me."

The journalist cleared his throat loudly.

Grandma Daisy glanced over her shoulder. "Oh, that's my granddaughter, Violet. She's a college professor."

"She's interrupting the interview," the reporter said. "We won't be able to use your last comment because of the noise." His voice was nasal and had a distinct Long Island sound to it.

"I'm so sorry," I said before I led Sadie around the corner of the old Victorian's wraparound porch.

As we walked away, the reporter asked my grandmother, "Now, can you repeat your last answer?"

"Violet, you must help me," Sadie said barely over a whisper when we were safely out of the reporter's view.

"I am trying to help you, Sadie. That's what I have been doing all this time."

She finally let go of my arm completely to wipe away her tears. "I know that, and I'm so very grateful. But things are worse now." She removed a tissue from the sleeve of her ruffled blouse and patted under her eyes.

"How could they possibly be worse?" I asked.

"All of these reporters are here because they learned that Anastasia was Evanna Blue." She lowered her voice even more. "But I already knew."

"You what?" I hissed.

"I knew that Anastasia was Evanna." She whispered it again as if it was still a secret worth keeping.

"How long have you known?"

"A few months." She squinted at me as if she feared my reaction.

"And how did you find out?" I buttoned up my jacket against the cold breeze wafting off the river. From this side of the house, we had a clear view of the corner where River Road turned to follow the Niagara's path. Sadie should have been freezing in her ruffled pink blouse, but it appeared that she was too agitated to notice the chill in the air.

"The last time I was there to water her plants when she was out of town, it was late at night. I went then because I had forgotten to water," she began.

This sounded eerily similar to my predicament last night with the birch tree and my clandestine run for fresh springwater.

"When I got to the second-floor sitting room, where most

of her plants are, I noticed light shining from behind the bookcase in that room before I turned on the overhead light. I went over to investigate with the light still off and when I reached behind the bookshelf, I hit the latch, and the book-shelf swung open. It took a second for me to realize what I'd found. When I did, I couldn't believe it."

"You said the light was left on in that room?" My brow wrinkled. Something about that sounded off to me.

"I guess Anastasia forgot to turn off the light the last time she was in there."

I frowned. That didn't sound like Anastasia to me. She had carefully kept this secret for over a decade; why would she leave the light on in a room that she so strictly protected like a national security secret? "Did you tell anyone? Anyone at all what you discovered? Did you tell Grant?"

"No, I never told anyone, not even Grant. I promised Anastasia I never would tell, but I don't think she believed me. She needed reassurance."

The pieces fell into place in my head. I had been right about Sadie holding back information when she talked to Grandma Daisy and me the night before. "Was this the reason she was so determined to find some dirt on you and how she learned about your plagiarism?"

She nodded miserably. "Yes. I promised her I would never tell, and I've kept that promise. Instead of believing me, she threatened me."

Sadie was right; this was bad for her. The police would think this was just extra ammunition for her already convincing motive to kill Anastasia.

As if she had read my mind, Sadie asked, "What if the police find out I knew? Wouldn't that be worse?"

That was a good question. If Rainwater found out that Sadie was hiding something more from him, it might convince him that much more that she had something to do with Anastasia's murder.

"What should I do?" she whimpered.

I knew the right thing to do was tell the police and reveal everything that she knew about Anastasia and how she'd learned it. The problem was, I didn't know if that was the smart thing to do. This might be a case where it was prudent to do the smart thing over the right thing.

"Why don't you go over to your shop while I think about it? I need to find out if anyone else knew about Anastasia's pen name before we divulge this information to the police."

"Oh, Violet." She clasped my hands in her smaller ones. "You don't know how much it means to me that you say 'we.' I know I can survive this if I have someone to lean on."

Not for the first time, I wondered where Grant was in all of this. He should be the one that Sadie was leaning on right now, not me. I didn't say any of this to her, though. "Of course, you can lean on me, Sadie. We'll get through this and soon it will all be a distant memory."

Tears sprang to her eyes again. "Not for Anastasia, it won't."

She had me there.

"Why don't you go over to your shop and make a few sales while I check on some leads. You might as well be making money with all these extra people in the village."

"I can't." She choked on the words as if they pained her. "I'm closed for the day. The place is surrounded by as many reporters as Charming Books."

"You can't let them impact your business."

"Who's going to want to buy a dress from a potential murderer, especially one who killed someone with a dress?" She looked like she was on the brink of tears yet again.

"Do the reporters know that was the murder weapon?"

"Yes," she choked out in a sob. "I'll be ruined."

I wrapped my arms around her. "How did they find out about the dress?"

"I don't know," she moaned. "David told me he would keep it out of the press, and I know you and Grandma Daisy wouldn't have said anything."

From the lawn, I saw Officer Wheaton scowling at me. I rubbed her back. I was happy to be comforting Sadie, but she needed Grant. When I did run across her no-good fiancé, I planned to give him a piece of my mind whether he wanted to hear it or not.

TWENTY-SIX

After some coaxing, I convinced Sadie to go inside Charming Books and wait out the worst of the reporters. I noted that at least two of the news vans were gone from the street. Three still remained, but I was happy to see some progress.

As I came around the side of the wraparound porch back to where I'd left my grandmother and the reporter, I found my grandmother was gone. In her place in the rocker and sitting across from the same rumpled man was yet another man I didn't recognize. He was about forty, I would guess, with short brown hair divided into a deep side part. He wore perfectly round glasses, which perched on his tiny round nose, and reminded me of Harry Potter.

"All of this must have come as shock," the reporter said in a soothing voice.

The man with the Harry Potter glasses nodded. "It has. It has. I had no idea my sister was this famous author."

Sister? This must be Coleridge, Anastasia's brother, whom Trudy had mentioned.

Coleridge placed a hand over his heart. "You don't know how much it pains me to have learned it after she was gone."

"You didn't know before?" the reporter asked.

"No!" Coleridge cried. "I had no idea. I wished she would have told me. I hate to think of how difficult it was for her to keep this secret for so long. As her only sibling, I could have been there for her through all of this."

Coleridge seemed to be playing the caring-brother card a little too heavily in my opinion.

The reporter asked Anastasia's brother a few more questions about the siblings' growing-up years. Coleridge answered with elaborate stories about how close he and Anastasia were. If they were so close, why hadn't she mentioned her brother at a Red Inkers meeting? I wondered.

Finally after what seemed like an eternity, the reporter said, "Thank you so much, Mr. Faber. We give you our deepest sympathy."

Coleridge bowed his head as if receiving a blessing rather than condolences on the passing of his only sister. His mannerisms seemed to be so over the top that they rang false.

The reporter clapped his hands on his knees and stood. "We got what we need," he told his cameraman. "Let's clear out and we can make the midday news. I don't know about you, but I'm ready to leave this strange village."

Strange village? If only he knew that he was standing in front of a magical bookshop.

Grandma Daisy stood in the doorway of Charming Books and called to the reporter, "Remember to mention us as Charming Books on River Road in Cascade Springs."

"I'll remember," he said. He walked over to his camera guy, and the pair spoke in hushed, excited tones.

"Grandma!" I hissed. "What are you doing?"

"An interview," she said simply. "Isn't it exciting? He's from a cable news channel, you know the one with that darling Rachel Maddow. Isn't that something?"

"Grandma, you gave him a sales pitch for the store when I assume that the interview was supposed to be about Anastasia."

She adjusted her scarf around her neck. Today she was wearing one that was decorated with leaves and pumpkins. "I don't see anything wrong with that. Anastasia was a regular customer. I would think that she would want the store to flourish."

I rubbed the spot between my eyebrows. I could feel a headache forming there. "Are you going to do every interview you are asked?"

She shook her head and her silver bob brushed her cheeks as she moved. "Certainly not, and there won't be an opportunity to. You will notice that now that I gave that interview, the other news crews are leaving too. They know that they have been scooped." She said this with a twinkle in her eye.

In front of the shop, I found that she was right. The other reporters, cameramen, and sound technicians loaded their equipment into their news vans, which had dozens of antennae coming out of the roof. Okay, perhaps Grandma Daisy knew more about the press than I did.

Grandma Daisy smiled. "See what I mean?"

"But the police chief wouldn't want you to talk about the investigation," I said.

"Who said that I spoke about the investigation?" she asked. "It was a personal interest piece. I shared what I knew about Anastasia the person, not the murder victim, and her place in our community."

I arched an eyebrow at her.

"Oh, all right, it will be a kinder and gentler view of the person Anastasia really was. No matter how awful that woman could be, I can't speak ill of the dead on the national news."

I gave her a hug. "You're a good person, Grandma Daisy. Do you know that?"

She hugged me back. "I've been told that a time or two." Before she let me go, she whispered, "Her brother is leaving. If you want to talk to him, this might be your only chance."

I stepped back from my grandmother to find Coleridge already on the lawn, heading toward the gate.

I launched down the steps. "Coleridge," I called.

He turned in surprise as if he hadn't expected anyone to know his name.

As I hurried over to him, I spotted a black-and-white cat stalking through the lawn. Emerson. The sneak got outside after all. I would have to worry about my mischievous cat later. "Can I speak to you for a moment?"

He frowned, which wrinkled his tiny nose. "Who are you?"

"I'm Violet Waverly. I'm a friend of Anastasia."

"A friend?" he snorted. "I wasn't aware that my sister

had friends." His entire demeanor changed from the grieving-brother persona that he'd portrayed during his television interview to someone I could easily see as Anastasia's blood relative.

"She did," I said, mentally adding "sort of." I went on to say, "I knew her through the Red Inkers."

"The red who?" he asked.

I was surprised that he didn't know. Anastasia had been a loyal member of the group, attending almost every meeting, since it began years ago. Wouldn't her brother know about such a large part of her life? Maybe he didn't know her at all. "Did you know about your sister's pseudonym?"

"No." His answer made it clear that he was tiring of our conversation.

"You never asked her how she could afford to live in such a large house?" I asked.

"Unlike some people," he said pointedly, "I'm not one to pry. I knew my sister was wealthy, yes, but I didn't know about her being this famous author, who frankly I never heard of."

Grandma Daisy joined us and cocked her head. "Have you heard of J. K. Rowling?"

"Who?" he asked.

"Look her up. She might have borrowed your glasses. You might want to take it up with her."

Ah, Grandma Daisy had also caught on to the Harry Potter glasses. I shot her a disapproving look. I didn't believe that Coleridge was the type who liked to be teased.

"Coleridge, my boy," Trudy said as she came through the front gate. "I haven't seen you since you were learning to tie your shoes."

He blinked at her as if he knew that he should recognize who was speaking to him, but couldn't quite place her.

"It's me, Mrs. Conner, your first-grade teacher." Trudy smiled. "I know first grade is a distant memory to you."

"Oh" was his response. Apparently Coleridge didn't find that fact to be especially impressive.

Trudy gave him a grandmotherly hug, which he stiffly accepted. "I'm glad you were able to meet Daisy and Violet here. I know they are absolutely heartbroken for you and so sorry Anastasia died in their bookshop. It's a terrible shame and a shock how it all happened."

He spun and faced Grandma Daisy and me. "You're the owners of this bookshop?"

I considered denying it for half a second, but Grandma Daisy straightened her spine and said, "Yes, we are, and Trudy is right. We are absolutely heartbroken over your sister's death."

His lips curled into a sneer, making him look less like Harry Potter and more like Snape. "You will be heartbroken after I'm through with you." He pointed at Charming Books. "You think you're so smart, don't you? I doubt you will feel that way when I hand you a lawsuit that will bury you and your great-great-grandchildren in debt for the rest of their lives." With that, he stomped away.

If Coleridge was anything like his sister, I knew that wasn't an idle threat.

~⦿~

TWENTY-SEVEN

~⦿~

After the news crew and most of the pedestrians blocking the street moved on, Grandma Daisy and I opened Charming Books for the day. Customers flowed into the shop and business was brisk. I saw more than one book fly off the shelf and hit an unsuspecting shopper. The shop's essence was working overtime.

I left Grandma Daisy with the customers and went to find Sadie. She was curled up in the children's loft in one of the beanbag chairs made to look like a boulder. Not much larger than a child herself, she fit snugly in the chair. In her lap, she had a copy of *Winnie-the-Pooh*.

She closed the book when I reached the landing with Emerson close on my heels. I wondered how he'd gotten back in the shop. I supposed I should just come to accept that I couldn't control my cat's comings and goings. He took independence to a new level.

She chuckled. "This was my favorite book growing up. I thought reading it would make me feel better."

I sat in the beanbag across from her. Unlike Sadie, I was not a perfect size for the small chair. My long legs were forced to bend, and I looked like I was a floor gymnast who got caught in a pose. "Did it work?"

Her lips, lined in bright red lipstick that complemented her black hair, curved into just a hint of a smile. "I think so. You must think I'm silly to turn to a children's book in a time like this when I should really be trying to see how to escape this mess that I'm in."

"I don't think it's silly at all," I said. "I'm a bookseller, remember, and a literature professor. I make sense of the world through books." I could feel the volume of Poe sitting in the back pocket of my jeans as I said this. I knew Sadie wouldn't take my statement as literally as I meant it. "I read everything, and children's books are just as well written as novels for adults."

She hugged her book to her chest. "I should have known you'd understand. I know Daisy would too. She and you are really the closest people I have to family in the village. I'm so grateful for you both."

"What about Grant?"

Her brow furrowed. "Grant is Grant."

I interpreted that to mean that Grant was a selfish jerk, but I could have just been projecting my own opinion of Nathan's younger brother. "Have you heard from him at all?"

"Oh yes, he's texted me that he's very busy at the winery's booth because of the festival. He just can't get away right now. His parents rely on him so much, and this is just an important week for their business."

It was an important week for all businesses in the village, even mine, but I was still doing my best to help my friend. Again, I said none of these thoughts.

She started to put the book she held back on the shelf that was in arm's reach of her.

"Keep the book," I said, stopping her. "It's a gift."

"I would like to keep it." She held it on her lap. "But you have to let me pay for it."

"Don't be silly. The book is yours. It's meant to be yours. I'm certain of that."

She hugged the book a little more tightly. "All right. Thank you."

After a couple of tries I climbed out of the beanbag chair and stood, without an ounce of grace, I might add. Sadie was far too polite to comment on this. "What are you going to do now?" I asked.

"I think you're right. I can't let what has happened ruin my business. I've done nothing wrong." She easily rose to her feet as if it took no effort at all. "I'm going to go back to my shop and open for the day."

I gave a sigh of relief. "I'm glad to hear it. I really am." And it was true. I was relieved that Sadie wasn't going to allow the suspicion that surrounded her to beat her. That was the last thing that she should do in this situation.

My mother and grandmother had ingrained in me the will to fight for what I wanted, to fight for what was right, and to fight for those I cared about. That's what Sadie needed to do now. In my opinion, she needed to stand up to Grant about how he treated her, but I wasn't going to press my luck by mentioning that too, at least not yet.

Sadie held her volume of *Winnie-the-Pooh* and walked down the stairs to the main floor of Charming Books with her head held high.

I reached the first floor a few seconds later. There were at least a dozen customers milling around the bookshelves. It did my heart good to see it.

My grandmother stood with a young couple looking for some parenting books. Grandma Daisy directed them to the right section. After the couple was engrossed in the books, I joined my grandmother. "If it's all right with you, I'd like to go to the Food and Wine Festival and check it out."

Her blue eyes twinkled behind her cat's-eye glasses. "And maybe do just a little bit of snooping while you're at it."

"A little. At the moment, I'm more concerned about finding Grant and telling him off over how he's treating Sadie." I balled my hands into fists at my sides. "After she stood by him this past summer, it's horrible."

She patted my arm. "I agree with you, but Sadie's relationship with Grant is Sadie's battle. She's never going to earn his respect if she doesn't stand up to him herself."

"She is too upset by Anastasia's murder to do that right now."

She nodded and looked as if she wanted to say something more and stopped herself.

I scanned the room. Emerson was nowhere to be seen, but Faulkner was in the front window, quoting from "The Raven." The crow had a small audience for his performance. "Are you sure you'll be all right without me? The place is really busy."

She smiled. "Violet, my dear, what do you think I did during the Food and Wine Festival when you were off finding yourself the last twelve years?"

Her comment, although true, caused a tiny pang of guilt in my chest.

She made a shooing motion. "Now, go. Sadie needs your help."

I left the shop and gasped when I saw who was clomping up the sidewalk leaning heavily on his cane. Charles Hancock, the octogenarian who had an irrepressible crush on Grandma Daisy. As much as I would jump into the bushes to escape Nathan, Grandma Daisy would jump off a cliff to avoid Charles.

"Violet, my dear," the elderly man said in his signature booming voice. "Is your grandmother at the shop? I've been out of town, and I just heard the news about Anastasia Faber's untimely demise. Terrible, terrible shame. I'm so sorry to hear it happened in Charming Books. Daisy has had enough to contend with these last few months since that scoundrel Benedict died. I am here to offer her the comfort and support that she needs in this difficult time." His gray bushy eyebrows knit together in concern.

I suppressed a grimace. I didn't doubt that Charles was there to support Grandma Daisy in her supposed time of need, but I also knew that his support was the last thing that she needed or wanted.

I cleared my throat. "Charles, that is so thoughtful, but now isn't the time to bother my grandmother. I have a better way that you can help her."

"Oh?" he asked. The impressive set of eyebrows rose. "How is that?"

I thought a moment. I needed to think of something fast that would take Charles a good deal of time to do. Then, it hit me. "I suppose you heard about the reporters who were gathered outside Charming Books earlier this morning."

"I did. Terrible," he said.

"Well, one journalist in particular mentioned Charming Books as the place where Anastasia died in his article. Grandma Daisy would like to talk to him. His name is Daven York. We think he's staying somewhere in the village," I said, even though I had no idea where Daven was. He could be halfway to New York City by now. "Grandma Daisy would really like to find out where, so that she could talk to him about the article."

"I cannot believe that he slandered my love so!" Charles's voice shook with fury. "I will find him and I will run him through." He brandished his cane as if it were a sword. "I will check every bed-and-breakfast and inn in the village. Do not worry. I will find the rogue if it takes the remainder of my days."

I jumped out of the way of the cane. The rest of the week would be fine with me. Then, I would have to think of another excuse to keep Charles out of my grandmother's hair.

"When I do, I will deal with him myself for her honor!"

"Bad idea! You know Grandma Daisy. She doesn't want a fuss made with this man. She would like to talk to him herself. She wouldn't want you to run him through or do anything that might get you into trouble."

He nodded. "You're right. Daisy is so kind she would always think of me first before herself. I will find this scoundrel and report back to her as soon as I learn his whereabouts. Rest assured, young Violet."

"No," I said. "No, report back to me about it. It's just too upsetting for Grandma Daisy."

"Yes, of course. Our goal is to make this as painless as possible for Daisy."

"That's right," I said, nodding.

"I shall go on my mission at once." He spun on his heels and headed down the sidewalk at a pace much faster than I would have thought possible for a man on a cane. I watched Charles turn the corner and hoped that I wouldn't come to regret the assignment that I'd given him.

With Charles no longer in sight, I continued on my way to the Food and Wine Festival. River Road was close to empty when I walked toward the Riverwalk. When I left Charming Books, I had half expected to find Emerson following me to the festival. He wasn't there. If anything, the cat was unpredictable. I suspected that he got that from me.

Before heading straight to the festival, I swung by La Crepe Jolie and collected my bike from where I'd left it the night before. I was grateful it was still there, and again I expected to find Emerson sitting in my bicycle basket waiting for me. Again he was MIA.

I knew from my visit to the Riverwalk the night before that Morton Vineyards had the first booth inside the Food and Wine Festival. Last night, Mrs. Morton had been in the booth. When I climbed off my bike and chained it to a rack a few feet away at the edge of the park, I was, if not happy, at least pleased to see Grant Morton in the booth, not his mother.

Grant was just as handsome as his older brother. But where Nathan was blond, tall, and lean, Grant was broad shouldered, somewhat squat, and brunet. He was at least five inches shorter than Nathan, which caused him to live in his older brother's shadow both figuratively and literally his entire life, and he made no secret of his resentment for Nathan. The brothers had been at odds since they were in grade school. I believed that the beginning of Grant and Nathan's problems stemmed from their parents. The elder Mortons had always pitted their sons in competition against each other. The brothers were only thirteen months apart in age, and I wouldn't have been the least surprised if that practice hadn't gone all the way back to when they were toddlers.

Grant wiped fingerprints off a bottle of ice wine with a clean white rag and raised his dark brow. "Vi, to what do I owe this regal visit? My, I haven't seen you in person in weeks."

An elderly man took one of the plastic wineglasses with its sample of ice wine from the Mortons' table. Grant nodded to him to acknowledge that he saw him.

The man backed away with his glass, not buying anything.

I decided to cut right to the chase. "I assume you heard about the murder and that Sadie is a murder suspect."

"I have, and I feel absolutely horrible for Sadie. She's a sweet girl."

My frown deepened. A sweet girl? He sounded like he was talking about a virtual stranger, not the person who was supposed to be the love of his life. "Where have you been? Sadie needs you right now."

"I'm sure you're doing just fine comforting her, since you are such a pro at meddling in other people's business." He set down the bottle, picked up another, and resumed polishing.

I ground my teeth. "I'm not her fiancé."

"Neither am I," he said.

I took a step back. "What do you mean?"

He set the bottle down and something between annoyance and amusement played across his face. "I'm not her fiancé either. Sadie and I broke up a week ago. In fact, I believe it was a week ago today."

"But why?" I asked. *And why didn't she tell me?* I wondered to myself.

"I realized I'm not in a good place in my life to be in a serious relationship, much less thinking about marriage. Right now, I need to begin thinking about my career and advancing my family's business." He folded the cloth in his hand and set it on the worktable behind him. "My parents have put a lot of trust in me to let me back into the business. I can't have any distractions right now."

I doubted he would ever be in a good place to get married, but I was so sorry Sadie had been hurt in the process of his coming to that obvious conclusion. If Grant and Sadie broke up a week ago, that meant that it wasn't long before Anastasia's death. "I understand why you haven't been around since you and Sadie broke up, but have you reached out to her at all? She could really use a friend right now. I know she would love to hear from you."

"I think you are doing more than enough in the friend

department for the both of us. Am I right? There is a rumor going around the village that you broke into Anastasia's house last night. Gutsy move. I suppose you believe that you can get away with anything, since my brother, the mayor, is still in love with you. Why he is remains a mystery to me and I suspect to most of the village."

I grew very still. How did Grant know about last night? I tried to remember everyone that I'd told. Grandma Daisy and Sadie, but I doubted either of them would say anything to Grant about it. Chief Rainwater and his officer knew of course. Rainwater would never tell, but I wouldn't put it past Wheaton. Then I remembered that I'd told Lacey and Adrien too. Could my well-meaning friends have half accidentally let the news slip? I hadn't specifically asked them not to tell anyone.

In front of me, Grant poured ice wine into the line of plastic wineglasses. He picked up one and held it out to me. "Would you like to try it? It's our best vintage."

I was just about to tell him exactly where he could put that wineglass when I caught movement out of the corner of my eye. I turned to see a man in a suit making his way back to the tent area with a cell phone attached to his ear. I blinked when I realized it was the same man I'd seen outside Charming Books during the sidewalk sale the day Anastasia died, the one who claimed to be her friend. He was heading toward the back of the festival in the direction of the La Crepe Jolie booth and the large dining tent.

"Keep the wine," I said, and backed away from him.

"Suit yourself," Grant said, tossing back the glassful as if taking down a shot of tequila.

~e

TWENTY-EIGHT

~e

I followed the man in the suit. It was midafternoon and business in the festival area was picking up. Not only were the tourists there, but there were also the local residents of Cascade Springs who were coming to the festival on their lunch breaks. I wove between and around laughing couples, moms with their hands grasping their small children's, and serious shoppers with cloth bags that were full to bursting with cheese, fruits, veggies, wine, and baked goods from the many vendors across the Riverwalk. For a moment, I lost sight of the man with the phone. I stepped around an elderly woman who seemed intent on squeezing every last one of the melons in the produce booth, and spotted him again at a table in the dining tent.

"I understand, I understand. I know this doesn't look good." He was silent for a moment. "Yes. The police are looking into it. Think of the postmortem sales. Her backlist is going to fly off the shelf. . . . Yes, sir, I understand that comment was inappropriate. But—" Whatever he was about to say was cut off by the voice on the other end of the line. After a full minute, he said, "Yes, yes, I will find out. You will be the first to know."

Could it even be possible that Anastasia was killed for publicity reasons? Could her publisher or someone else be that demented to kill her to increase overall sales of her books? It didn't make sense. They would have to know any increase the notoriety of her death garnered was only temporary.

The man slid his phone inside his jacket.

"I'll take a white wine please," the man said, sounding exhausted. "Whatever you have."

I frowned. "I'm not a waitress."

He looked up from the white linen tablecloth. "You!"

"Me?"

"Yes, you, you are the one from the bookshop, aren't you? You're the one who told me that Anastasia was dead." He buried his face in his hands. "I can't . . ."

Behind me there was the faintest clicking sound. I turned around to see a middle-aged man holding a selfie stick in front of his face as he took a photograph of himself with the New York man and me in the background.

Anastasia's friend jumped out of his seat as if he had been struck by lightning. "What do you think you're doing?"

The man with the selfie stick stepped back. "I heard you speaking on the phone about Evanna Blue—I mean Anastasia Faber. I could tell you really knew her, so I took a photograph with you." The man trembled slightly.

"Without my permission," the other man said through gritted teeth.

"I'm a huge fan of Evanna Blue, and I came to the village to see the places she visited in her last days and the people in her life. It's my tribute to my favorite author."

He turned to face the selfie stick, sucked in his gut, and took yet another photo with the other man and me in the background.

Anastasia's friend yanked the selfie stick out of the man's hand and broke it over his knee. He handed the two halves back to the man.

The tourist stared at his broken selfie stick. His bottom lip quivered. "You broke it. How could you do that?"

"Easily," Anastasia's friend said. His face must have appeared menacing enough because the tourist backed away without another word.

The man in the suit's cell phone rang again and he answered the phone. "Eaton speaking."

Eaton? Where had I heard that name before? Then it hit me: the printed e-mail that I had found in Anastasia's secret office. The last name of the person who wrote the e-mail was Eaton. I pulled my phone out of the back pocket of my jeans and scrolled through my e-mail until I found the one with the photograph of Anastasia's e-mail attached. I was so glad I'd had the foresight to send myself a copy before I showed it to Chief Rainwater, who erased the original photo from my phone.

The man barked an order to someone on the other end of his call, and then Edmund Eaton slumped back into the chair. "Wow, it felt good to break that stick. I hate those things. They are a menace."

I wasn't a huge fan of the selfie stick either. Nowadays they were a common accessory at Niagara Falls while tourists were overlooking the falls. They were especially popular with the foreign visitors, and it wasn't uncommon to get smacked in the head with one while trying to enjoy the majestic scenery of the falls.

"How long have you been Anastasia's agent?" I asked.

His mouth fell open. "How did you know?"

"I saw an e-mail between the two of you." I didn't mention *where* I had seen the e-mail and hoped he wouldn't ask.

He scowled. "What does it matter now?" He removed a white handkerchief from his jacket pocket and patted his sweaty brow with it. It was a cool day with a chilly breeze coming from Canada across the river, which was just on the other side of the thin tent wall.

"Do you know how the news got out that Anastasia was Evanna?" I asked.

He pointed to the seat across from him at the round table. "If you are going to interrogate me, you might as well sit down. I do not appreciate being loomed over."

I sat on the folding chair, crossed my arms on the tablecloth, and waited.

"I have no idea how the news leaked about Evanna's identity. That's what I'm trying to figure out. I assumed you were eavesdropping on my conversation earlier. The conversation was with her publisher, who was less than pleased by Anastasia's death and by the revelation of the pen name."

I wanted to ask him what the publisher was more upset about, but I was afraid that I would be disappointed by the answer. "What did you tell him?"

"The same thing I told you, that I don't know how the

word got out. We only know of one person who knew Evanna Blue's true identity."

"Who's that?"

"Her name is Sadie Cunningham."

My heart sank. That was what I was afraid he'd say.

He shook his head. "But I would be surprised if it were her, to be honest. Anastasia was so certain that she had found a way for this Sadie to keep quiet. I have worked with Anastasia for a very long time. If she did something to keep a person quiet, it should have worked."

In Sadie's case, it was with the threat of exposing Sadie's earlier transgressions in life.

"What about her literary works?" I asked. "The Anastasia I knew dreamed of being published in literary fiction. In fact, she went out of her way to disparage popular and genre fiction."

He sighed. "I know. Trust me, I know."

"Was there any chance of her literary work becoming published?"

"Quite frankly, no." He took a deep breath as if he knew he needed to fortify himself for what came next. "It's something to write for the love of it; it's another to write for profit. The lucky authors are the ones who write for both. Anastasia was not one of the lucky ones, at least in that sense."

"Did Anastasia threaten to stop writing as Evanna?" I asked.

He started to stand up. "I have said too much."

I jumped to my feet. "You need to talk to the police about this. They will want to know what you've told me."

"No, thank you. I have no interest in becoming involved

in any of this. I plan to be on the next plane to New York City just as soon as I check into a few more things."

"Like what?" I asked in my most innocent voice.

"That is none of your business." With that, he stomped out of the tent. As he left, I saw a figure standing in the shadow of La Crepe Jolie's tent. There was a long line of tourists waiting to order a crepe from Adrien. The shadowy figure wasn't in line for a crepe. He was just staring at me.

Fenimore.

TWENTY-NINE

I stomped over to him. I'd had just about enough of the troubadour skulking around me. It seemed in the last two days, he was everywhere, or at least everywhere I was, which only made it seem that much worse.

"Why are you following me?" I demanded.

"I need to talk to you," the man said in a raspy voice as if it had gotten worn out by years of smoking or singing. Perhaps a combination of both.

I hadn't expected that answer. "What about?"

He glanced around at all the festival activity. "I need to talk to you in private."

Like that was going to happen. I folded my arms. "Whatever you have to say to me, you can say to me out here in the open."

He adjusted the strap of his guitar on his shoulder. "I

don't think that's true. I believe you would like to hear what I have to say when we are alone."

If this stranger seriously thought I would be willing to be alone with him when a murder had just been committed in the village, he was cracked. "Does this have something to do with Anastasia?"

"Who?" he asked, appearing genuinely confused by the question.

"Or you might know her as Evanna Blue. Does that name mean anything to you?"

He furrowed his brow. "I don't know who you are talking about." He removed an e-cigarette from the pocket of his flannel jacket. I saw the amber liquid slosh back and forth inside of it.

I interrupted him. "What's that?"

He stared down at the piece of plastic in his hand. "I'm trying to quit smoking. It's not good for my singing voice. I suppose at my age it's a little late now to save it completely, but I am trying. There are so many things that I want to make better. You should know that."

"Why should *I* know that?"

He fiddled with the e-cigarette in his hand and didn't answer my question.

I took a step toward him. "So you don't know anything about Anastasia's death, even when you hold that"—I pointed at the e-cigarette—"in your hand. Don't you know how foolish it is to flash that around after what happened?"

"What are you talking about?" Fenimore stared at me as if I had two heads.

"Everyone in the village knows what happened, even

the tourists, and you're not really a tourist, are you, Fenimore?" I balled my fists at my sides. "You have been to our village many times before."

His mouth hung open. "You're as fiery as your mother. I should have expected you to be so. It's like looking at her caught in a time capsule. It is almost too much to bear."

I stumbled backward as if he had slapped me across the face. "Stay away from me," I whispered.

Unable to process what he had just said to me, I started to walk away. How would this man, who was only in the village for the festival, know my mother? I didn't want to know. Clearly, he was using it as a diversionary tactic to distract me from the e-cigarette in his hand. Well, he could talk to Chief Rainwater about that if he refused to speak to me about the matter. I turned to go.

"I wanted to talk to you about Fern," he called after me.

I spun around. There was only one Fern in my life, and that was my mother—my mother, who died when I was thirteen. What could this man possibly say about her? "What did you say?"

He held out his hands with the palms facing up. One hand was empty. The other held the e-cigarette.

"Violet, is this man bothering you?" Nathan walked up beside me and glared at Fenimore.

I tore my eyes away from Fenimore's face. "Nathan, I'm fine." I refocused my attention onto Fenimore. "What do you have to say about my mother?"

"Now is not the time." He turned and ambled away with the e-cigarette clasped in his fist so tightly I was surprised that it didn't snap in two.

I took a step after him, but Nathan reached out and grabbed my hand. "Violet, where are you going?"

I jerked my hand from his grasp. "I have to know what he was going to say."

The two seconds that Nathan held me back were just long enough for Fenimore to melt into the growing crowd of festivalgoers and disappear. I looked left and right. All I saw were people carrying plastic cups of wine and dishes of steaming food. Fenimore was gone.

My heart thumped in my chest.

"Violet, what's wrong?" Nathan asked.

His voice was so full of concern that I turned to look at him. The concern that I had heard in his voice registered in his eyes as well. "He said something about my mom."

Nathan's eyes narrowed. "What did he say about her?"

Nathan had known my mother from our growing up together, but I was still angry at him for stopping me from learning what Fenimore had to say. I might not have another chance. "That I was fiery like she was."

His expression cleared. "I can vouch for that," he teased. "Why are you so upset by it?"

"I don't know exactly. It was just how he said it. It's just—" I searched for the right words. "How would he know what my mother was like? How would he know her at all?"

"Let me find him. I'll find out what he knows about your mother." He took two steps in the direction in which Fenimore had melted into the crowd.

This time, I grabbed his wrist to stop him.

A slim woman with steel gray hair and a serious-looking clipboard stood a few feet away. "Mr. Mayor, we need you to judge the ice wine dessert contest now."

Nathan looked from the woman to me and back again.

"Go," I said, releasing his wrist. I hadn't realized until that moment that I had still been holding it. I dropped my arm to my side. "I'll be fine."

"If you need—"

"Mr. Mayor?" the officious woman repeated.

I gave Nathan a small smile. "You should go. Your public awaits. Thank you, though."

His eyes lit up with just enough hope in them that it worried me, making me wish I could take my gratitude back, not because I didn't mean it, but because I didn't want to hurt him. For the first time, I realized that was exactly what I might be doing, and I wondered if I was hurting myself in the process too.

THIRTY

Nathan went off with the woman, who I could only assume was his secretary although we weren't formally introduced.

"You look like you've seen a ghost," someone said to the right.

I turned to find Chief Rainwater at my side, and the thumping resumed in my chest, which had nothing to do with my encounter with Fenimore and his saying my mother's name. I swallowed. "I'm fine. Have you spoken to Fenimore about Anastasia's murder?"

His eyes narrowed. "Who?"

"Fenimore. The troubadour who is in the village for the Food and Wine Festival. I couldn't tell you if Fenimore was his first or last name. No one I've spoken to seems to know the answer to that either."

"Is that the guy with the guitar and harmonica?" he asked.

I nodded.

"I've seen him around town." Rainwater rested his hand on his duty belt just in front of his gun. "Why should I talk to him about Anastasia's death? Did he see something?"

"I don't know that," I admitted. "But I think he might have something to do with it."

"Why's that?"

"I saw him with an e-cigarette," I said, and waited for Rainwater to praise my detective work.

"A lot of people smoke e-cigarettes, Violet. It's become very popular in recent years," he said, and disappointed me in the process.

"Yes, I know that," I said, biting back my irritation. "But why would he flaunt it in front of me so soon after Anastasia's death?" I described how Fenimore pulled the e-cigarette out of his pocket.

"That doesn't sound like flaunting to me," he said, and before I could protest, he asked, "What motive does he have?"

I frowned. It was an obvious and reasonable question. I couldn't just say the man was crazy. Fenimore might be a tad eccentric, but that didn't make him a murderer, especially in Cascade Springs, where everyone had his or her own flavor of eccentricity. "I don't know," I said finally.

"Are you sure that's all of it, just you seeing him with an electronic cigarette?" Rainwater asked. He searched my face with his piercing amber eyes.

My mother's face came to my mind's eye. As always in my memory, it was somewhat fuzzy, as if covered with a piece of clouded glass that softened her face into impressions more than features. Many times, I wondered if I would forget what she looked like if it weren't for the photographs that I had, which had been taken throughout her life. Without those, would her face continue to fade into a blur of color before disappearing entirely from my memory?

"Violet?" Rainwater asked, taking a step toward me. There was still a good two feet of space between us, but it felt so much smaller.

I licked my lips, which felt terribly dry. "That was all."

How was it that I was able to tell Nathan what Fenimore had said about my mother, but I wasn't able to tell the police chief? Because Nathan knew my mother, I told myself, and Rainwater never did. He never would.

The words about my mother caught in my mouth. "That was all," I repeated.

He took another step toward me, and now only one foot of space separated us from each other. "I don't believe you."

Before I could answer, there was a high-pitched squeal, and a pink-and-purple blur raced toward the police chief and catapulted into his arms. Rainwater let out an "umph" upon impact.

The girl in Rainwater's arms appeared to be about five or six, and she flung her arms around Rainwater's neck. "Where have you been? We have been looking for you *everywhere*!" the child admonished him.

The girl was Native American like Rainwater and had

the same amber-colored eyes. For the briefest of moments, I thought it might be his daughter. The thought that Rainwater had a child made my pulse quicken.

The girl looked at me. "Who are you?"

Somehow I found my voice. "I'm Violet."

"Violet!" She beamed. "Uncle David talks about you."

Uncle. I blew out a breath. The girl was Rainwater's niece. I should have known. He had spoken of her often at Red Inker meetings and always fondly. Seeing how the girl clung to her uncle's neck, the fondness went both ways.

"I'm Aster Cloud," she said proudly.

"Hello, Aster," I said. "I've heard so much about you from your uncle."

Her face split into a grin, and she pointed behind me. "That's my mom."

A small Native American woman smiled shyly at me. She was just over five feet tall and her long hair cascaded down her back in a black sheet. I was immediately envious of her gorgeous hair.

Rainwater adjusted his niece in his arms. "Violet, this is my sister, Danielle, and"—he smiled down at his niece—"you've just met Aster, the troublemaker in the family."

"Uncle David!" the child cried in outrage.

He laughed at her pint-sized annoyance. When he recovered, he said, "Danielle and Aster have been staying with me for the last few months."

His comment took me back to when I first returned to Cascade Springs and heard a woman's voice in Rainwater's house. At the time, I had assumed that it was a girlfriend of the police chief's, but I realized now that it was much more likely his sister. I couldn't help but admire Rainwater for taking his sister and her daughter in when they needed a place to stay. There were a lot of siblings in the same predicament who wouldn't do that.

"Just until I can get back on my feet," Danielle interjected, and then lowered her voice. "I'm in the middle of a divorce. My ex-husband . . ." She trailed off.

I noticed Rainwater's jaw tighten when Danielle mentioned her ex-husband even for the briefest of seconds.

Aster wriggled out of her uncle's arms. "It's ice cream time." She took hold of his large hand in her tiny one and pulled. "You promised."

He laughed again, and his eyes sparkled. "Okay, okay." Rainwater stopped despite Aster's persistent tugging on his hand. "Violet?"

"Yes?" I asked.

"Would you like to join us for ice cream?" the police chief asked me.

I would, I wanted to say, but instead, I said, "I had better get back to the bookshop. Grandma Daisy has been there alone for too long."

He nodded. I could be mistaken, but I thought I saw disappointment in his amber eyes.

I waved to Danielle and Aster. "It was nice meeting both of you."

Danielle gave me a shy smile.

I turned to go.

"Violet," Rainwater said.

I turned to face him again.

"I'll talk to Fenimore," he said.

I nodded.

Aster yanked on Rainwater's hand. "Come on! You promised to buy me an ice cream."

The police chief laughed. "I did indeed." He gave me a half wave as he allowed Aster to drag him away.

Danielle nodded to me before following her daughter and brother in the direction of the homemade ice cream tent.

It wasn't until the trio disappeared around the side of one of the white canvas tents that what Aster had said hit me. "Uncle David talks about you." Rainwater spoke of me with his family? Was that good or bad?

THIRTY-ONE

B y the time I returned to Charming Books, I felt like I
had swum the length of the Niagara River. I was emo-
tionally wrung out. When I entered the shop, the downstairs
was still busy with customers. Grandma Daisy stood at the
sales counter grinning from ear to ear with every swipe of
a credit card. The shop had lost at least a half day of income
with Anastasia's death, but it seemed that its notoriety as
the place where a famous person had been killed more than
made up for any loss. It made me wonder if anyone would
have cared that Anastasia had died if it remained a secret
that she was Evanna Blue. Something about that made me
terribly sad. No life should be more valued above another,
but I knew that didn't hold true in reality.

Trudy handed a middle schooler a copy of *Alice's
Adventures in Wonderland*. "This is the book you've been
looking for."

The child nodded and danced over to who I assumed was her father with the book hugged to her chest.

"You on the payroll now?" I teased Trudy.

She laughed and it sounded like the chime of church bells. "Not quite yet. I'm just lending a hand where I might be needed. You know I like to make myself useful. When I stopped in to pick up my book order for the week, I saw how busy Daisy was and decided to pitch in." She gave me a beady look. "I was surprised to find you not here. Where had you wandered off to?"

"I was down at the Food and Wine Festival, talking to a few people."

"About what?" She raised one eyebrow.

"Anastasia. I'm trying to find out who might have known Anastasia was Evanna Blue before she died."

"And how did that go for you?" Again the eyebrow went up.

I sighed. "It's a long story."

She smiled. "Those are the best kind." She began to cough and reached in her pocketbook for a tissue. "Excuse me." She coughed into the tissue. The cough was deeper in her chest this time.

I touched her arm. "Trudy, are you all right? That cough sounds bad. Are you sure it's just allergies? Maybe you should get it looked at."

She waved away my concern. "It's just allergies," she said, sounding a bit hoarse.

I wanted to argue with her more, but she went on to say, "Speaking of long stories, I really should be working on my book, you know," she said. "I'm about three chapters from the end."

"Congratulations!" I glanced around the shop. "Have you seen Sadie?"

Trudy smiled. "Last I saw her, she was inside her shop doing a brisk business. I was glad to see it. It's important she go on with business as usual. You should never let your circumstances hold you back from living your dream. Ever. You have to fight for everything you have."

She said it with so much ferocity that I blinked. Recovering quickly, I said, "I'm glad. Maybe I should go over there and check on her."

She shook her head. "No, dear, she needs to get back into the swing of things, so that life will become normal for her again. You going over there and talking about the murder will just upset her."

I frowned. "I don't think . . ."

"Trust me on this. Has your first-grade teacher ever steered you wrong?"

"No," I admitted.

"That's right. Now, I see a young woman over there in the mystery section eyeing a collector's edition of Agatha Christie. Go close that sale." She gave me a little shove, and I did what I was told.

The remainder of the day was uneventful. I helped Grandma Daisy with sales and in between customers, I marked the response papers from my morning class, which seemed like a lifetime ago. Just before the shop closed, I was able to sneak away across the street to Midcentury Vintage. I was hoping to find Sadie and ask her about her breakup with Grant, but when I went over to the shop, I found it closed and Sadie nowhere to be found.

After closing Charming Books, Grandma Daisy went home, clearly tired from the busy day. It wasn't every day that she was interviewed by cable television, and I was grateful for that. She asked me if I wanted to stay with her for another night because I might feel odd sleeping in Charming Books, where Anastasia had died. I opted to stay in my own apartment in the bookshop. Just like Trudy said about Sadie, my life needed to get back to normal too.

When the shop was quiet, I sat on the spiral staircase that wrapped around the birch tree. Emerson was at my side, not telling me what he had been up to all day, and Faulkner loomed over us both in the white branches. I held the bent copy of Edgar Allan Poe's works that I had carried around in the back pocket of my jeans all day, and set it on my lap. "All right, what should I read?" I asked the shop. My voice echoed off the open staircase.

Nothing happened.

I sighed. I shouldn't have expected the essence would work on command. I was just about to lift the book from my lap and open it myself when pages began to flutter. I held my hands suspended over the book, not touching a thing. The fluttering slowed and the book fell open again to "The Purloined Letter."

Like "The Murders in the Rue Morgue," "The Purloined Letter" was one of Poe's detective stories featuring the detective C. Auguste Dupin. Thinking of that made me remember Chief Rainwater in his Dupin costume the day before, and even though I was completely alone in the bookshop except for the animals, I found myself blushing. It might have been the tweed.

"Nevermore," Faulkner chided.

I shot the large black bird a look.

I needed to understand why the shop insisted on this story. The only way to do that was to read.

"At Paris, just after dark one gusty evening in the autumn," the story began.

As I read the line silently to myself, the wind picked up outside, and I could hear the wind chime that hung from Charming Books' front porch jingle and clank as the metal pieces knocked against one another.

I bent my neck back, looking up into the tree's silvery boughs. "You can't control the weather too? Can you? Because that would just be freaky."

As usual, my question was met with silence, and so I turned back to the story. I was so engrossed in Poe's tale that I didn't hear someone knocking on the front door of Charming Books until Emerson smacked my hand with his paw and then leaped from the staircase to the floor.

Pound, pound, pound, the knocks on the door came.

"Nevermore," Faulkner said hauntingly above my head.

I swallowed and stood. Was I living out my very own "Raven" moment just like when the narrator thought someone was there and it turned out to be the wind . . . or so he tried to convince himself?

Pound. Pound. Pound.

That was most certainly not the wind.

The moonlight poured through the skylight above the tree. The light reflected off the tree's white bark, giving it a ghostly silver sheen.

I looked through the small four-paned window in the front door and found Chief David Rainwater standing there. I threw open the door. Behind him, leaves that had been stripped from the trees by the fierce wind swirled in little cyclones. "Come in and get out of the wind."

He stepped across the threshold. "Thank you. The weather is certainly changing. I expect we may have snow by Halloween."

"That will be no fun for the trick-or-treaters, including your niece. What is she going as?"

His face softened when I mentioned Aster. "Joan of Arc. She read about her in school, and now Joan is Aster's heroine. Somehow my sister has to find child-sized chain mail by Halloween night or we are going to have a very upset girl knight on our hands."

I chuckled. "I know I only spoke to Aster for a couple of minutes, but that doesn't surprise me in the least."

He smiled. "She liked meeting you. Both she and my sister did."

His comment brought back Aster saying that the chief spoke about me. Did he say good things about me? I was too chicken to ask.

"Thank you for being so kind to them." His face clouded over. "Danielle has not had an easy time of it. Her husband isn't being reasonable as far as the divorce is concerned, and she's having a hard time finding a job. This week has been better for that. She worked for the village helping set up the tents for the festival."

"I'm sorry," I said. "Is there anything that I can do to help your sister? Maybe I can ask around to see who is hiring."

His face broke into a smile. "Just you offering is enough."

I wasn't so sure about that. I wished there was something that I could do for his sister and his niece.

"I'm sorry to be barging in on you like this," he said, plucking a leaf from the shoulder of his coat. "It's late and I should have called."

"It's fine." I held up the book in my hand. "I was just reading."

His smile widened. "I wouldn't expect anything less."

"Do you want something to drink?" I asked. "I can make tea or I'm sure that Grandma Daisy has something stronger in one of the cupboards. She's partial to Baileys."

He shook his head. "Water's fine. Nothing stronger than that. Thanks. I'm still on duty. A police officer's work is never done."

"And I suppose that is especially true for a police chief in the middle of a murder investigation."

He frowned. "Yes."

"Have a seat on the sofa and I'll grab your water."

Without waiting for a reply, I hurried into the kitchen with Emerson on my heels. The police chief didn't stop me although the kitchen was still technically part of the crime scene. The swinging door closed shut behind us, and I grasped the granite countertop to steady myself. What was Rainwater doing here? It had to be about the murder. There could be no other reason. "Get a grip, Violet," I told myself.

On the other side of the room, a bright yellow X of crime scene tape blocked the doorway that led to the back stairs of the house. A garish reminder of the location of Anastasia Faber's death.

Emerson leaped onto the kitchen stool and cocked his head to me, dropping the black side of his face lower than the white. His markings were such that when he closed his left eye, it made him look like a pirate with a black eye patch.

I took a glass from the overhead cabinet and filled it with cold tap water, straightened my shoulders, and went back into the main part of the shop.

Rainwater sat in the middle of the couch closest to the cash register. I handed the water glass to him.

"Thank you," he said.

I stepped back and took in my seating options. The other couch seemed too far away for a serious conversation, but I couldn't bring myself to sit next to Rainwater. Finally, I perched on the edge of the coffee table directly across from him. The coffee table was a good two feet from the couch. He smiled as if he had read every last thought that flashed across my mind during my momentary dilemma.

He sipped from his water. "I stopped by because I wanted to tell you that I spoke with Fenimore, the troubadour, about Anastasia."

I forgot my awkwardness and leaned forward. "What did he say?"

"He clearly didn't know who I was talking about. He doesn't know who Evanna Blue is either."

"Maybe he killed her at random, then?" I said even though I knew I was reaching. "Or it was an accident."

He shook his head. "If Anastasia had died in an accident or a random act of violence, I might believe that it was possible, but her death was planned, premeditated, and personal."

I shifted away from him. "It's still possible he might have done it," I said, refusing to give up on my theory.

"He has an alibi," Rainwater said. "At the time of her death, he was playing his guitar in the middle of the Food and Wine Festival. Dozens of people saw him. I asked around and already half the vendors at the festival I spoke to confirmed he was there."

"But you yourself said that the nicotine could have been placed on the dress at any time. An alibi doesn't really hold up in a case like that."

"Can I ask you a question?"

My gaze met his amber eyes. "Sure."

"Why did you suspect Fenimore had anything to do with the murder? When you told me about it at the festival today, you actually appeared frightened." He smiled. "And in full disclosure that's why I stopped by tonight. I could have told you everything I'd just said during a simple phone call. I just had to see with my own eyes that you were all right."

My pulse quickened. "As you can see, I'm fine."

He studied me as he sipped from his water glass. "What is it about Fenimore that bothers you so much?"

Again, I was unable to share with the police chief what the troubadour had said about my mother.

He broke eye contact with me as if he was disappointed with my lack of an answer and set the water glass on the coaster on an end table next to him. "Well, I should let you get back to your reading, then."

He stood up, and I stood at the exact same time. We were face-to-face, mere inches from each other. For a half second that seemed like a year, we just stared at each other. All I could hear was my blood pulsing in my ears. All I could see was his eyes. This close, I could see they were more than amber. There were also tiny flecks of gold in his irises.

"Nevermore!" Faulkner cried, breaking up the moment. I didn't know if I was relieved or disappointed by the crow's interruption. Perhaps a little bit of both.

Rainwater slipped out of the tight place, brushing across my body as he went. He moved over to the foot of the birch tree as if he wanted to put some distance between us. "Has anyone ever commented on how unusual it is to have a tree like this growing indoors?"

I found my voice. "All the time."

"How old is it?"

"Over two hundred years," I said. "It was here when my ancestress Rosalee built the house. She wanted to save the tree, so she built her home around it."

His brow creased. "That is unusually old for a birch tree."

"Oh," I said, internally kicking myself for revealing the age of the tree. It wasn't a secret, or at least I hadn't thought it was until Rainwater made that comment. "I don't think it's that uncommon. My family has nursed and watched over the tree for so long. It seems natural that it would remain alive with such good care and protection from the elements."

He stared up into the boughs. "Maybe."

I swallowed. Did Rainwater suspect something about the tree? "You know Sadie didn't do this. She was framed."

"If I thought Sadie killed Anastasia, I would have arrested her already." He looked at me. "I have more than enough evidence to do it. I agree with you that she was framed. Unfortunately, I must find an alternative suspect relatively fast or I might have to arrest her no matter what I believe."

I folded my arms around my waist. "You can't. Not when you know she is innocent."

"If the county DA tells me to, I don't have much of a choice. Thankfully he's allowing me more time because of Sadie's relationship with the Mortons. No one wants to upset the Morton family unnecessarily, as you know."

Oh, I knew better even than he did. I didn't tell him that Grant and Sadie broke up a week ago, long before the murder.

Rainwater walked to the front door. "You know birch trees are sacred to my people," he said when he reached the door.

I nodded, unable to speak.

He gave one last look to the tree. "It makes you wonder, doesn't it?"

I forced a laugh. "Wonder about what?"

He shook his head. "Good night, Violet." He went out the door.

"Good night," I said as I closed and locked the door after him.

THIRTY-TWO

The next morning, I woke with sunshine streaming onto my face, which was pouring in through the skylight above the tree. I lay on my back on one of the couches that flanked either side of Charming Books' enormous fireplace. Emerson lay on my stomach, kneading my breastbone. I rubbed sleep from my eyes. After Rainwater left the night before, I'd fallen asleep on the couch while researching Poe's work.

"Up and at 'em" Faulkner cawed.

I groaned and rolled over to my stomach, causing Emerson to jump onto the back of the couch.

The volume of Poe's works was splayed open on the floor. I had been up into the wee hours reading the entire book from cover to cover, and I still didn't know what the shop's essence was trying to tell me by directing me to read "The Purloined Letter." The lesson had to be to look for the obvious. But in the case of Anastasia's death what was the obvious? It all appeared to be unclear to me.

Then, it hit me.

"Her brother!" I cried, sitting straight up. "Her brother, who now stands to inherit the fortune she made as Evanna Blue." I jumped off the couch. "I need to find Coleridge Faber and find out what he knows."

Coleridge must still be in the village. Cascade Springs, being a tourist town, had no shortage of places where he could be staying. The village boasted at least twenty bed-and-breakfasts, and he could even be staying in Anastasia's home. I couldn't eliminate that as a possibility.

Faulkner flew over my head and landed on his favorite branch in the birch tree.

I ducked. "Cut that out. One of these days you're going to hit me."

He cackled in reply.

Emerson hissed at the bird. At least I had my tuxie in my corner.

It was a little after seven in the morning. The shop didn't open until ten, but I knew Grandma Daisy would arrive just before nine to start the day. That gave me a little less than two hours to track down Coleridge. It would take all day to call every bed-and-breakfast and inquire if he was a guest there, and that was assuming they would tell me, when I knew most, wanting to protect their guests' privacy, would not. I did have another idea. It was a long shot, but if it panned out, it would save me a great deal of time.

I grabbed my phone from the coffee table and found the battery was almost dead. I had forgotten to plug it in the night before, not surprising seeing how I had forgotten to go to bed at all. I scrolled through my contacts until I found the number for La Crepe Jolie. I prayed that Lacey would answer. I knew she was just beginning her breakfast rush, which must be even bigger than normal because of the Food and Wine Festival. Business would be brisk, and she might not have a spare moment to answer the phone.

"La Crepe Jolie, how may I help you?" Lacey asked in a breathless voice in my ear.

"Lacey, it's Violet," I said.

"Violet, it's so good to hear from you. How are you this morning?" Her voice was bright and cheery as always. No one calling La Crepe Jolie would have guessed she had been up since four baking the fresh cookies and pastries for the café.

"Fine. What about you?"

"It's bedlam over here," she said, clearly out of breath. "I can hardly keep up."

"Maybe you should take a break when this week is over. You and Adrien should treat yourselves with a weekend away," I said. "The Food and Wine Festival week must be absolutely swamped for you."

"To be honest, it's not just the festival. Our business has grown leaps and bounds over the last year since Adrien started the catering side of the business."

"Are you looking to hire more staff?"

"I think it's time. It's just taking some effort to convince Adrien. He loves the café being just our little place, but if we want to continue to grow, we're going to need more help." She chuckled. "Don't tell me you're asking because you're looking for a job. Don't you have enough to do already?"

I glanced at the tree. "More than enough. I asked because I know Danielle Cloud is looking for work. She's the chief's younger sister."

"Oh, I know Danielle. I didn't know she was looking. Has she had food service experience?" she asked.

"I have no idea," I admitted.

"Experience helps, but it's not a deal breaker. We can always train people to do the work. We can't train them to have a welcoming personality, which is required for the restaurant business."

"Same goes for the bookseller business."

She laughed. "I suppose it does. I'll talk to Adrien about it. He likes the police chief, and we both know Danielle. She's quiet but a sweet girl. I certainly would want to hire someone to bring calm to work." As she spoke, her excitement grew. "Thanks for the suggestion. Why are you calling so early? Do you need to put in a breakfast order? I know how fond Daisy is of Adrien's quiche."

My mouth watered at the mention of Adrien's quiche. I pushed thoughts of breakfast aside, and focused on the reason that I called. "I'm not ordering breakfast. I just called for a little information."

"Oh?" she said, sounding immediately perky. "What information is that?"

"Do you know Anastasia's brother, Coleridge?"

"I know of him. Why do you ask?"

"I'd like to talk to him about his sister, and I was wondering if you knew where he was staying."

She was quiet for a moment. "I don't know."

"Oh." It had been a long shot, but still I was disappointed. I had been so excited about tracking Coleridge down that morning that the idea it would take some time deflated me. "Could he be staying at Anastasia's house, do you think?"

"Definitely not," Lacey said. "A customer just told me that the police have the place under guard. Everyone is talking about you being chased out of the place two days ago."

I shifted uncomfortably in my seat. "You don't say." I guessed I was right in assuming that Lacey had been talking about my nighttime encounter with Daven York.

She clicked her tongue in disapproval. "It's horrible what's happening in the village. It makes it feel unsafe to even sleep in our own beds, you know?" A buzzer went off in the background on Lacey's end of the line. "Those are the quiches. Violet, I have to go, but I will tell you what. I'll start asking around. Someone who comes into the café today is bound to know where Anastasia's brother is staying if he's in the village. You know how the people in Cascade Springs talk."

I certainly did. "Thanks, Lacey. I really appreciate that."

"No problem. What are friends for?" The buzzer went off again. She shouted, "Gotta go!" in my ear and ended the call.

So it looked like, as far as the Coleridge angle in the case was concerned, I had hit a dead end. I ran my hand through my tangled hair, and pulled at my sweater. I was wearing the same clothes I had worn the day before, but I still wasn't ready to give up investigating just yet.

I fell back onto the couch. I needed to think this through. Rainwater had said the night before that he was getting pressure from the county DA to arrest Sadie because of the evidence, and the only reason the DA wasn't forcing the issue was that he believed she was still engaged to Grant Morton. The DA didn't want to upset the influential family. It was only a matter of time before Rainwater or the DA learned, like I did, that Sadie was no longer engaged to Grant. When they learned of the broken engagement, her time would run out, because there would be no reason for the DA to make Rainwater wait to arrest her. I was running out of time and so was Sadie.

I needed to remind myself that Coleridge wasn't my only suspect. Yes, Fenimore had been eliminated from the list, with no connections to Anastasia or her writing as Evanna Blue. The police chief was right to tell me his guilt was very unlikely. But I did have other suspects. There was Daven York, the reporter who broke the story about Evanna Blue's identity, and there was Anastasia's literary agent, Edmund Eaton. Of the two, I thought Edmund was the most likely of the pair. He had the most to lose if Anastasia refused to write any more novels as Evanna Blue. He wasn't going to be any easier to track down than Coleridge was. I stopped myself from calling Lacey back and asking her about Edmund as well, when I knew she was so busy at the café.

I stood. I would just have to find Edmund Eaton myself. There were many B&Bs in Cascade Springs, but I had an immediate suspicion of which one the agent would be staying at, and I had just enough time to run over there and prove my suspicions before my grandmother arrived at the shop for the day. Just in case the trip took longer than I expected, I scribbled a little note for my grandmother, and set it in the open cash register drawer where she wouldn't miss it.

I looked down at my clothes. No New York City native would take me seriously in my current state. I looked more like a college kid who'd been out all night than a responsible and successful bookseller.

I ran up the stairs to my apartment to get ready for the day.

Twenty minutes later I came down the stairs dressed in my best pair of jeans and a printed blouse under a wool suit jacket. I knew it wasn't NYC business attire, but it was just about as good as it got in Cascade Springs, at least in my case. Perhaps Grandma Daisy was right, and Sadie did need to give my wardrobe an overhaul. If I could keep her out of jail, I just might let her do it.

The shop's telephone rang. It was a little before eight and the shop wasn't open yet. Typically, I would have let the call go to voice mail, but for some reason, I felt compelled to answer it. "Charming Books, where the perfect book finds you," I said, repeating the greeting that my grandmother had drilled into me since I was a small child. Grandma Daisy always said people don't truly remember something without repetition, so repeating the Charming Books tagline was essential. What I didn't know as a child was how literally true the tagline was.

"Yes, hello, this is Charles Hancock. To whom am I speaking?"

I should have let the call go to voice mail. I put more

warmth in my voice than I felt. "This is Violet. How can I help you?"

"Violet? Very good," he said in his powerful voice. "I have fulfilled my mission and tracked down the rogue who had the audacity to slander my sweet Daisy and thrust her business into a media circus. He should be banned from the village, no, from the state."

"You've done what?" I asked, confused.

"I found Daven York. I'm following him down River Road as we speak."

"You're what?" I cried.

THIRTY-THREE

"The rogue has the nerve to walk around our village as if it was his God-given right. As soon as I catch up to him, I plan to give him a piece of my mind and my cane."

"Don't do that!" I said.

"Whyever not? He has dishonored my beloved Daisy. There is nothing I wouldn't do for her."

I couldn't let an eighty-year-old man with a Don Quixote complex knock Daven silly with his cane before I had a chance to speak to the reporter myself. "I know that, Charles, and as her granddaughter, I appreciate that," I said, hoping that statement didn't come back to haunt me. "But I think to save Grandma Daisy any more public scrutiny, we need to deal with this delicately. That means no giving anyone a piece of your cane."

"I wasn't going to hurt him." He paused. "Too badly."

"Where are you? I'll come to you. Are you still on River Road?"

"Yes. He's just come out of La Crepe Jolie with a muffin and coffee. I don't know how he can live with himself let alone eat after what he's done."

"Stay there! I'll be over as soon as I can."

"Don't you think I should follow him?"

"No! Please stay. It's what Grandma Daisy would want."

"If you're sure . . ." He trailed off.

I ended the call, shoved my phone into the back pocket of my jeans, and ran for the door.

This early in the morning, the traffic at the Food and Wine Festival was light. There were only about a dozen pedestrians on the Riverwalk, as the festival tents wouldn't officially open until ten, although the vendors were already there for the day setting up their stations. I spotted both Grant and his mother in the Morton Vineyards booth, unpacking crates of ice wine. I sped by them on my bike, hoping I could pass without being seen.

I slowed my pedaling as I closed in on La Crepe Jolie, but Charles was nowhere in sight. Lacey stepped out of the café and shook out a tablecloth onto the sidewalk. Tiny crumbs flew in the air like confetti. "Violet, what are you doing here? I didn't expect to see you here after our conversation this morning."

"I didn't expect to come," I said as I straddled my bike. "Have you seen Charles Hancock? I was supposed to meet him here."

"Charles Hancock?" she asked. "Yes, he was here. When

he said that he was planning on meeting you, I thought he was confused. You know he is getting up there in years. Personally, I'm not sure that he's all there anymore."

"I think Charles might know what's going on in this village more than the rest of us do. Do you know which way he went?"

She dusted some flour off her sweater sleeve. "He said that he was going to the arts district. He said to tell you that his quarry—whatever that means—was staying there."

I put my right foot on the bike pedal, preparing to kick off. "Thank you so much, Lacey. I have to go. I'll see you later." I pushed my left foot off the sidewalk and rolled my bike onto the street.

"Whatever you are up to, be careful," she called after me.

I raised my hand to acknowledge that I heard her, but I was too focused on finding Charles Hancock to reply. Despite how annoying he could be, if Charles got hurt while on a mission that I'd foolishly given him, I would never forgive myself. Thankfully, I knew exactly where to go. There weren't many bed-and-breakfasts in the arts district, and I knew just the one a journalist from NYC would choose for his lodgings.

Puffin Lane B&B was in the arts district of Cascade Springs. The small touristy village had attracted many artists and craftspeople over the decades as they collectively settled in the Bird neighborhood. I only called it that because all the streets in that section of the village were named after birds. There was Puffin Lane, Sparrow Street, Lark Avenue, and several more that wove through the west side of the village on the opposite end from the river and the natural springs.

The B&B was on the corner of the street at the entrance to the rest of the neighborhood and looked like it would be more suited for the streets of New Orleans with its wrought ironwork and numerous terraces than for a Western New York village.

Before I even reached the front door to the B&B, I spotted Charles standing on the corner with a pair of binoculars pointed at the B&B's second-floor terrace.

"Charles!" I called.

He dropped his binoculars from his eyes and lifted a finger to his lips. "Shh!" In a hushed voice, he went on to say, "The scoundrel is up there. He might hear you."

I jumped off my bike and leaned it against a tree. I removed my bike helmet and hung it from the handlebars. "Can I see?"

Somewhat reluctantly, Charles handed me the binoculars. I held them in front of my eyes. Daven York was on the second-floor terrace. He sat at a white ironwork table and faced away from me, but he wasn't alone. I could just make out the shadow of another person on the terrace with him. Daven hadn't been my quarry when I awoke that morning. I had been determined to track down Anastasia's brother, Coleridge, but now that I saw Daven, I couldn't let the opportunity go by. I hadn't seen him since he'd chased me from Anastasia's house two nights ago. Honestly, I was surprised he was still in town. I would have thought he'd fled the moment his story broke to the press. He hadn't been seen anywhere when Charming Books was surrounded by reporters the day before.

"What shall we do? Shall we storm the B&B?" Charles asked.

I found the excitement in his voice more than a little alarming. "We aren't storming anything. He's not alone on the terrace, but I don't know who's with him. I'll see if I can get close enough to overhear their conversation. You did a good job, Charles, and I will be sure to tell Grandma Daisy that, but I can take it from here."

He tapped his cane on the sidewalk. "Are you mad? I am not going to run away now, not moments before battle."

I grimaced. Maybe Lacey had been right and Charles was a little bit confused as far as reality was concerned. "There will be no battle. You can stay," I conceded because I couldn't see any way of ridding myself of him without attracting the attention of Daven, not to mention every sleepy resident of the arts district.

The arts district was a drowsy place in the early morning. Many of the artists who lived there preferred to wake up midday and work on their masterpieces late into the night. At the same time, it was too far from the Riverwalk to have any overflow festival traffic this early in the day. Because of this, the street was empty. There wasn't even a jogger or a dog walker to disturb the quiet. "But please follow my lead."

He sniffed. "Typically, I am the one at the front lines, but I will permit you take the lead just this once."

"Thanks so much," I muttered with as much grace as I could muster, which admittedly wasn't much. I handed Charles the binoculars back. "Keep watch. I'm going to cross the street to see if I can get close enough to see who Daven is talking to."

He nodded and accepted the binoculars without further complaint.

I crossed the street and positioned myself underneath the terrace. I stood just below where Daven sat and pressed my back against the whitewashed brick wall of the building.

"I write for a trade magazine, not the *New York Times*. I'm not willing to go to prison for this," Daven snapped. He did nothing to modulate his voice as if he didn't care who heard him.

"No one's asking you to go to prison, but I see no reason to reveal my name to the police. What will that get you?" a second man's voice asked.

I pressed my body harder against the cool brick and listened.

"It's your fault that I'm still here. I stayed to talk to you, and now I'm trapped in this storybook reject of a village because the police won't let me leave."

Storybook reject? I thought that was a tad harsh.

Daven went on to say, "The village police chief thinks that I might have had something to do with her murder. I have already been charged with breaking and entering. I don't work for a newspaper where committing a crime in the name of the press earns me street cred. Believe me when I say that my editor and publisher are not amused, even though my story has single-handedly increased their circulation and views online by eighty percent in the last week. They threatened to terminate me."

There was a banging sound as if Daven brought his hand down on the tabletop where he and the other man sat. "That's all the thanks I get for doing good work." Daven's voice shook with anger.

"I understand, but just give me a little more time," the second man pleaded. "I promise I will give you the story that will make your publisher not only forgive you, but kiss your feet."

Daven said something else I couldn't hear.

I stepped back from the wall and craned my neck back, hoping to get a good look at the two men. Although I could see the back of Daven's head, I couldn't see the man that he was talking to, and I needed to know who it was. He might just be the key to breaking open this entire case, and at the very least he was Daven's informant, which meant that Chief Rainwater needed to talk to him.

The scraping of chairs echoed as the two men stood up to leave. *No, I haven't seen the informant yet.*

"Wait," the informant said. "Just give me two minutes more."

"Two minutes is more than you deserve," Daven said. "But fine."

Two minutes. That's all the time that I had to spy whomever the journalist was talking to. I had to see who it was. Because whomever Daven was speaking to had to be the person who'd told him Anastasia's true identity and how to find the secret room in Anastasia's mansion.

I tried the front door of the B&B. It was locked. Apparently, guests were required to enter with a key or knock. What was I going to say when I knocked on the door? *Oh, hi, I just need to run upstairs to have a look at one of your guests so that I can reveal his identity to the police.* That would never work.

Charles waved at me from across the street.

"What?" I mouthed.

He used his cane to point to the corner of the B&B where a trellis covered in ivy was tethered to the side of the whitewashed building. It was roughly three feet wide and extended all the way to the second-floor terrace where the men spoke.

"Bad idea," I whispered.

Charles kept pointing at the trellis like his life depended on it. Maybe it did, because his face was impossibly red from the exertion.

"You have one minute left," I heard Daven say to his companion. He might as well have said it to me, because his comment made me spring into action.

I waved to Charles, hoping that he would relax some, ran over to the trellis, grabbed it with both hands, and shook it. It didn't budge. I saw that it was bolted to the side of the brick building. As I fit my shoe in the bottom rung of the trellis, I thought that this was going to be one of those ideas that I would come to regret.

As the trellis held with every rung I climbed, I gained confidence, climbing faster. Finally, I climbed far enough up the trellis to peek through the ironwork onto the terrace. Daven's back was still toward me, but I could clearly see the man facing him. It was Anastasia's literary agent, Edmund Eaton.

The only problem with such a clear view of Edmund was that he also had a clear view of me, or at least of the top of my head.

His face paled. "There's someone watching us."

Daven spun around. "You!" Daven pointed at me.

I yelped and my body jerked back. The trellis made a terrible cracking sound as the wooden frame broke away from the building.

I landed on the sidewalk below in a heap, and the broken trellis fell on top of me.

THIRTY-FOUR

EMT Keenan's white teeth flashed against his dark skin as he smiled at me from the B&B's white ironwork chair, which was identical to the one in which I sat. "I didn't expect to see you again so soon." The smile grew even wider. "Then again from what David tells me, I should have known that we would be seeing each other again."

Rainwater paced on the other side of the hotel. He looked like a caged tiger and an angry one at that. I guessed I was the one he was so mad at. Daven York and Edmund Eaton stood a few feet away being questioned by Officer Clipton. Daven scowled at the officer, and Edmund scanned the area as if looking for escape routes. Charles regaled a bored-looking Officer Wheaton with a play-by-play of the morning's events, ending dramatically with my tumble from the B&B's trellis.

"You took quite a nasty spill there." Keenan removed the blood pressure cuff from my arm.

"I'm fine," I insisted. "I don't know why everyone is making such a fuss." I glanced over at the broken piece of trellis. "I'm a lot better off than the poor trellis."

I had already spoken to the B&B owner about the broken trellis and promised to pay for her to have a new one installed and to have any ivy that was injured in my fall replanted as well.

Thankfully the owner was an old friend of my grandmother's and would let me pay for the damage outright and promised not to file trespassing or damaging-property charges. It didn't hurt that Grandma Daisy was so well liked in the village. I was grateful for that.

Keenan lifted my elbow, moving my right shoulder in the process.

"Ow." I winced.

"I thought you said you were fine." He wiggled his thick black eyebrows.

I gritted my teeth against the pain. "I am."

He started to pack up his medical kit. "What you are is lucky. You fell ten feet. It could have been so much worse for you."

I knew that.

Keenan stood. "I still think you need to go to the hospital, but since you have refused, I can't force you to go. You're going to have to at least go to the nearest clinic and have that arm x-rayed. I think I'm right in my assessment that it's only bad bruising localized in your right shoulder where you landed, but you shouldn't take chances with these sorts of injuries. Only an X-ray will be able to tell you whether or not it's more serious."

"All right," I agreed grudgingly.

He laughed. "Don't sound so happy about it."

Rainwater paced back and forth ten feet behind Keenan. Back and forth. Back and forth. I would have run away to escape the tongue-lashing that I knew I was about to receive from him if my shoulder didn't hurt so much.

Keenan walked over to the chief and spoke to him. Rainwater watched me over Keenan's shoulder as he listened to what his friend the EMT had to say. Finally, Keenan clapped him on the shoulder. "She's all yours."

I grimaced. I was toast.

Rainwater sat in the chair that Keenan had just vacated.

For a moment, I wondered if I should play up the shoulder injury, but I was afraid that would backfire by causing Rainwater to ship me off to the hospital with Keenan.

"Do you want to tell me what happened?" the police chief asked.

I thought better than making a smart remark and told him everything that had happened since I arrived on Puffin Lane. "When I heard Daven speaking about the article that he wrote about Anastasia, I wanted to see who he was talking to. I climbed the trellis, and you know what happened after that."

"I do." His voice was deceptively neutral. "Keenan said you refuse to go to the hospital."

"I have a bad bruise. I don't really want to be stuck in the emergency room for the rest of the day. We're in the middle of the Food and Wine Festival. I need to return to the shop and help Grandma Daisy open."

"Not until you get that X-ray, you won't. I'll take you to the clinic myself," he said, leaving no room for argument.

I hesitated. "Don't you need to question Edmund and Daven? What about Charles? I know he must have a lot to say about it. I'm perfectly capable of going to the clinic by myself."

"My officers will take care of it." He was stone-faced. "And I don't know if you're perfectly capable of making your way to the clinic after that stunt you pulled."

I frowned. "What about my bike?"

"Officer Clipton will take your bike back to Charming Books."

I didn't move.

He stood. "Do you need help standing up?"

"No," I said, and with as much dignity as I could muster, I rose to my feet. It took everything within me not to cry out in pain as I moved.

At his departmental SUV, Rainwater held the passenger door open for me while I climbed in. He shut the door behind me, and Officer Wheaton came over to him. "Chief, where are you going?" The sound of Wheaton's voice was muffled, but I could clearly make out the words through the car door.

"I'm taking Miss Waverly to the clinic for some X-rays. Finish your questioning. I expect a report on my desk by the time I return to the office."

Wheaton folded his arms across his muscular chest. "Shouldn't the EMTs be taking care of her? Why do you need to take her?"

"I don't *need* to take her. I'm choosing to take her." He turned and walked around the SUV.

Wheaton scowled at me through the SUV's wind-shield. I didn't know what I had ever done to the buzz-cut officer, but whatever it was, it wasn't good.

Rainwater didn't speak on the short drive to the clinic, and my shoulder hurt too much to bother with small talk. When we entered the clinic, the receptionist gave me a clipboard with at least forty documents I needed to fill out clipped to the front of it. Rainwater and I took seats next to each other in the empty waiting room.

I was right-handed, so filling out the forms was no picnic. However, I refused to ask Rainwater for help, since he seemed set on giving me the silent treatment.

I was only halfway through the forms when a nurse appeared in the doorway leading to the back office. "Miss Waverly, we're ready for you."

I stood up and handed the nurse my clipboard. To Rainwater, I said, "You don't have to wait. I can call a friend or Grandma Daisy for a ride back to the shop."

"I'll wait." He leaned back in the uncomfortable plastic chair as if he planned never to move.

Okay, then, I thought, and followed the nurse back into the examining room.

Nearly an hour later, the medical staff at the clinic had bent and twisted my body in so many ways to capture all the X-rays they needed, I felt like a pretzel that had been broken into a thousand pieces and then stomped on for good measure.

When the X-rays were done, a nurse directed me back to the waiting room. As promised, the police chief was right where I had left him. He held his cell phone next to his ear. "That sounds fine, Clipton," he said into the phone. "We can discuss it further when I get back to the office."

The nurse stood beside me. "Violet should be fine," the nurse told Rainwater without prompting. "She has some deep bruising on her right shoulder and her right hip, but both will heal in time. We gave her some Tylenol for the pain. The doctor wrote her a prescription for something a little stronger to take at night, so that she can get some sleep."

Rainwater nodded. "Are you ready to go, Violet?" He no longer sounded mad.

I was so relieved that he was no longer giving me the silent treatment that I said, "More than ready. Let's get out of here."

Again Rainwater opened and closed the SUV's passenger side door for me. When he climbed in, he asked, "Do you want to swing by the pharmacy to pick up those pills?"

I shook my head. "I'm going to tough it out with Tylenol. I hate to take anything stronger. In fact, I hate taking medicine of any kind."

He raised his eyebrows. "And why's that?"

I laughed. "I just like to have all my working faculties."

His eyebrows rose a little higher.

What I didn't tell the police chief was I didn't like to take medicine because of my mother's illness. The number of drugs she had been on the last two years of her life was staggering, and none of them helped, not really. She still died.

I struggled with my seat belt. A stiffness had settled into my muscles and bones.

Rainwater took the seat belt buckle from my hand and clicked it into place.

"I'm not an invalid."

A smile played on the corners of his mouth. "I never said you were, but I do need to get back to work and don't have time to watch you prove that you can do absolutely everything on your own right now."

I leaned back in my seat feeling all of four years old.

He started the car and pulled out of the parking lot. "While you were getting your X-rays, my sister called."

"Oh?"

"She said that Lacey Dupont offered her a job at the café. She starts tomorrow. You wouldn't know anything about that, would you?" He glanced at me before returning his attention to the road.

"I'm sorry if you think I was meddling, but when I spoke to Lacey this morning, she mentioned she and Adrien needed extra help at La Crepe Jolie and Danielle immediately came to mind. I suggested that Lacey talk to her. I didn't know she would out-and-out offer her the job, but I'm glad she did."

He gripped the steering wheel. "I don't think you were meddling. In fact, I wanted to thank you for Danielle and myself."

I let out a breath. "You don't have to thank me."

The village was small, and we were already moving down River Road. It was midmorning now, and the merchant district was picking up. Rainwater rolled the SUV to a stop in front of Charming Books. With the number of text messages on my phone, I knew my grandmother was wondering what had become of me.

The SUV idled in front of the bookshop.

"Thank you for the ride," I murmured, but before I had a chance to unbuckle my seat belt, Rainwater did it for me.

"You need to learn that you can ask for help." His voice was low.

"It's a hard lesson for me," I said quietly. "I've been taking care of myself for a very long time."

He shifted in his seat to face me. "Why is that exactly?"

I stared at him. It was a loaded question, and the answers were many. Because I never had a father, because my mother died when I needed her the very most, because I was accused of murder when I was seventeen. Those were all good reasons; I could have told Rainwater any one of those answers, and it would be enough.

Even though the movement made my sore body scream in pain, I leaned across the seat and kissed the police chief on the cheek.

His tanned skin changed into a burnt red shade.

"Thank you," I said, and opened my own door and stepped onto the tree lawn in front of Charming Books.

From the grass, I gave Rainwater a little wave through the SUV's window. He smiled at me and finally pulled the car away from the curb. It wasn't until Rainwater's tail-lights disappeared around the corner of River Road that I realized I wasn't alone on the sidewalk.

THIRTY-FIVE

Nathan Morton, in another mayoral suit, stood ten feet away from me on the sidewalk in front of my bookshop.

"Nathan," I said, taken aback. "What are you doing here?"

"I heard about what happened this morning and came to see if you were all right." He glared in the direction of where Rainwater's car had disappeared. "I see that you are."

"Yes, I'm perfectly fine." I took a step back from him.

He balled his fists at his sides. "Tell me one thing."

"What?" I asked, guessing that I wouldn't like whatever he had to say.

"Are you and the police chief seeing each other?"

"Nathan, don't be ridiculous. He gave me a ride home. That's it." I opened the gate that surrounded Charming Books' front yard.

"I saw you kiss him, Vi." He was hurt and angry.

I spun around. "Were you spying on me?"

"It's hard not to see it, since you did it in front of God and everyone," he snapped.

I placed my hands on my hips, forgetting about my injured shoulder. The sharp movement sent a jolt of pain up my right arm, but I refused to let Nathan see I was hurt. I had only kissed Rainwater on the cheek. It hadn't meant anything, but I wasn't going to tell Nathan that. It was none of his business. Nothing in my life was his business. Just because we had been in love once, he thought he had some claim on my heart. Well, he didn't.

"Do you have anything to say for yourself?" Nathan wanted to know.

I refused to speak.

"Fine." Nathan stomped down the sidewalk in the direction of the festival and Riverwalk.

To my surprise, part of me wanted to run after him and explain. Why, I didn't know. Maybe it was to re-create the friendship that we'd had before Colleen died. Nostalgia for another time before our lives became so complicated could be the only reason for the impulse. But that time was past, and there was no getting it back. I didn't owe anyone an explanation, least of all Nathan Morton.

I was about to step through the gate when I saw Sadie making her way up the sidewalk toward Midcentury Vintage. This October morning, she wore a cashmere sweater, a black-and-pink poodle skirt, and saddle shoes.

On anyone else, the outfit would look like a Halloween costume, especially with the holiday just one week away, but on Sadie it worked. Despite how adorable the vintage clothier looked in her outfit, it was evident that not all was well in her world. She moved up the sidewalk dragging her feet as if there were glue stuck to the bottoms of her saddle shoes. Even the poodle embroidered on her skirt seemed to droop.

"Sadie," I called.

She looked up from her shoes and gave me a small smile.

I walked over to her. "Are you on your way to open Midcentury Vintage?" Her shop should have been open by now. I didn't like how Sadie was letting what had happened to Anastasia impact her business.

She pulled on the end of her long black ponytail. "You're moving strangely. Are you hurt?"

"I'm fine. I had a little tumble this morning." That was one way to describe it. "I'll be fine."

Her mouth fell open. "A tumble? What happened?"

I gave her a short version of the morning's events.

"Violet, you could have been killed!" she exclaimed.

"Naw," I said. "The trellis wasn't that high."

She shook her head and her ponytail swayed back and forth. "I can't believe you did that for me. I can't believe you teamed up with Charles Hancock for me either."

"Trust me—Charles was not part of the plan."

She laughed, and I was so relieved to hear her good humor had returned. The fall had been worth it. Almost.

Her good cheer made it even more difficult to ask what I had to ask her next. "Why didn't you tell me that you and Grant already broke up?"

She looked up at me. Tears gathered in her big blue eyes. "How did you find out?"

"Grant told me." I held on to my right arm with my left hand, hoping that would alleviate some of the pain. I had told Rainwater that I wasn't interested in any strong drugs to help me through my injury, but that prescription in my pocket was sounding pretty good right about now. "This is the reason he hasn't been around since Anastasia died, isn't it?"

She nodded miserably.

"Why did you let us, even Nathan, continue to believe that you and Grant were still together?" I asked.

A single tear slid down her face. "Because I was hoping that it wasn't true. Grant and I have broken up before and we always got back together. I thought this time it would be just like that." Another tear followed the trail of the first. "I want to be with him. I love him."

I stopped just short of asking her why. Considering my own love life dilemmas—if I could even call them that—I was in no place to point fingers.

Despite the pain in my shoulder, I gave her a hug. "And you just might get back together, but I want you to think long and hard about being engaged to Grant again. Do you really want to be with someone who will break your heart so easily?"

"He is what I want," she said with as much conviction as I had ever heard her use.

"Then, okay," I conceded gently. "Soon this mess surrounding Anastasia's death will be behind all of us, and we will be able to move on with our lives. Will you be at the Red Inkers meeting tonight at Charming Books?"

"Will there still be a meeting, considering . . . ?" She trailed off.

"I think we should have it. It'll give everyone a chance to talk about what happened. In the village, we knew Anastasia the best of anyone. Sure, we didn't know her as Evanna Blue, but we knew Anastasia Faber, and I think it would do us good to talk about her and what happened."

"I don't know if I should come. What if they think I really did pour that nicotine on Anastasia's dress?"

"Please," I scoffed. "Not one of the Red Inkers could think you were behind Anastasia's death. They know you. They're your friends." I took a step back in the direction of the still open gate that led into Charming Books' front yard. "Now, no more arguing. The Red Inkers meeting will go on as planned, and I'm expecting you there."

She nodded. "All right." And with that, she crossed the street to her own shop.

I watched her go before I retreated to my own shop. As soon as I walked through the door to Charming Books, my grandmother was in front of me, and she wasn't happy. I could tell by the way she held the end of her cobweb-printed scarf in a stranglehold.

"Violet, what on earth happened to you?" my grandmother wanted to know. "I only sent you fourteen text messages. None of which you took the time to answer."

I rubbed my shoulder. "I know, Grandma Daisy, and I'm sorry. I had a bit of a spill." I gave her a brief version of the morning's events, but I thought it would be best to leave Charles Hancock from my tale at least until she calmed down a bit.

"Why on earth would you climb that trellis?" She

flailed her arms, and the scent of lavender, which I always associated with my grandmother, wafted around me. Usually I found it comforting, but it didn't have the same soothing element when I was being reprimanded even if I deserved it.

"David wanted to know the same thing," I admitted. At my feet, Emerson purred as he wove around my legs. At least one of them was happy to see me in one piece.

"I should think so. I'm surprised David didn't throw you in the village jail for sheer stupidity."

At her mention of Rainwater, I felt my cheeks heat up.

My grandmother studied me and opened her mouth to say something before snapping it closed again.

"What do you need me to do?" I asked, looking around the shop. There was one customer in the cookbook section, but other than that, the shop was empty save for the usual suspects: Grandma Daisy, Emerson, and Faulkner.

"You're covered in dirt. Go upstairs and clean yourself up. You can tell me more about it later." She made a shooing motion with her hands.

I didn't even attempt to argue with her and headed up the staircase to my apartment. Once inside, I sat on my bed and pulled my cell phone out of my jacket pocket. I called Richard at Springside. The English professor was in his office and picked up on the first ring.

"Richard, I was wondering if I could ask you a favor," I said.

There was a shuffle of papers on the other end of the line. "How can I help you, Violet?"

"Can you cover my class today?" My American Literature I class was taking their midterm today. If it was canceled, it would put grades and everything on my syllabus behind, but at the rate I was moving, there was no way that I would make it there in time to administer the exam. Briefly, I told Richard about my fall and asked him if he would be willing to give the exam to my students that afternoon.

"Of course, Violet, I would be happy to proctor your exam later. The quiet while they are taking the test will give me time to mark my own midterms. I should have finished them last night, but I got caught up on a bit of interesting research. I think I'm onto something with the article I'm working on—"

"Thank you, Richard." I cut him off. Typically, I loved hearing about Richard's research, but I knew from experience the conversation could go on for hours if I allowed it. I didn't have time for that, and neither did Richard if he was going to administer my midterm. "I owe you big-time," I told my department chair. "The department secretary has the exams. All you will have to do is hand them out. If you could bring the finished tests to the Red Inkers meeting tonight, I'd appreciate it. If not, I can pick them up tomorrow."

"Are we still having the Red Inkers meeting?" he asked uncertainly.

"I think we should," I said. "It will give us all a chance to talk about what happened." I essentially repeated what I had just told Sadie a little while ago outside the shop.

"You're sure you will be up to it if you're not feeling well?"

"I'll be fine in a few hours," I reassured him.

"Well, if you insist, I will let the others know."

I thanked him and said good-bye as I headed to the shower.

I stood in the shower until the water ran cold, which wasn't long at all for a house of Charming Books' age. Back in my bedroom, I dressed quickly, and I was in the middle of drying my long, wavy hair, which was a time-consuming process when I was completely healthy. With an injured shoulder, it took twice as long. I was almost done, or as done as I was going to be under the circumstances, when Emerson batted my right hand with his pristine white paw.

I turned off the hair dryer. "What's wrong?" I asked the tuxedo cat.

With the hair dryer off, I could hear the ringing of my cell phone on my dresser. I leaped up to answer it and groaned with the effort. I snatched up the phone just before it went to voice mail.

"Violet, thank goodness you answered," Lacey said breathlessly on the other end of the line. "He's here at the Food and Wine Festival."

"Who?"

"Coleridge! Anastasia's brother. If you want to talk to him, you had better get your behind down here to the festival quick. I heard him just tell someone he planned to leave the village as soon as he finished eating his lunch."

"On my way," I said, and ended the call without saying good-bye.

THIRTY-SIX

Grandma Daisy wasn't thrilled when I said I planned to go back out again after just returning from my battle with the trellis. However, I didn't give her a chance to argue, because I was out the door before she finished her first complaint about it.

Emerson followed me out the door. I pointed at the lawn. "Stay here."

He meowed. Whether it was in agreement or protest, I couldn't be sure.

Officer Clipton still hadn't brought my bike from Puffin Lane B&B to Charming Books, so I was forced to walk to the festival. It was probably for the best. I didn't know if I could get a firm grip on the bicycle's handlebars with my shoulder hurting so badly.

Emerson sat in the middle of Charming Books' lawn just like I had told him to do. Was I hallucinating or was the cat starting to listen to me? I hurried down the street toward the Riverwalk. The closer I came to the festival, the more crowded with pedestrians the street became. As I wove through the crush of jovial people who had already partaken of the many wines that the local wineries had to offer the tourists, I kept my eye out for Fenimore the troubadour. I didn't want to run into him again. Rainwater claimed the musician didn't have anything to do with Anastasia's murder, and that might be true. However, he had mentioned my mother, and I was going to avoid having a conversation about her with a stranger at any cost.

I turned my thoughts away from Fenimore and back to the murder itself. I had three remaining suspects: the journalist, Daven York; the agent, Edmund Eaton; and the brother and Harry Potter doppelgänger, Coleridge Faber.

The shop's essence had directed me to read "The Purloined Letter," and if I was right in my interpretation, then the books were trying to tell me the killer was the most obvious suspect. Coleridge had to be the killer. It was the scenario that made the most sense if the books were right, and I had no reason to doubt them.

Lacey was in La Crepe Jolie's tent and waved at me wildly from across the green. If she didn't want to draw attention to my arrival, she was failing miserably. "Violet, over here!" she called.

I waved back to acknowledge I'd seen her. I hoped it would put a stop to her crazed-pageant-queen-on-a-float wave, but it didn't.

"Violet!" she called again.

Some of the festivalgoers turned to stare at me.

I ducked my head and hurried over to her tent.

Adrien was at the crepe station again, whipping up delicious crepes. My stomach rumbled, and I wondered when I had last eaten. However, this wasn't the time to think about food.

Lacey slid out from behind the booth. "You got here fast." She gave me a tight hug.

"Eee," I cried.

She stepped back. "Are you all right?"

I rubbed my shoulder. "I'm fine. I fell this morning."

"Yes!" she said. "I heard you jumped from the second-floor terrace of Puffin Lane B&B."

"I didn't jump," I said, and left it at that. If I spoke any more about the morning's events with Lacey, we would be there all day. "Where's Coleridge?"

She pointed in the direction of the big dining tent. "He's in there."

I followed her line of sight and found Coleridge in the far corner of the tent, sitting alone. Half a dozen plates of food surrounded him. "He must have a big appetite," I said.

"I heard him say he would leave after he was done eating. I didn't know how long it would take you to get here, so I went from booth to booth gathering up samples of the food and wine from the other vendors and gave it to him. I told him it was a gift from the village in memory of Anastasia, who was such a prominent member."

"I'm impressed."

She grinned. "I learned all my tricks from you and Colleen in high school. You two could convince just about anyone to do what you wanted. Remember when you

talked Coach Bryant into canceling gym class because
he needed to take time to relax and strategize before the
big football game that night?"

I laughed at the memory. Colleen had really been the
one that sweet-talked the coach out of teaching class, not
that it had been much of a challenge really. It was the first
time that I recalled a memory that involved Colleen without the black cloud of loss that I had associated with her
since the day she died.

"Does he look like Harry Potter to you?" she asked.
"I think the resemblance is uncanny, but then again if he
wore a red-and-white-striped shirt, he could just as easily
look like Where's Waldo. It's the glasses, I think."

She had a point.

She grabbed a small plate of madeleines from her
table. "Here, take these. You can use it as a cover."

I took the plate from her hand and thanked her.

I smiled at people eating in the big tent as I carried the
plate of cookies to the back where Coleridge sat. Now
that I stood right next to his table, I could see there was
even more food piled across the table than I had been able
to see from La Crepe Jolie's booth. Clearly, Lacey had
taken her job seriously in keeping Coleridge at the festival
until I showed up.

Coleridge peered at me with red eyes over his Harry
Potter glasses. "I really don't need any more food. I have
more than enough as you can see."

"Everyone in the village feels terrible about what happened to your sister." I set the plate of cookies in the one
empty spot on the edge of the table. "We just want to
show you how much we care."

He snorted. "That's a load of crap. I know very well that everyone in Cascade Springs couldn't stand my sister. I can't blame them. She was a pretentious snob, and I couldn't stand her either." He spoke with so much venom that I took a step back. Perhaps I was right in thinking that Coleridge was the killer. He certainly had strong feelings where his sister was concerned.

"Do I know you?" He studied my face. He wagged his finger at me. "You're the owner of the bookstore. I'm going to sue you for everything that you have."

I froze. I had forgotten about his threat of a lawsuit. It was a very real threat, I was afraid. Anastasia did die from falling down the back stairs of Charming Books. She might have been made unsteady from the liquid nicotine soaked into her dress, but it was the fall that actually killed her.

"Or I would." He swayed in his seat. "If I had any money to do it, which I don't." He swallowed what was left in the wineglass in his hand. "Do you know my sister didn't leave me a blasted thing? She had all that money and every last penny is going to charity?" He set the empty glass back on the table and reached for another full one.

I sat across from him at the table, shifting some of the plates aside so that I could rest my hands on the edge of the table.

He took a big gulp from the glass in his hand.

I wondered how many glasses of wine Lacey had given him to keep him from leaving. The only saving grace was it was unlikely he had gotten to the festival by car, so he wouldn't be driving.

"Do you know when I heard that my sister died and

was rich, I thought that I would quit my job? I sent my boss a scathing e-mail and told him just what I thought of him, the scum. There is no going back to that office." He took a swig from his wineglass.

"Maybe you should eat something," I said, noting that although Coleridge was surrounded by empty wineglasses, most of his plates were still filled with food. "You need to soak up the alcohol."

"I don't need to do anything. Except to get out of this horrid little village and salvage what is left of my life."

"When did you find out that Anastasia didn't leave you any money?"

"This morning. I met with her lawyer. Pompous jerk. I think he almost enjoyed telling me the news that I had been written out of her will."

"And did you know your sister was Evanna Blue?" It was a question that I knew he'd been asked many times over the last few days, but I still needed to ask it.

"No, I had no idea. It's just like my sister to keep a secret like that." He sipped from his glass again.

"If you had known and thought you would stand to inherit her money, it would be a very convincing motive for murder."

He slammed his glass on the table, and I was relieved it was plastic. If it had been anything else, it would have shattered. "If you think that I killed my sister, you're wrong. I was working ten- and thirteen-hour days for my troll of a boss back in Newark. If you don't believe me, ask the police chief. He confirmed it with my boss, and I have even more proof." He reached into the inside pocket of his jacket and removed a piece of folded paper. He set the plane ticket on the edge of the table. "Read it. Don't be shy now."

I reached across the food and picked it up. The date on the ticket stub was the day that Anastasia died, which coincided with his story. If he was in Newark until after her death, then there was no way that he could have poisoned her dress. I set the plane ticket back on the table. Whether he was on the plane would be easy to verify, and I knew that Rainwater already had by this point.

He picked up the ticket and tucked it back into his coat pocket.

"What can you tell me about her literary agent, Edmund Eaton?"

"Nothing," Coleridge said. "I just met him this morning. He was at the meeting with the lawyer too. The lawyer said he had to be there in order to know how to handle Anastasia's contracts and royalties with her publishers. He didn't seem too happy about Anastasia's will either."

"What charity did she leave her money to?"

"What charity didn't she leave money to? She left money to children's charities, the poor, the elderly, libraries, animal rescues, and environmental groups. You'd think she would be willing to leave a million or so to her only living relative," he said bitterly.

Knowing what Anastasia had done with her wealth made me like her a little bit more. Perhaps she'd had a soft heart underneath her tough exterior and superior demeanor. If she had, it was a secret that she'd kept well hidden, and if anything, Anastasia Faber could keep one whopper of a secret.

Coleridge struggled to his feet and held on to the table to steady himself.

"You're not driving, are you?" I asked just to be sure.

"No." He blinked at me from behind his round glasses. "I don't even have a car in this village."

"Good," I said, relieved. "I suggest you go back to wherever you are staying and take a nap."

He nodded dumbly. "A nap sounds good."

I stood. "Do you need help getting there?"

"No," he said. "My B&B is just up River Road a bit. I need the walk. It will help me think."

I took a step back. "Okay."

I watched Coleridge stumble away, bouncing off people in the crowd as he went, and with him left my hopes of solving Anastasia Faber's murder.

THIRTY-SEVEN

Before I left the dining tent, I cleared Coleridge's table. The local teenagers who were in charge of keeping the festival pristine were running in all directions. They certainly didn't have the time to take care of that many plates of food and empty wineglasses. I kept the small plate of madeleines for myself and ate them as I walked back to La Crepe Jolie's booth.

"How did it go?" Lacey wanted to know, as breathless as ever. The lunch crowd was beginning to finally taper off, and Adrien was making some fresh crepe batter before the next onslaught of tourists.

"He's not the killer," I said, unable to hide the disappointment from my voice.

She smiled. "Cheer up, Violet. Eliminating a suspect moves you one step closer to who actually did it."

If only that were true, and I wished I had Lacey's optimistic outlook on life. I hadn't appreciated it as a teenager, and I was embarrassed to remember that Colleen and I would sometimes snicker behind Lacey's back about her over-the-top happiness. What a waste that was. A little over a decade later, Lacey had a thriving business and a gorgeous husband who adored her. It seemed happiness wasn't so bad after all.

Despite the dull ache in my shoulder, I gave her a hug. "Thank you for that. I needed to hear it."

Lacey beamed from ear to ear. "Anytime," she said, and I knew that was true. Whenever I needed picking up from a dark mood, Lacey would be there, and I needed a friend like that in my life. It made me want to be a better friend to her. And I would be, I vowed if only to myself.

"I should be getting back to Charming Books, or Grandma Daisy is bound to send out a search party for me."

She laughed. "Not before Adrien and I feed you. He would never recover from it if you left La Crepe Jolie's booth hungry."

"I am a little hungry," I admitted. More than a little actually, I thought.

"I know," she said. "I can hear your tummy rumbling."

Twenty minutes later, I polished off what was left of my mushroom and ham crepe, and thanked Lacey and Adrien for another excellent lunch. As usual, they refused to let me pay for the meal.

Adrien shook his head. "We can't accept your money. We owe you for telling us Danielle Cloud was looking for work. She will be such a welcome addition to La Crepe Jolie. We're so excited for her to start working for us tomorrow."

Lacey nodded agreement and beamed up at her husband. He smiled down at her with such tenderness that I thought what they had was a happiness I could live with if I ever found it for myself.

Finally, I said good-bye and left the Duponts in their booth. In my left hand, I carried a care package of food to take back to Grandma Daisy. It weighed as much as the *Compact Oxford English Dictionary* and I knew it contained all my grandmother's favorite treats from the French café.

I turned the corner on River Road where it veered away from the river and into the shopping district of the village. The blue Victorian that was Charming Books and my home stood on the corner just as it had for the last two hundred years. Afternoon sunlight sparkled off its windows. As I stared at the house, it wasn't too much of a stretch to believe that magic could be found there.

"I've always thought this was a beautiful house," a voice said.

I jumped, nearly dropping my grandmother's bag of goodies. I spun around to find Fenimore standing behind me.

His harmonica wasn't around his neck, but he had his guitar slung over his right shoulder. "When your mother told me this was where she lived, I could hardly believe it. It's like a place out of a fairy tale."

I headed toward the gate. "I need to get back to work."

"Violet, wait." His voice held so much pain in it that I turned to face him again even though every thought in my head was screaming for me to run away from this man.

He held his hand out to me. "Can I have just two minutes of your time? I will tell you what I need to say, and then I'll be out of your life forever if that's what you want. I'm heading to my next village later today. This will be the last time I have a chance to talk to you for a very long time."

"You want to talk to me about my mother?" I set the bag of food beside me on the sidewalk and folded my arms. It wasn't until I made the movement that I remembered my injured shoulder. I dropped my arms to my sides.

He nodded. "Yes."

"Fine. Go ahead. If you know so much about my mother, then just say it," I snapped.

"I know so much about your mother, Violet, because I'm your dad."

The air drained from my lungs in a whoosh, and I had to grasp onto the fence surrounding Charming Books' front yard to remain upright. "What did you say?"

"I'm your dad." He said it almost apologetically.

"I have to go." I threw open the gate, completely forgetting my grandmother's food. I had to get away from this liar. How dare he say something like this to me?

"Wait." He held out his hand.

I froze.

"Will you let me explain?"

Explain what? I wondered. What a terrible prank this all

was? I had no idea who my father was. My mother refused to tell me, and the father line on my birth certificate was even left blank. When I reached middle school and an age when I really was beginning to become curious and wanted to know who my father was, Mom had been diagnosed with cancer. She was so sick those last two years of her life, I never pressed her to find out the truth, but that didn't mean the scruffy troubadour standing in front of me was my father. It didn't.

When I didn't say anything, he went on to say, "I didn't know I had a daughter until you were almost grown. Fern wrote me a letter before she died and sent it to the last known address she had for me. Since I move around so much, I didn't receive the letter until months after she had passed."

"Why are you just coming forward now?" I asked.

"Because I couldn't deal with the idea of having a daughter, at least not at that point in my life. I wasn't in a stable place." He forced a laugh. "I suppose you could say I'm not stable now, but I'm better off. I even have a house over in Niagara Falls. It's the first roots that I have ever put down."

He had a house in Niagara Falls, just twenty minutes from where we stood now, and he'd never once come to Charming Books to find me.

"And," he went on, "I didn't want to barge in on you in your grief. I knew you were just a kid then. I thought me getting involved in your life at that point would just be a disruption."

"Why didn't she tell me?" I asked, still not able to absorb what he was saying. "And how do I know that you aren't lying?"

He removed a crumpled yellow envelope from his flannel coat pocket and held it out to me. "This is the letter from Fern."

Even from a distance, I recognized my mother's distinctive swooping handwriting.

He shook the letter at me. "Here, take it. It has the proof you need."

I didn't move to take the envelope from his hand. I didn't want it. I didn't want any of this. "Why are you here now? Why not go about your life as you always have, pretending that you don't have a child?" I could hear the tears in my voice. I didn't fight them. I didn't care.

"I've come back to the Food and Wine Festival every year for the last ten years, hoping to catch a glimpse of you. This was the first time that you were here. You looked so much like Fern—you acted so much like Fern—well, recognizing her in you gave me the courage I needed to tell you. I hadn't planned to. I just wanted to see you, but when I did, I couldn't run away again without you knowing the truth."

"Does my grandmother know any of this?" I asked.

He shook his head. "No. In the letter, Fern said that she never told anyone about me." He took a step toward me. "You look so much like her."

I backed away. "How dare you even say that? You don't know that!" I was shouting now, and the tourists closest to the corner stared in my direction. I lowered my voice. "You have a one-night stand with my mother and now you want to be part of my life."

He shook his head sadly. "It wasn't like that. I loved her. We were together an entire summer. I was here working a summer job, and we met at one of the village fairs they have in the summer. She was the one who broke it off. She broke my heart, and I fled Cascade Springs, which is why I knew nothing about you."

"Why would she do that?" I couldn't believe my mother would do such a thing.

"She said that it was her destiny to be alone, and if we stayed together, both of us were bound to become more hurt than we already were."

The Caretaker role. By the time my mother would have met Fenimore, she would have already known she was to be the shop's next Caretaker. She would have known from our family history that all the Waverly women ended up alone one way or another to take on their duties. I refused to believe that it had to be that way.

"If you loved her, why didn't you argue with her? Why didn't you insist on staying?"

"It wasn't my way," he said sadly. "I'm a nomad, Violet. My life is on the road. It always has been, and it always will be. Even though I own a little house in Niagara Falls, I'm hardly ever there."

"Is Fenimore your first or last name?" I had to know.

"It's my first name."

"So what's the rest of your name?"

"Fenimore James," he said.

Fenimore James was my father. It was still too much to believe.

He adjusted his guitar on his shoulder. "I've told you what I needed to say." He held out the letter to me. "I'd like you to have this. I have carried it with me for too long. It belongs to you now."

I still made no move to take the letter.

He set the yellowed envelope on the fence post. "I will leave this with you. You will know what to do with it when you're ready." He nodded, and just like he walked away from my mother thirty years ago, he walked away from me.

THIRTY-EIGHT

❧

"Violet, you don't look well," Grandma Daisy said. "Are you all right? Are you in pain from the fall?"

It wasn't from the fall. After Fenimore's bombshell, the fall was nothing.

"I'm fine," I said. "Maybe a little tired." I plastered a smile on my face. "I see the shop is filling with customers. I think we should get to the business of selling books, don't you?"

She gave me a curious look. Her silver bob covered half her face as she tilted her head. Finally, she nodded. "All right."

For the rest of the afternoon and into the early evening, Grandma Daisy and I focused on our job as booksellers. During that time, I pushed thoughts of fathers and murder to the very back of my mind. Not that the shop was happy with my need of avoidance at the moment. Every book that I touched became a volume of Poe's works.

"I'm not in the mood," I whispered to the essence, to the tree, to the shop itself. The last thing in the world I wanted to think about at the moment was Anastasia's murder. All I wanted to do was concentrate on my job as a bookseller. The shop's essence seemed to get the message after I refused to look at the works of Poe that it presented, because after a while it stopped directing me to certain books. Part of me worried whether I had scared it off altogether, but a larger part of me was too overwhelmed by what Fenimore had to say to me outside the shop to care.

Grandma Daisy and I were closing up for the night when Sadie came into the shop. She carried a tray of cupcakes decorated in Halloween colors and looked happier than I had seen her since before Anastasia died.

"Hi, Sadie." I waved at her from behind the sales counter, where I was counting out the cash drawer for the night. "Can we do something for you?"

Her face fell. "Aren't we having a Red Inkers meeting tonight?"

I smacked myself on the forehead. "I'm sorry. I completely forgot. I don't even have the chairs set up yet."

"If it's not a good time, we can meet in Midcentury Vintage." Her eyebrows pinched together.

"Don't be silly," I said. "It's a fine time. We were just so busy today that it slipped my mind. Of course the Red Inkers meeting can go on as planned."

Her face broke into the bright smile that I had missed so much over the last few days.

I started to move around the counter. "Just let me grab the folding chairs from the storage room."

She set the cupcakes on an end table and waved me away. "You keep doing what you're doing, and I will set everything up. Just because we meet in Charming Books doesn't mean that you have to do all the work."

I smiled my thanks. As I closed the cash drawer, Grandma Daisy put on her coat. "It's been quite a day. I think we sold more books today than all last month." She grinned.

"Quite a week," I said.

She nodded. "I'll give you that. Well, I'm off. I'm looking forward to putting my feet up and curling up with a novel of my own."

"That sounds nice," I admitted. "I'll be doing the same just as soon as the Red Inkers meeting is over."

She searched my face. "Are you all right, my dear?"

"Don't I look all right?" I smiled.

"No." She pressed her lips together as if in thought. "You look stricken."

That was a perfect word for how I felt. I was stricken, but I wasn't going to tell my grandmother that. Fenimore's announcement would be just as much a bombshell to her as it had been to me. I had to come to terms with it myself before I told anyone, even my grandma Daisy, whom I loved more than anyone else on this earth.

I laughed it off. "It's just the strain from the week, I'm sure. It's not often that someone dies in our shop, is it?"

"Thank heavens for that." She shook her head, sending her silver locks swaying back and forth around her cat's-eye glasses. "If you say so."

She left not long after that.

I finished closing up the shop and helped Sadie set up the chairs for the meeting. "Sadie." I unfolded one of the chairs. "Have you thought about who might have gone into your apartment and taken your liquid nicotine?"

She frowned as she unfolded a chair of her own. "I don't know who could have done it. My apartment is so small. It's just a studio. I hardly ever have anyone over other than Grant."

I opened my mouth.

"And before you say anything, Grant didn't take it. He didn't know about me smoking e-cigarettes—I made sure of that. Besides, he would have no reason to kill Anastasia."

I frowned. I guessed she had a point no matter how much I didn't want to admit it. "So Grant was the only one in your apartment?"

"I didn't say that. Sometimes, I have fittings there when people can't make it to the shop."

I straightened the folding chair in front of me. "Who comes to these fittings?"

"Regular clients. They don't happen often. The shop is much more comfortable to have a fitting in, but Trudy was there about three weeks ago when I was fitting her for her dress for the Poe-try reading."

"Trudy?" I asked.

She nodded.

"So Trudy knew about all the costumes before you unveiled them the night before the reading?"

"Maybe not all of them, but I was working on the three dresses—yours, Trudy's, and Anastasia's—at my apartment at night after work. You know, while I watched TV."

"I thought you said Anastasia's dress never left your shop before you gave it to her."

"I might have fibbed to David about that. I just didn't

want to give him more reason to search my apartment. I already felt exposed when he and his officers searched my shop."

There was a knock on the front door.

"I'll get it." Sadie ran to the door.

There was so much more that I wanted to ask her, but before I could, Sadie threw the door wide open for Richard and Trudy to enter.

Rainwater was going to have to miss the meeting because of his police chief duties. Honestly, I was relieved he wasn't going to be there. I didn't know what he thought about my boldness of kissing him on the cheek the last time I saw him. I didn't even know what I thought about it, and I wasn't in the mood for any more emotional turmoil that day. I had already been given more than my share.

My mind was buzzing over my conversation with Sadie. I had to be wrong.

The four of us sat on folding chairs in a circle under the birch tree. As if by a force of habit, Sadie had set up six chairs for the meeting. Two stood empty as a constant reminder as to what had happened. One was for Chief Rainwater, and one was for Anastasia. Only one of those seats would ever be filled again.

Richard cleared his throat, pulling me from my thoughts. "Violet, I brought those exams from your American Literature class. I put them on the sales counter for you when I came in."

"Thanks, Richard." I smiled gratefully, hoping that I was acting normally. "I'll be back on campus tomorrow to teach all my classes. I really appreciate you covering for me today."

Sadie passed around the tray of cupcakes. "I thought we all needed a little treat after the week we've had," she said.

She was right. I was tempted to take two, but I restrained myself and selected the largest cupcake from the tray.

Richard cleared his throat. "We're a little off schedule because of recent events. Did anyone bring a writing sample to read to the group?"

"Are we not even going to mention Anastasia's death?" Sadie asked, returning to her seat and taking a cupcake for herself. "Should we have a moment of silence or something to remember her by?"

"Why?" Trudy snapped. "Is she worth remembering?"

The three of us stared at Trudy, and my heart began to beat faster. Maybe I wasn't wrong.

Trudy licked icing off her index finger. "She got what was coming to her."

Richard stopped his cupcake halfway to his mouth. "Trudy, how can you say such a thing?"

She glared at him over her own cupcake. "How can you not? You know how she has treated all of us over the years. She ridiculed our choices to write fiction for fun and enjoyment, and all this time she was doing it herself and making money hand over fist at it. Doesn't that steam you?"

Richard pulled at the cuffs of his oxford shirt, looking uncomfortable. "I'm sure we were all surprised when we heard the news, but I wouldn't say I'm angry at Anastasia. I suppose I am more hurt that she didn't trust us with her secret. We're a close-knit group here, and I thought we shared all of our literary endeavors and accomplishments with each other."

Trudy wiped her mouth with a napkin. "The moment I found out she was Evanna Blue, I knew she was a hypocrite, and it just wasn't something I was going to stand for. I told her so too." She took a big bite of her cupcake as if to seal her point.

The room grew very silent at her announcement. She told Anastasia she was a hypocrite. That meant she knew Anastasia was Evanna Blue before she died. I wasn't wrong. I wasn't wrong at all.

Sadie spoke first. "You knew she was Evanna Blue before the murder? I wasn't the only one who knew?"

Trudy's face turned a dark shade of red as if she just realized her grave mistake.

"Hidden in plain sight," I whispered. That's what the shop's essence was trying to tell me. It didn't want me to peg Coleridge as the killer because he was the most obvious choice and served to gain the most from Anastasia's death. The essence wanted me to suspect Trudy, because she was the murderer hiding in plain sight right in front of me all this time.

My heart dropped to the soles of my shoes. Trudy? Could it really be Trudy who killed Anastasia? No, that wasn't possible. Trudy was Mrs. Conner, my first-grade teacher. First-grade teachers don't kill people, they just don't. Even with that in mind, I had to know. I had to know for certain.

"What did you say, Violet?" Richard asked me.

I swallowed. "Nothing. I was just talking to myself."

"I would be curious to hear what you said too," Trudy commented with an edge to her voice.

I felt rooted in the folding chair. "It was nothing."

Trudy slowly set her plate, with what remained of her cupcake on it, on the table beside her folding chair. She moved her expansive pocketbook to her lap and removed a gun from its depths. Cocking the small gun, she pointed it directly at me. "This is a derringer. It was my great-grandmother's. I inherited it from my father, but I can assure you that it works just fine." She adjusted her grip on the handle. "Now, what did you say, Violet?"

My mouth grew dry. The words, they wouldn't come.

"Trudy!" Richard cried. "What on earth are you doing?"

She didn't even glance in his direction and kept the gun trained on me. "Stay out of this, Richard." With her eyes boring into me, she said, "I asked you a question."

My voice returned. "I said the answer was in plain sight. You, you are the killer, and you were in plain sight of me this entire time."

"How long have you known?" Trudy asked.

"Trudy?" Sadie asked as it dawned on her what was really happening.

I glanced at Sadie and Richard, willing them to run to call for help, but neither of them moved. If I moved, I would surely be shot, and they might be as well. "I only just figured it out," I said.

"You killed her?" Richard was aghast. "Why?"

Trudy's gaze flicked in his direction just for a moment. "I didn't mean to kill her. She was supposed to make a fool of herself at the Poe-try Reading. I never thought she would die. I only wanted to teach her a lesson. The nicotine was meant to disorient her, that was all. I wanted her to be humiliated over it. Afterward, I would tell her that I was the one who caused her humiliation. I knew then she would take me more seriously."

"By poisoning her with liquid nicotine?" I asked. "How does that teach anyone anything? Why would she take you more seriously because of it?"

Trudy glared back at me. "It would teach her to keep her word! When I found out she was Evanna, I told her I would keep her secret if she'd help me. She said that she would, but she lied."

"How did you find out her secret?" Sadie's voice trembled.

"I dropped in on her one day with some soup. This was over a year ago when she'd had the flu. I thought I was doing the neighborly thing by taking care of her. I knocked on her door and there was no answer. It was unlocked, so I went inside. I found her asleep at her desk in her secret office. Trust me when I say that she was furious with me when I found out."

"You've known for a year?" Sadie asked. "You've kept her secret all this time? Why would you keep her secret if you hated her so much?"

While Sadie asked her questions, I glanced around the shop, looking for some means of escape. I tried to catch Richard's eye to signal to him to run for help, but he was too busy gaping at Trudy.

"I needed her. I wanted to get published so desperately,

you see, and I was running out of time. I asked her to talk to her agent about me and make him help me get published. I know my work is just as good as Evanna Blue's, if not better." She took a breath. "She claimed she talked to him and he said he wasn't interested in my work. I knew she was lying. I have twice the talent she did."

"But, Trudy, you would have been published eventually. All the Red Inkers have always said that—well, maybe not Anastasia, but the rest of us have," Richard said.

"I don't have time for eventually. Don't you understand that I'm dying?" She coughed as if to emphasize her point. "I have lung cancer, you see, from years of smoking, smoking to cope with the death of my dream. Anastasia's agent was my last hope!"

"But why did you frame me?" Sadie asked in a small, childlike voice. "I'm your friend."

"I told you already that I didn't intend for her to die. I only wanted to embarrass her. I was searching for a way to do it when I went to your apartment for the fitting. When I saw the liquid nicotine hidden in your linen closet—"

"You went through my linen closet?" Sadie gasped.

I glanced at Sadie. Now was not the time to take up the invasion of privacy with Trudy, especially when Trudy was holding a gun pointed at me. I swallowed. "What happened when you found the nicotine?"

"I saw my chance. I, of all people, know how poisonous nicotine can be and I knew that liquid nicotine could cause confusion if a large amount is absorbed through the skin. I saw the nicotine, and I remembered her dress. I knew what I had to do. It seemed poetic in a way that Anastasia's humiliation would come from the same substance that was killing me."

"But the dress wasn't wet when you left my apartment that night," Sadie said.

"Of course not," Trudy snapped at Sadie.

I appreciated that Sadie had her spunk back after the tragic events of the week, but I prayed that she didn't push Trudy too far with her questioning while the gun remained in Trudy's hand.

"I waited until later that week when I knew the dress was in your shop. I waited until the shop closed, broke in, and poured the liquid on the dress. I even used a hair dryer to dry out the dress before I left. It wasn't that hard to do." Trudy said all this as if she were rattling off the steps to make a perfect cake, not how to poison someone.

Sadie, Richard, and I all stared at her.

"You don't understand. I can tell from your faces that you don't. Is it better to die with a dream unfulfilled than try one last time to make that life's dream come true? I spent my life trapped in a classroom giving my all to children. I was good at it. The children loved me—you loved me." She stared at me.

I had loved her. She had been my favorite teacher. A lump caught in my throat.

"But teaching wasn't my passion." She was shouting now. "It wasn't the dream that I wanted. I wanted to write. When I retired, I promised myself I would finally write and publish a novel. It was finally my time to live my own dreams."

"You still can," I said, thinking a lot of people write in prison, where she was surely destined to go.

"There's no time left now." She coughed again. "The doctors have told me I have six months at best and that was a month ago. I suppose I could say that I have five months now. Five months to reach my dream of being a published author. It will never happen now." Tears ran down her wrinkled face.

I looked her in the eye. "So what are you going to do with the time you have left? Kill all of us? How is that reaching your dreams?"

She licked her lips. "Do you want to see me spend the last few months of my life in a prison cell? Is that what you want to become of your old teacher?"

"No," I said. "But I don't want to die either."

A great caw rang out in the shop, and Faulkner swooped down from the birch tree and onto Trudy's head. He dug his talons into her pin curls.

The retired teacher screamed out in pain. "Get it off me." She waved the gun around wildly.

While Faulkner did a number on her hair, Emerson went after her right ankle, biting down hard.

Richard, Sadie, and I hit the floor to escape the line of fire. I covered my head, and the gun went off. I lifted my head and saw the bullet had missed everyone in the room. I pushed myself up onto my hands and knees and gasped. The bullet had hit the birch tree and embedded into the trunk. My heart stopped. The tree. The tree had been shot. I had no time to absorb this realization because Trudy shot again, driving a bullet into the stone fireplace just over my head.

I crawled behind one of the couches. Richard ducked behind the sales counter, and Sadie didn't move. I felt like I might throw up. Had she been shot? I didn't know it for sure.

Sadie finally struggled to her feet and ran behind the sales counter with Richard. I gave a sigh of relief.

Somehow while I was distracted with Sadie, Trudy escaped the clutches of the crow and the cat. Her hair sprang wildly out of her head in all directions.

Faulkner was flapping his wings, obviously perturbed, but otherwise okay. Emerson was crouched low beneath an end table. I prayed he was fine too.

I started to get up, but before I could, Trudy stood above me with the gun trained on my chest.

"I'm sorry that I have to do this, Violet—you always were one of my favorite students—but I can't go to jail. I can't." She aimed the gun at me, and I squeezed my eyes shut, waiting for the bang.

There was a great crash. I opened my eyes just in time to see a full bookcase topple over and land on Trudy. She screamed. There was no one even near it when it fell. Sadie and Richard were on the opposite side of the room. The shop itself was defending me. Trudy cried out in pain as the heavy bookcase pinned her on the floor.

I scrambled to my feet and kicked the gun out of her hand. It slid across the room and under one of the couches.

I crouched by Trudy, wondering how many of her bones were broken. Her right hand stuck out from under the bookcase.

Despite everything, I reached for it and held it delicately in my own. "It's going to be okay, Trudy. It's going to be okay." I wondered how many times when I was a child she had comforted me in the same tone of voice.

I heard the sirens blaring up River Road. Rainwater was coming. I gave Trudy's hand another reassuring squeeze.

EPILOGUE

A week later on Halloween night, I came through the back door of Charming Books, taking a moment to stare at the staircase, which was no longer surrounded by crime scene tape. Trudy was out on bail, awaiting trial. The last I heard, she had a good chance at an insanity plea, claiming that she had been driven crazy by her jealousy of Anastasia and her own devastating diagnosis. I hoped that she wouldn't go to prison. I knew what she did was wrong, but despite everything, I didn't want my first-grade teacher to spend her last days on earth in a prison cell.

"Violet? Is that you?" I heard my grandmother call me from the other side of the kitchen door. "Hurry up and water the tree if you want to do it before the trick-or-treaters arrive."

"On my way!" I called back.

Emerson waited for me on the other side of the swinging door that led from the kitchen into the shop. I hurried over to the birch tree with my watering can.

Grandma Daisy clicked her tongue. "It's not doing well. I've never seen it like this in all my days."

Some Caretaker I was. The birch tree was dying and on my watch too.

As part of gathering evidence over what had happened at the last Red Inkers meeting, Rainwater had dug Trudy's stray bullet out of the tree's trunk with a pocketknife. Since then, the tree had not been doing well. Every morning, I came downstairs to find leaves on the floor, and those still clinging to the branches were turning brown. I knew I had to do something.

"I hope this works," I muttered to my grandmother.

"There's only one way to find out," she replied.

I took a deep breath, lifted the watering can, and poured the springwater into the bullet hole. It was the only thing I could think to do to save the tree. The water bubbled and fumed like a potion boiling in a medieval cauldron. It did that for a full minute, and then the bubble evaporated. The trunk was smooth in the spot as if nothing had ever happened. The tree was whole again. I bent my head back and stared in amazement as the leaves turned from a sickly brown to a vibrant green right before my eyes.

Faulkner, who had avoided the tree ever since the shooting, swooped from his perch at the front window and flew into the tree. He settled on his favorite branch near the top and began to clean his feathers.

Tentatively, I touched the spot where the bullet hole

had been. It was cool to the touch and felt no different from any other place on the tree's trunk. "Wow," I whispered.

"I second that," my grandmother whispered. "Things are mended."

I poured what water was left into the dirt around the tree, shaking the final few droplets from the can. "Some things are mended," I murmured, thinking of the letter from my mother to Fenimore hidden away in my sock drawer upstairs in my apartment. I'd yet to read it, and I hadn't breathed a word of it to my grandmother.

"Are you thinking of Nathan and David?" she asked.

I hadn't been, but now that she mentioned it, that was another thing that needed to be mended—if not mended, then decided. Nathan hadn't spoken to me since he saw me kiss Rainwater on the cheek outside Charming Books. After I'd avoided him for so many months, now he was avoiding me and I was surprised to find that I missed him.

Grandma Daisy touched my cheek. "I don't know which one you will choose, Violet, my dear. I just want you to be happy. Your heart will guide you to the right decision. Both of them are worthy of you."

She said this as if it were only up to me. I suspected Nathan and Rainwater had to have a say in any decision, if there was even one to make now that Nathan was avoiding me. Thinking of my mother and the choice she'd made to push the man she loved away because she knew that she was the next Caretaker, I said, "Is there even a point? Don't all the Waverly women end up alone?"

A pained expression crossed my grandmother's face, but before she could argue, the doorbell rang.

I set the watering can on the closest table. "Those must be the trick-or-treaters." I grabbed the bowl of candy from the sales counter and sprang for the door, so grateful for the distraction.

I threw open the door to find Minnie Mouse, Little Bo Peep, and Captain America on my doorstep. The children held out their pillowcases to me. "Trick or treat!" they cried in unison.

After that, the trick-or-treaters came in droves, and there was no time for Grandma Daisy to resume our conversation about Nathan and Rainwater.

I was just dropping a Snickers bar into Frankenstein's bag when I saw a tall man and a pint-sized knight come up Charming Books' steps. Chief David Rainwater grinned at me, and my stomach flipped inside my body.

In front of him stood a glorious knight. Rainwater hadn't been kidding when he said that his niece, Aster, planned to trick-or-treat as Joan of Arc. Aster had the complete ensemble from the helmet to the shield and the thankfully plastic sword to the chain mail.

I dropped a piece of candy into her bag. "Where's your mom?" I asked.

"Mom had to work," Aster said. "She really likes it."

I smiled. "I'm so glad."

"I'm glad too," Rainwater said. I could feel him watching me.

Grandma Daisy pushed me aside. "Come in out of the cold for a moment," she insisted. "Aster, I was saving a stash of king-sized bars just for you. They're in the kitchen. Let's go check them out."

Joan of Arc pumped her tiny fist. "Yes!"

Grandma Daisy and Aster hurried back to the kitchen, leaving the police chief and me standing alone.

"I see Danielle found the chain mail," I said.

"Just in the nick of time too." He chuckled. Rainwater wandered over to the tree and stared at it. "Where's the bullet hole?"

"Ummm . . ." I couldn't think of anything to say. I had been so focused on saving the tree, I hadn't thought about covering up the evidence of the tree's miraculous healing. Now I realized my mistake.

The police chief ran his hand up and down the tree's trunk. "Where did it go? This isn't possible."

I shrugged. "I guess the tree healed itself."

He studied me. "I'm beginning to wonder if there is a lot more to this than a self-healing tree."

I swallowed and was saved by the return of Grandma Daisy and Aster. Aster tugged on her uncle's arm. "Uncle David, come on. I need more candy."

He laughed. "All right."

The little girl spun around, and her chain mail clinked together. "Violet, you should come with us. It will be so much fun!"

"You should," Rainwater agreed with a smile.

I hesitated. "I should stay here and help Grandma Daisy pass out the candy."

"You don't think I can do it myself?" my grandmother scoffed.

"I wasn't saying that," I protested.

"Go on, Violet," my grandmother urged, her eyes sparkling. "Emerson and I will do a fine job of passing out what's left of the Halloween candy."

Aster jumped up and down, her chain mail jingling together like a collection of tiny bells as she hopped in place. "Please!"

I glanced at Rainwater.

"I could use the company," he said. "I'm completely outnumbered out there by pint-sized ghosts and goblins. I could use an adult at my side for backup."

My face broke into a smile. "Okay," I said, and followed Joan of Arc and the village police chief out into the crisp autumn air on the most beautiful Halloween in my memory.

Read on for an excerpt from the first
Magical Bookshop Mystery
by Amanda Flower . . .

CRIME AND POETRY

Available now!

ONE

"**G**randma! Grandma Daisy!" I called as soon as I was inside Charming Books. There were books everywhere—on the crowded shelves, the end tables, the sales counter, and the floor. Everywhere. But there was no sign of my ailing grandmother.

Browsing customers in brightly colored T-shirts and shorts stared at me openmouthed. I knew I must have looked a fright. I had driven from Chicago to Cascade Springs, New York, a small village nestled on the banks of the Niagara River just minutes from the world-famous Niagara Falls. I'd made the drive in seven hours, stopping only twice for gas and potty breaks. My fingernails were bitten to the quick, dark circles hovered beneath my bloodshot blue eyes, and my wavy strawberry blond hair was in a knot on top of my head. Last time I caught sight of it in the rearview mirror, it had resembled a pom-pom that had been caught in a dryer's lint trap. I stopped looking in the rearview after that.

A crow gripping a perch in the shop's large bay window cawed.

I jumped, and my hands flew to my chest. I had thought the crow was stuffed.

The bird glared at me with his beady black eyes. He certainly wasn't stuffed. "Grandma Daisy!" he mimicked me. "Grandma!"

I sidestepped away from the black bird. I thought parrots were the only birds that could talk. The crow was the only one who spoke. None of the customers made a peep. A few slipped out the front door behind me. "Escape from the crazy lady" was written all over their faces. I couldn't say I blamed them.

A slim woman stepped out from between packed bookshelves. She wore jeans, a hot pink T-shirt with the bookshop's logo on it, and, despite the summer's heat, a long silken scarf. Silk scarves were Grandma Daisy's signature. I could count on one hand the number of times I had seen her without one intricately tied around her neck. Today's scarf was white with silver-dollar-sized ladybugs marching across it. Her straight silver hair was cut in a sleek bob that fell to her chin. Cat's-eye-shaped glasses perched on her nose. She was a woman in her seventies, but clearly someone who took care of herself. Clearly someone who was not dying.

My mouth fell open, and I knew I must look a lot like those tourists I'd frightened. "Grandma!" The word came out of my mouth somewhere between a curse and a prayer.

"Violet, my girl." She haphazardly dropped the pile of

books she had in her arms onto one of the two matching couches in the middle of the room at the base of the birch tree, which seemed to grow out of the floor. "You came!"

I stepped back. "Of course I came. You were *dying*."

More customers skirted for the door. They knew what was good for them. I wouldn't have hung around either. The only one who seemed to be enjoying the show was the crow. He was no longer in the front window, but on the end table to my right. Great. A crow was loose in my grandmother's bookshop. I wished I could say this surprised me, but it didn't.

Grandma Daisy chuckled. "Oh, that."

"'Oh, that'? That's all you can say?" I screeched. "Do you have any idea what you've put me through? I left school. I left my job. I left *everything* to be with you at your deathbed."

Grandma had the decency to wince.

"Look at you. You look like you are ready to run a marathon. When I spoke to you on the phone last night, you were coughing and gasping. You sounded like you were at death's door."

Grandma Daisy faked a cough. "Like this?" Her face morphed into pathetic. "Oh, Violet, I need you. Please come." Fake cough. Fake cough. "The doctor said I don't have much more time."

Heat surged up from the base of my neck to the top of my head. I couldn't remember the last time I had been this angry. Oh yeah, I did—it was the first time I'd left Cascade Springs, twelve years ago. I had promised myself that day I would never come back, and look where I was, back in Cascade Springs, tricked by my very own grandmother.

"You were dying," the crow said.

"Quiet, Faulkner," Grandma Daisy ordered.

The large black bird sidestepped across the tabletop. Seemed that the crow was a new addition to the shop. It'd been twelve years, but I would have remembered Faulkner. I wondered why Grandma Daisy had never mentioned the bird. I would have thought a talking pet crow would have made a great conversation piece.

Grandma Daisy searched my face. "I may have fibbed a bit. Can you forgive me?" she asked, giving me her elfish smile. It wasn't going to work, not this time.

I spun around, ignored Faulkner, who was spouting "You were dying!" over and over again, and stomped out of the shop.

Behind me the screen door smacked against the doorframe. I stumbled across the front porch and gripped the whitewashed wooden railing. Charming Books ("where the perfect book picks you") sat in the center of River Road in the middle of Old Town Cascade Springs, a historic part of the village that was on the National Historic Landmarks list. Every house and small business on the street was more adorable than the last, but none were as stunning as Charming Books, a periwinkle Queen Anne Victorian with gingerbread to spare and a wraparound porch that was twice the size of my studio apartment back in Chicago.

The tiny front yard was full to bursting with blooming roses and, of course, daisies—Grandma's personal favorite. On the brick road in front of me, gas lampposts lined the street on either side and prancing horses and white carriages waited at the curbs, ready to take tourists for a spin around the village and along the famous Riverwalk at a moment's notice. The horses' manes were elaborately braided with satiny ribbons, and their drivers wore red coats with tails and top hats.

It was charming. It was perfect. It was the last place on planet Earth I wanted to be.

I had half a mind to jump in my car and head west for Chicago, never looking back. I couldn't do that. My shoulders slumped. I was so incredibly tired. Coffee wouldn't be any help. Coffee had lost its ability to keep me alert my third year of grad school. And as much as she vexed me, I couldn't leave Grandma Daisy without saying good-bye. For better or worse, she was all the family I had left in the world. And then, there was the whole pom-pom hair situation, which could be tolerated for only so long. I'd need a hairbrush and maybe a blowtorch to get that under control.

The screen door to the Queen Anne creaked open. I didn't have to turn around to know it was my grandmother. The scent of lavender talcum powder that always surrounded her floated on the breeze. "Violet, I know it wasn't right for me to lie to you."

I folded my arms, refusing to look at her. I knew it was childish, but I was going on two hours of sleep and tons of betrayal. Being a grown-up wasn't on the top of my priority list.

She placed her hand on my shoulder. "It was wrong of me. Very wrong, but it was the only way I could convince you to come back here."

She was probably right in that assumption, but I wasn't going to make it easy for her. "So you pretended to be dying?"

She let out a breath. "What I said about needing you to come back was true. I do need you here. I want you to stay."

She had to be kidding. She knew what had happened to me in this town. She knew why I'd left the day after I graduated high school. She knew better than anyone. "Well, that's too bad," I said. "I'm not staying."

"Can't you stay a little while? For me?"

I felt a pang in my heart. I didn't want to leave Grandma Daisy, and despite the whole lying thing, it was wonderful to see her, but I couldn't stay. It was too hard. "I'll wait until tomorrow, but I'll leave in the morning."

Of course that last statement came to be known as "famous last words."

TWO

"Well, then," Grandma Daisy said, her face breaking into a smile. "You should come inside, and I'll fetch you a cold drink."

My shoulders slumped in defeat. She got me, and she got me good. "Okay."

I followed Grandma Daisy back inside the shop. We were the only ones there besides Faulkner the crow.

I nodded at Faulkner. "What's up with the crow?"

She chuckled. "He showed up in the garden during the winter with a broken wing. He was a young bird then, barely more than a chick. I nursed him back to health, and he decided to stay. Every bookshop needs a mascot."

"What's wrong with a cat?"

"You know I'm not a traditionalist," she said with a smile.

I frowned as I looked around the shop. "I'm sorry I scared away all your customers."

She smoothed her silky bob. "It's no matter. If they needed something, it would have found them."

My eyes slid to her. "You mean they were just browsers?"

She gave a small smile. "You could call them that."

I wanted to ask her what that meant, but she scurried away, muttering about lemonade. As Charming Books was an old converted house, there was a full kitchen in the back. I almost followed her, but my surroundings stopped me. Charming Books was, well, charming. There was something about it that was beguiling. I had been to dozens of other bookstores in my life and never felt the same jolt of wonder as I did while in my grandmother's shop. It was a feeling of warmth and understanding I got as I looked around the room, like the books were alive and old friends. I knew that was ridiculous, and I would never say that aloud to anyone. The villagers of Cascade Springs thought I was a lot of things. I didn't need to add peculiar to an already lengthy list.

Now that I wasn't blinded by the fear I would find my grandmother dead, I was able to take in my surroundings. The bookshop looked exactly as I remembered it. A vaulted ceiling spanned half the room, stopping in the center of the shop at a metal spiral staircase that led to the second floor. The staircase wrapped itself around a live birch tree with three trunks, each as thick as a grown man. Once a year, grandmother had a tree service come in to prune the tree so that it didn't break through the historic building's slate roof. Currently, its branches stopped six inches from the ceiling.

Sunlight poured into the shop from the windows and the large skylight on the second floor and reflected off the birch tree's white, silver-flecked bark. The tree, just like the house, had belonged to my family for generations, since my ancestress Rosalee Waverly built the home at the beginning of the nineteenth century. Although the structure had shifted over the last two hundred years, the most notable change occurred at the turn of the twentieth century when one of Rosalee's descendants transformed the home into a Queen Anne Victorian, as was the fashion at that time.

At the top of the staircase, I could see through the black iron railing into the children's room, which was decorated as a wood sprite's palace that would have put Tinker Bell to shame. It had been the perfect place to hide during my mother's chemo treatments.

For the moment, I would have to wait to visit the fairy room. Faulkner the crow stared at me from one of the tree's branches as if daring me to climb the stairs. I wasn't up to facing him. I hadn't been the least bit surprised that my grandma had nursed Faulkner back to health. When I was a child, she had a revolving door of injured and sick animals going through her house. She was just kind-hearted. I sighed. If she was that kindhearted, why would she lie to me, her own granddaughter, about being sick? What was so important that made her want me to move back to Cascade Springs? Part of me was afraid to ask, because Grandma Daisy could be very convincing when she wanted to be, and apparently, after the "I'm dying" speech over the phone, she could be quite an actress too.

It was beginning to ebb, but adrenaline still pulsed in my veins from fear that Grandma Daisy was ill. Even though I hadn't been back to Cascade Springs since I was seventeen, I saw my grandmother at least twice a year. She visited me in Chicago for Christmas, and every year we met somewhere in the world for our annual girls' trip. People might think it was odd I vacationed with my grandmother, but those people didn't have a grandmother like mine. I was the one ready to call it a day at eleven. Grandma could party the whole night through. Last year, she drank me under the table in São Paolo.

The front bell jangled, notifying the shop that someone had entered. Grandma Daisy rushed past me with a tray holding a lemonade pitcher and glasses. She shoved a sweaty glass of lemonade into my hand on her way to greet her customer.

As beautifully crafted and enchanting as the shop itself was, the books were the most eye-catching aspect. They were everywhere. Along the walls, bookshelves rose eleven feet high. In the middle of the room, much shorter shelves held even more volumes, and soft chairs were tucked in every corner for a quiet place to get lost in a book.

I walked around the shop, sliding my finger across the spines of all the lovely books. Charming Books had been the place where I had fallen in love with literature. When I was a child, I ran here every day after school, eager to see what new novels and plays my grandmother had in stock. Back then, I daydreamed of running the shop myself one day, and helping shoppers find the perfect book for themselves and their family or friends. That was before. Now I poured my love of the written word into my PhD program in American literature. After years of scholarship, I was one dissertation away from my culminating degree, and after that, who knew what would happen? I'd started submitting my vita to colleges and universities, but as of yet haven't yielded much more than a lukewarm reception to it. In the world of academe, a PhD in literature was easy to come by and the competition was fierce for the few open professor jobs in the country. I wasn't panicking. Or at least I wasn't panicking yet.

I heard muffled voices as Grandma Daisy chatted with the shopper about a book, and I smiled at the sound of her energetic voice. Nothing made my grandmother happier than talking about books. I stepped out from the bookshelves and found Grandma with a white-haired man in riding pants and a red jacket with tails. His riding boots were polished to a high sheen, and he tucked his black top hat under his arm. His and my grandmother's heads were suspiciously close together, much closer than in a typical bookseller-and-buyer transaction.

I cleared my throat.

Grandma Daisy jumped back from the man. "Oh, Violet, you gave me a start."

The man beamed at me. He had straight white teeth that sparkled against his tanned skin. "You're Violet. I've heard so much about you. I'm so glad to finally meet you. My, aren't you the spitting image of Daisy?"

I wasn't so sure about that. I still had the crazy pompom do on the top of my head. It couldn't have been more different from my grandmother's sleek and smooth bob. I frowned. "I haven't heard about you." Usually, I was a much friendlier person, but it was hard to be polite with a crow looming over you.

He laughed. "I see you get your spunk from Daisy too." He held out his free hand. "I'm Benedict Raisin, the best carriage driver in Cascade Springs or on either side of the Niagara River. Don't let anyone else tell you different."

I shook his hand and smiled despite myself. "Nice to meet you." Self-consciously, I touched my hair. "I have to apologize for my appearance. I just arrived."

"Aww, what's to apologize for? I thought that's how all the young girls wear their hair nowadays," he said, releasing my hand.

I laughed.

"There, now, I see you have your grandmother's beautiful smile too."

I glanced at Grandma Daisy, and her cheeks pinkened. My suspicion returned. Who was this guy, and why was my grandma acting like a twelve-year-old girl with a crush around him?

"How do you two know each other?" I asked.

"He's a customer," Grandma Daisy said a little too quickly.

A customer? Just a customer? I wasn't buying it.

Benedict chuckled. "Seems to me you've been in the big city far too long. Everyone knows everyone in our little village." He dusted off the top of his hat. "I'm one of Daisy's *best* customers. I'm here to restock on my reading material. Being a carriage driver means that ninety percent of my time is spent waiting for the next tourist. It's good to have a book handy for the slow times of the day."

"What are you looking for?" I was always interested in what people were reading.

He cocked his head. "I'm not sure. I do like action. A good thriller keeps the blood pumping in my old ticker." He rested a hand on his chest. "Poor old thing doesn't work quite as well as it used to, but I get by."

Grandma Daisy smiled. "Don't let Benedict fool you; he

is the picture of health." She turned back to her friend. "Why don't you browse a bit? Would you like some lemonade?"

"I never turn down your lemonade, Daisy."

Again, I looked from Benedict to my grandmother and back again. There was definitely more to their relationship than my grandmother wanted me to know.

Grandma Daisy went to the tray on the counter and poured Benedict a generous serving of lemonade.

"Your grandmother tells me you're studying literature," he said.

I nodded. "At the University of Chicago. I'm working on my dissertation in Transcendentalist literature."

He frowned as if he wasn't sure what I was talking about. I got that look a lot when speaking about my dissertation. I supposed it wasn't a good time to share my interpretation of *Walden*.

"You must have gotten your love of books from Daisy," he said.

I smiled. "I did. In fact, if it weren't for Gran—"

A book flew off the shelf and nailed Benedict on the kneecap and fell open.

"Ouch," he cried.

"Where on earth did that come from?" I searched the room for Faulkner. I half expected the crow to be responsible for the projectile book. I was wrong. Faulkner sat silently in the tree, not moving a feather. He made eye contact with me, and I was the one who looked away.

Benedict leaned over to pick up the book. "Oh my. Emily Dickinson. You know I used to be a bit of a poetry buff as a young man. Here's my chance to brush up a little.

I have always enjoyed Dickinson. 'The Carriage,'" he said, reading the poem that the book had fallen open to. "Doesn't that sound like the perfect poem for me?"

"I'm a fan of Dickinson myself," I said. "She was a contemporary with many of the Transcendentalist writers."

He cocked his head as if he considered that bit of information. "It will do me good to get some culture, then. It's been a long time since I read anything without an explosion in it. This seems to be a good place to start." He read from the book:

Because I could not stop for Death,
He kindly stopped for me;
The carriage held but just ourselves
And Immortality.

He frowned. "It's not the most cheerful verse in the world."

"Emily wasn't all rainbows and sunshine," I said.

"Apparently not." He laughed.

Grandma Daisy abandoned the lemonade and hurried over to him. "This must be some kind of mistake."

Benedict and I both raised our eyebrows at her.

She cleared her throat and reached for the volume of poetry in Benedict's hands. "I mean, there are so many newer novels that you haven't read. Why don't we find something else for you? Dickinson is all right, but I'm sure I could find you something else that you would like even more."

Benedict stepped back from her. "But I want to read this one. Poetry is food for the soul."

Grandma Daisy took another step toward him. "What

about some Tom Clancy? James Patterson? I'm sure James has published five books since you were last in the shop. He's so prolific. I know those are both your favorites."

I set my lemonade on an end table. "Grandma, why are you trying to talk someone out of reading a classic American poet?"

She turned to me, and there was a strange look in her eyes. Was it fear? Fear of what? A book?

My grandmother may have claimed to be the image of health, but maybe she wasn't. Maybe she wasn't right in the head if someone buying a collection of Emily Dickinson's poetry freaked her out. The thought made me shiver.

"Daisy, don't be silly. I have always wanted to read this. It will keep me company as I wait for my customers." He lifted the book in his hand. "Considering its size, it will keep me occupied for some time. I'll just take this one today."

Grandma Daisy chewed the pink lipstick off her lower lip. "If you're sure."

"I'm sure." He smiled good-naturedly. "Now, I must be returning to my post. Let's ring this up." He wagged his finger at Grandma Daisy. "And before you say it, I insist on paying for the book."

My grandmother and Benedict moved across the huge Oriental rug that covered two-thirds of the shop floor. He had a bounce in his step, and Grandma Daisy dragged her feet.

After she'd rung him up, Grandma Daisy watched him stroll out of the store. She bit her lip, and I might have been mistaken, but I thought I saw tears in her eyes.

Connect with Berkley Publishing Online!

For sneak peeks into the newest releases, news on all your favorite authors, book giveaways, and a central place to connect with fellow fans—

"Like" and follow Berkley Publishing!

facebook.com/BerkleyPub
twitter.com/BerkleyPub
instagram.com/BerkleyPub